JIM ANTHONY
Super-Detective

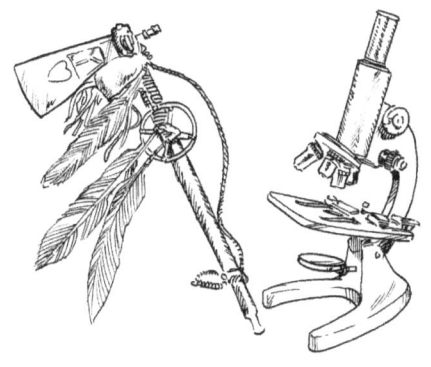

AIRSHIP 27 PRODUCTIONS

AN AIRSHIP 27 PRODUCTION

Jim Anthony: Super-Detective, Volume Four

The Scream Hammer © 2013 Joel Jenkins
Under a Commanche Moon © 2013 Frank Byrns
Neighborhood in Peril © 2013 Erwin K. Roberts
The Resurrected Killer © 2013 Mark Justice

An Airship 27 Production
www.airship27.com
www.airship27hangar.com

Interior illustrations © 2013 Michael Neno
Cover illustration © 2013 Eric Meador

Editor: Ron Fortier
Associate Editor: Gordon Dymowski
Production and design: Rob Davis.
Marketing and promotion: Michael Vance

ISBN-13: 978-0615896335
ISBN-10: 0615896332

Printed in the United States of America

10 9 8 7 6 5 4 3 2 1

Volume Four

CONTENTS

THE SCREAM HAMMER

by Joel Jenkin

Tom Gentry piloted the Cierva Rota Mark 1 gyrocopter over the verdant jungle hills of Nayarit Mexico, the one-hundred-forty horsepower Genet Major motor throbbing and the double-bladed rotor slicing the air over his head. To the west rose the last snow-capped peaks of the Sierra Madre Occidental, their broad bases swallowed up in the thick greenery of the creeping jungle. Below them the turbulent blue waters of the *Rio Grande de Santiago* cascaded down precipitous falls. Above, the summer sun glowered in the sapphire sky, overhanging the blunt peaks of the Ceboruco and the Sanganguey volcanoes—the Ceboruco churning out a whispy trail of vapor to the west.

Gentry twisted in his seat and shouted at the passenger behind him, the hot Mexico wind tugging at his light brown hair and his freckled face turned in a frown even while his white-knuckled hands gripped the yoke of the autogyro. "I don't like the looks of that volcano, Jim."

"It hasn't erupted for nearly seventy years," answered the passenger, a tall man with broad, muscular shoulders tapering to a narrow waist and dark eyes that peered hawk-like from a sun-bronzed face. Hair as black as midnight escaped the leather pilot's helmet as he fixed his eyes on the trail of vapor that escaped the hollowed dome of the Ceboruco. "There's little chance that it will happen again, today."

Gentry shrugged his hulking shoulders. "I'm just saying, Jim, that something doesn't look copacetic, and ain't we supposed to be on the watch-out for things that don't look copacetic?"

"Indeed we are," replied Anthony, but his words were lost in the cacophony of the gyrocopter's beating blades. His sharp eyes caught a glimpse of something out of place in a grassy clearing over a stand of vine-draped camachile trees, and he motioned for Gentry to swoop in and take a closer look.

As they neared the clearing both Gentry and Anthony could easily make out the form of a battered jeep half-hidden among the tall stalks of the tropical grass.

"Let's check it out," shouted Anthony. "Can you bring the autogyro safely down?"

"One way to find out," responded Gentry, and he wheeled the aircraft in a tight turn, and brought the autogyro down toward the uneven field. He made a pass over the terrain, scanning for fallen logs or other debris among the tall grasses, and determining that his intended landing field was unobstructed he sent the Rota Mark into a sharp descent that soon had him nicking the grass tops so that the seed laden pods on their bending blades billowed clouds of parachute-shaped seed behind the path of the autogyro. Then the Rota Mark plowed a furrow through the field and the front landing gear contacted the uneven earth, jouncing the autogyro through the tall grasses even while the front rotor mowed through it.

However, Tom Gentry had brought them through many a tight spots before—he'd lost track of how many disasters he had narrowly averted by virtue of his piloting skills—and this case was no different. The autogyro finally came to a rest among the sea of swaying grass and while Gentry shut down the front and overhead rotors Anthony slipped back his goggles and removed his leather helmet, letting the dark curls of his hair spill out. Once the rotors had ceased beating, he stepped out onto the wing of the autogyro and watched the wind sweep away the clouds of seeds. Then he dropped into the thick grasses, gratified to find the ground beneath his feet, and the autogyro, firm and unyielding.

Anthony waded his way through the thick sward until came upon an overgrown roadway, the dirt ruts grown with vegetation that had been flattened only by the abandoned Jeep that he found hidden among the heavy grasses. Like many of the vehicles encountered in the back areas of Mexico, this one had seen better days. The body of the Jeep was bent and rusted, paint flaking off in numerous areas. A roll bar had been welded onto the vehicle, and it was apparent that the Jeep had actually been rolled over at least once before. The vehicle was empty except for a couple of spare gasoline cans, a canteen on the driver's seat, and a canvas duffel bag on the floor.

Anthony knelt and examined the bend in the grass and how it had sprung back up, and by this he was able to determine how long ago the jeep had come into the field. Some found Jim Anthony's ability to read tracks beyond belief or even attributed it to some supernatural ability, but Jim sprang from both Irish and Comanche descent—and from a young age his grandfather, Mephito, had taken him on hunts deep in the wilderness, and taught him the lore handed down from generation to generation. On those trips, young Jim Anthony had learned how to read a turned leaf or a bent blade of grass.

Anthony could hear the trudging footsteps of Tom Gentry's come up behind him. "What have we got, Jim?"

"The Jeep has been here for three to four weeks. There's no sign of human tracks on this side of the vehicle." The Irish-Comanche half-breed rose to his feet and circled around to the other side of the rusting hulk, and immediately he was able to spot tracks among the swaying grasses.

"A man weighing about one-hundred and sixty pounds left the Jeep. He walks with a slight limp in his left leg. He's got a crooked hobnail in the heel of his left boot."

"So why would he leave his Jeep here?" asked Gentry.

"That's the question," grunted Anthony. He began to wade through the tangle of partially bent grass, his keen eyes watching the ground. "Maybe we can pick up a few clues if we follow for a ways."

"Lead on," gestured Gentry. "I couldn't follow an elephant through swampland."

The field had a gentle roll to it and as they descended to a lower elevation the ground became softer and Anthony came upon a clear boot print, the edges decaying from erosion. He spent a few moments memorizing the pattern of the tread, and then continued on toward the edge of the forest. It was here that the trail ended.

When Gentry saw that his boss had come to a dead end, he squinted toward the sky. "Maybe a helicopter threw down a ladder and picked him up. There's enough clearance between the trees at the edge of the forest."

"I don't think so," responded his swarthy-skinned boss after a few moments of examination. "There are markings intersecting the path of the jeep driver. At one time the grass was pressed down in an odd winding pattern, as if it were pushed down by a snake."

"If the driver got bit by a snake, where is his body?"

"I said 'as if it were pushed down by a snake' because the pattern is very similar" replied Anthony. "But this pattern is much too large to be any snake that I'm familiar with. What ever it was appears to have swallowed the driver whole. If you look closely at the base of the grass stalks you'll be able to see some residual blood stains, so whatever it was sank its teeth into the driver first."

Gentry peered nervously into the wavering sea of grass. "Maybe it's not so smart for us to be wandering around without some heavy armament. I'll head back to the autogyro and grab the buffalo rifle."

"That might be a wise idea," agreed Anthony. "In the meantime I'm going to move ahead and follow the track of the beast that ate the driver."

While Gentry trudged back to the autogyro, Anthony forged further into the grasses, following the winding path left by the beast. The grass had since sprung back into place, leaving only a residual bend in the stalks—

but to the trained eye these subtle clues, which would go unnoticed by someone else, were clear evidence that something large had passed.

The spoor led along the forest line without venturing into it, and then meandered up to a rocky butte about a mile distant. The trail was simple enough for Anthony to follow and he pursued the track of the beast with long strides that carried him easily across the uneven terrain. Gentry still hadn't caught up to him by the time he reached the butte, but he could see his pilot's head and shoulders moving through the wind-rustled plains, a large-bored rifle slung over the left shoulder.

Anthony, however, turned his attention to the massive pile of feces atop the butte. He broke the boulder-sized stool apart with a heavy stick and found mats of hair among the remains. As he dug further he came across the partially-digested leather sole of boot. He scraped this clean and found that it did, indeed, match the pattern of the track he had earlier discovered.

About the time that Gentry came hiking over the crest of the butte, Anthony uncovered something hard and metallic among the clay-like mud of the beast's feces. He pulled out the object with a stick and wiped it down with a handful of grass.

"What have you got?" asked Gentry.

"Our friend from the Jeep definitely got eaten, but the only thing that survived ingestion was some hair, the sole of a boot and this." Anthony raised up the object he had been cleaning so that the pilot could make out the pitted black surface of a gun—a pistol with a boxy body and a slender snout offset by a fifty-five degree handle angle and a large ring of a trigger guard.

"That looks like a Nazi weapon," said Gentry.

"It is," replied Anthony. "It's a semi-automatic Luger P-zero-eight."

"Hmm, so you think that maybe *Ministro* Morales reports of Nazi activity in Nayarit are accurate?"

"I don't know about accurate—the reports seem to be based on second or third hand accounts of armed men in the area, but this Luger goes a long way in substantiating the rumors."

Gentry took the pistol and examined it closely. He dropped the clip and found that it was empty—perhaps fired at whatever had devoured the pilot. "If the Nazis have established a base of operation in Nayarit, that puts them uncomfortably close to the United States."

Anthony shrugged noncommittally. "Closer than I'd like to see, but they would have to gather a substantial force here, and that kind of troop movement would be much easier to spot than what we seem to be dealing with here."

"Still, best to nip it in the bud if we can. What about this thing that devoured the jeep driver?"

The half-Comanche grunted. "For the time being, let's leave well enough alone. It may well have done us a favor by eating this German fellow, and now it's got a snout full of lead—whatever it is, I don't think we want to mess with it when it's angry."

"Fair enough," said Gentry. "Then let's get to the autogyro before it wanders back and decides to make a meal of us, too. Besides, I have a feeling that you're anxious to see the *Ministro*'s daughter. How long has it been?"

"Too long," said Jim Anthony. "And what about you? I recall you taking some rather long walks with Maria's pretty little maid."

A sly smile crept across Gentry's freckled face. "Ah, Cipriana. I wouldn't mind taking a few more long walks with that doll."

Their take-off was more perilous than their landing, and Anthony was forced to clear a few logs from the path of the autogyro—inadvertently disturbing a large nest of red ants—before they were finally able to bump across the rough terrain and plow through the thick grass with enough speed to take to the air. As they soared into the sky, shedding bits of shredded grass from the front propeller and landing gear, Anthony looked down at the winding ribbon of the *Rio Grande de Santiago* and for a moment he thought he caught a glimpse of something large and sinuous rustling through the thick grasses of the field that lay far below them. He looked again, but the autogyro moved away so that sight of the field was lost to the grand verdure of the great Nayarit jungles.

Their flight took them past the dark depths of Crater Lake and the glowering bulk of the Sanganguey Volcano, over the bustling metropolis of Tepic and the stuccoed hovels that lay in the suburbs, and across the thick palm forests toward the warm waters of the glistering Pacific Ocean. Before they reached the rolling waves of Rincon Bay they came across a large sugarcane plantation and Gentry guided the plane in a gradual descent toward a dirt landing strip nestled among the tall stalks of cane.

Children playing with carved toys of wood looked to the sky when they heard the beating rotors of the autogyro and they scattered from the field, running toward the roofed verandas of the ranch house and the outlying quarters, crying out and pointing at the incoming aircraft. *"un helicóptero, un helicóptero!"*

This landing was much smoother than the previous and Gentry expertly settled the Rota Mark gyrocopter onto the runway for a smooth landing that cast up clouds of choking dust from the front and overhead rotors.

The freckled Irishman cut the motors and gradually the rotors spun to a halt.

Anthony leaped from the wing and stretched his cramped legs. If the gyrocopter lacked one thing, it was leg room for a tall man. He pulled away his goggles and doffed his leather flight helmet, and emerging through the dusty haze he saw a curvaceous form. A long hand-painted skirt flapped above bare ankles and feet and she wore a red peasant blouse, the bare flesh of her arms darkened to a dusky hue by the equatorial sun. Her hair, black as night, fluttered a dark fringe about her shapely shoulders. The long lashes of deep brown eyes blinked against the dust, and Jim Anthony's heart leaped as he saw the straight nose and overlarge mouth that lent a touch of sensuality to the beauty of the woman whose face had haunted his memories and his dreams for the past year.

When she saw him there among the roiling dust she gave a cry and leaped into his muscular arms, and ignoring the settling grit she rained kisses upon the face and lips of the large man—which he returned with an equal fervor.

Gentry came alongside them with a bemused expression and scanned the hazy field in the direction of the ranch house. He thought he caught a glimpse of her slender form standing beneath the eaves of the veranda, wrapped in a brightly colored *mantón* and holding a bundle in Cipriana's arms. The pilot's expression of bemusement turned into a frown when he saw that Cipriana had failed to exhibit the same enthusiasm about his return as Maria Morales had shown for his best friend's arrival.

Finally, Jim and Maria concluded their passionate greeting and with clasped hands they continued toward the ranch house, Tom Gentry escorting them with a heavy canvas duffel bag in his left hand.

"We're so pleased that the two of you could return for a visit," said Maria. "I only wish that it was your heart that brought you back instead of dire rumors of German soldiers tramping around in our jungles."

Anthony squeezed Maria's hand. "I assure you, my heart has never left. Unfortunately, since Japan decided to bomb Pearl Harbor Uncle Sam has kept me very busy on various errands around the globe. I was very pleased when I found out the latest assignment was sending me back into your arms."

"Me, too. I received your letter just a couple of days ago."

"Maybe we can prolong this assignment for a few weeks," interjected Gentry, his eye not leaving Cipriana's slender form as they neared the veranda.

"Yes," agreed Maria. "Perhaps you can be a little less efficient than is your habit on your usual cases."

"I'll do my best to be slothful and lazy," agreed Anthony with a smile.

"So what happens when you finish your assignment, here?" asked Maria. "Are you gone again, chasing Nazi spies and Imperial plots—leaving me to become an old spinster while you're off having grand adventures around the world?"

"Some adventures are less grand than others," said Anthony, and he recalled the torn corpses lying in French trenches and the horrible thing that feasted upon their festering flesh. "But I've made a decision that if you'll have me, and if Senior Morales will give his blessing, I'll not leave here without making you my wife."

Maria clutched at his arm and smiled brightly. "If that's your way of proposing then my answer is yes. I know we've talked of marriage in our letters, but you'd been absent for so long I didn't dare dream that it might become a reality. Still, we have my father to contend with. He thinks quite highly of you since the incident with the *chupacabra* last year, but I'm not so certain he'll like the idea of me marrying an American."

"That's what I'm afraid of. If I catch him in the wrong mood he may throw me off the ranch and bar me from ever entering Mexico again."

Maria turned and caught a glimpse of Gentry, his mouth hanging agape and his eyes wide. "What's the matter, Tom? It looks like you've seen a ghost. Didn't you think Jim was the marrying kind?"

"I guess I just...thought..." Gentry's words trailed off into nothingness.

"You thought what?" prodded Anthony.

"I just didn't know that you and Maria were so serious. I thought all those letters you were writing and sending had to do with maintaining your business interests—not with carrying on a hot and heavy long distance romance. Why didn't you tell me?"

Anthony shrugged. "You never asked. You were too busy prowling for pretty faces to pay much notice that I was keeping myself off the market."

"I guess you're right," said Gentry, his voice both bemused and befuddled.

"You know, Cipriana has talked of you a few times since your absence," said Maria to the bewildered pilot. "Perhaps a few kind words and some flowers might rekindle her interest. It's good for a man to settle down with a woman."

Gentry's eyes glazed over in an expression similar to those that Anthony had seen in shell-shock victims returning from the fields of war.

"Settle down?" gulped Gentry.

"*Hola, Senior* Gentry," greeted Cipriana, as the pilot came to the veranda—but her tone was frosty and her manner reserved. Her face was a dusky brown, framed by wild black hair and her cheek bones high, lips full. The only marring of her features was a slight crook to her nose, but it lent her an exotic aspect that some might argue increased her beauty rather than detracted from it.

"*Hola, Seniorita,*" replied Gentry, his heart leaping in his throat when he saw the baby that she held. "I hope the year has been kind to you since we last parted ways. It appears that it has, you're even more beautiful than I remember."

"Flattering words," replied Cipriana, "but despite what they say, absence does not make the heart grow fonder."

Maria interrupted the awkward moment by taking the baby from Cipriana's arms. "Jim, Tom, meet my new baby brother, Arturo."

"Pleasure to meet you, little guy," cooed Anthony, as Arturo curled tiny fingers around the adventurer's large forefinger. Though scarcely three or four months old, the boy had a shock of wild black hair and a few freckles across the bridge of his nose that showed he had already seen some sun. "Did your Father remarry since I was last here?"

"No," said Maria, a tinge of regret in her voice. "Since my Mother died he has made himself very busy with his work, too busy to look for another wife. Still, *poco* Arturo has helped ease some of his loss."

"*Ministro* Morales adopted the baby," explained Cipriana, "and Maria and I have been caring for him."

"One of the local girls got into trouble," said Maria, "But instead of letting her be put to shame, my father adopted the baby. He has always wanted a boy, and I like having a little brother."

Gentry breathed a sigh of relief, and gave an uneasy smile.

"Would you like to hold him?" Cipriana asked the pilot.

The broad-shouldered Irishman declined with a gentle wave of his hand. "Babies make me nervous."

Anthony laughed at his friend's discomfort. "You've strafed the German trenches in the teeth of machine gun fire from above and below. How is it that a little baby makes you nervous?"

"I was an only child. I never learned what to do with a baby."

"Where is *Ministro* Morales?" asked Anthony.

"He's away with a squad of soldiers, chasing some opium *banditos*," said Maria. "The jungle has been a strange place as of late. First there were reports of Nazi soldiers creeping around the jungles outside of *Laguna Agua Brava* and now there are reports of demonic screams echoing from the deep forest in the dead of night, that investigating scientist, Dr. Archuleta, disappeared, and hunters have been found dead—their hair turned white from fear, and bleeding from their ears."

"Not to mention that playing children have been disappearing and even babies have been stolen from their cribs," interjected Cipriana. She took Arturo and hugged him close, as if the threat might, even then, be creeping near.

"I didn't hear any of this in the OSS briefing," said Tom. "We were asked to investigate the possible presence of Nazi activity. They didn't mention any of the rest."

"These were all considered matters of local jurisdiction," said Maria. "However, once we begin receiving reports of German military activity I prompted my father to report this to an agent of your Office of Strategic Services at the American Embassy. Naturally, I hoped that they would send you to investigate."

"Resources have been spread thin during the war," said Anthony, "and the OSS has been using me and my business organization to investigate a number of affairs that are outside their normal purview or their current capabilities."

"I'm glad you're here," said Maria. "Even if it took a threat to the homeland of the United States to do it—is it wrong that I feel that way?"

Anthony chuckled. "I was hoping that the reports might be unfounded, but Tom and I did a survey of the surrounding area before we landed here, and we found something interesting near a plateau by the *Rio Grande de Santiago*."

Maria's dark lashes flickered. "Don't keep us in suspense, Senior Anthony."

Gentry lifted the canvas duffel that they had discovered in the abandoned Jeep, and placed it on the wooden table, which rested on the porch beneath the veranda. He unzipped the bag and extracted the pistol they had discovered in the digested remains.

"A pistol?" questioned Maria.

"A German pistol," clarified Anthony. "It does tend to indicate a German presence in Nayarit."

"You didn't find a human that went along with the pistol?"

"No, just the remains of a human that had been eaten by something very large that traveled on its belly."

"*La serpiente del monstruo*," breathed Cipriana, and she held Arturo even more tightly to her bosom.

Anthony spoke Spanish quite well, and Gentry had picked up a smattering of the language when they had visited a year prior—enough to understand Cipriana's words.

"So you do have a giant snake running around the *Rio Grande de Santiago*?" exclaimed the pilot. "Why, based on the path that thing cut through the grasses it must have been forty, fifty feet long and four or five feet in diameter."

"I wish that it was confined to just the areas along the *Rio Grande de Santiago*, but it seems to travel widely! It showed up about the time that the screaming in the wilderness began," said Maria.

"You think they are related?" asked Anthony as he wrapped the Luger in a rag and stowed it among his personal belongings.

Maria shrugged. "It could be just coincidence, and I've never before heard of a screaming snake—but there may be some connection."

"I've got another puzzle for you," said Anthony. He reached into the duffel bag and extricated a carved figurine with puffy features and slit-like eyes placed in a broad rectangular head. The figure was seated on a block, its shortened bulbous legs tapering to a point. "I found this in the duffel bag, and it looks like one of those Chinesco artifacts that we encountered in the tomb shafts last time we were here."

"Don't remind me." Maria shifted uncomfortably as she recalled the ordeal. "Perhaps *Senior* Eisler will be able to shed some light on the origin of the artifact."

She turned to a bare-chested boy in ragged knee-pants that had followed them on to the veranda. "Carlos, *traiga por favor Senior* Eisler."

"*Si Senioreta*," repled Carlos, and then he ran off toward a trio of stucco *cabinas*, bare feet slapping against the dirt road.

"So who is this *Senior* Eisler?" asked Anthony.

Maria sat down on the wooden bench next to the table and examined the odd figurine. "He and a couple of his staff are currently living in one of our outbuildings and heading an excavation on the tomb shaft we discovered—as well as two more that he's found since."

Anthony and Maria found plenty of easy conversation while they waited for Carlos to return, but Gentry found his attempt at dialogue with Cipriana rebuffed by cold, monosyllabic responses. So when Carlos came skipping up the path, with a solidly-built figure trudging along behind him, Gentry was glad for the interruption.

Mr. Eisler appeared to be in his early fifties, his head entirely bald except for a ring of iron gray around the temples and the back of his head. He was about the same height as Gentry, his torso thick and powerful, with wiry arms emerging from a short-sleeved shirt that was open, and revealed thick thatches of silver hair on his chest. He wore an engraved golden band on his ring finger.

"*Seniorita Morales*, Carlos tells me that you have some guests that you would like me to meet." Eisler's voice was thick with an accent that was long on vowels and vague on the r's.

"Are you German?" snapped Gentry.

"Happily, no," said Mr. Eisler, and he extended a hand, and exhibited a surprisingly strong grip. "I come from the neighboring country of Austria, which was—up until recently—a completely separate entity from Hitler's regime. I had a thriving import and export business in Austria until Chancellor Schuschnigg resigned his post in March of 1938 and let the National Socialists take complete control of the government."

"Please excuse my partner's lack of delicacy," said Anthony, and he shook Mr. Eisler's hand. "My name is Jim Anthony. Mr. Gentry and I have spent some time fighting the Nazis and neither of us have much tolerance for the Germans these days."

"Completely understandable," said Eisler, with a knowing smile. "My business was decimated when the Nazis took control of Austria. Fortunately, I had seen the writing on the wall. The National Socialist party had been gaining power for some time and I moved most of my assets out of the country and took a freighter out of Austria the day after Schuschnigg bowed to Hitler's threats of invasion and resigned."

"So what brings you to Nayarit?" asked Anthony. "Mexico is far afield from Austria."

"So true," agreed Eisler. "But since my enterprise became practically non-existent I thought I'd indulge an interest that I'd developed while doing importing and exporting. While I was in Austria I imported a few archeological artifacts for wealthy collectors, and even managed to collect a couple for myself. When I heard of the discovery of another tomb shaft here in Nayarit, I could not resist the idea of exploring it. I contacted *Ministro* Morales and gained permission for further excavations."

"What of your family?" Anthony pointed to Eisler's wedding band. "Did you bring your wife with you?"

"No, unfortunately. She was rather outspoken against the National Socialist Party in Austria and was killed in rioting. With Korrina dead, there was truly nothing left for me in Austria." He began rifling through his wallet and produced a gray photo that he passed to Anthony.

Anthony gave the photograph polite inspection. It showed Eisler in a dark suit and standing next to a statuesque blonde woman in a v-necked cocktail dress that was cut enticingly low. Her hair was pinned into place in an elaborate hairdo and she held the stem of a champagne glass with a firm resolve that was reflected in her cold gaze. Surely a trick of the light, reflected Anthony. Behind them were other couples, and it was clear that the photograph had been taken at some social gathering.

"Your wife was a beautiful woman." He began to return the photograph, but Gentry snatched it away so as to examine it himself. "Is she Austrian, also?"

"Thank you, Mr. Anthony. I met Korrina in Finland in 1932 when I was developing a business alliance with the Papenburg Trading Company. Not a day goes by that I do not think of her. But I do my best to distract myself with other endeavors so as to not too keenly feel the pain of her loss." He waved his hand toward the odd figurine that still rested upon the table. "If you don't mind me asking, where did you find this wonderful piece?"

"Why, this is the very reason I asked Carlos to fetch you," explained Maria. "We were wondering if you might be able to shed some light on the mystery that Jim and Tom encountered while flying over the *Rio Grande de Santiago.*"

"Does the mystery involve this example of tomb shaft artwork?"

"It does," said Anthony. "We came across an abandoned jeep. The driver appears to have been devoured my some local fauna, and we found this artifact among the driver's belongings."

Eisler hefted the artifact and examined it in the roseate light of the sun. "It really is a beautiful piece of artwork. It might bring four to six thousand dollars if the right collector was approached. Was there anything else of interest among the driver's effects?"

"Nothing quite so ancient," answered Anthony. "That was the only artifact, and there was little enough remaining of the driver, though the footprints indicated the weight and bearing of a male."

Eisler smiled. "Are you a hunter, Mr. Anthony?"

"Only when necessary. Can you tell me anything about the origins of the artifact?"

"I can tell you what I'm afraid has happened," said Eisler, his smile fading to a frown. "I and my men have been away from the dig for a couple of days while I located some supporting timbers for a shaft we've been

"That was the only artifact..."

excavating. In the meantime I'm concerned that some local *banditos* may have encroached on my diggings and made off with some contents of the tomb. The *banditos* have little concern for safety and at other discoveries they have lowered children down the shaft and had them collect whatever treasures they find. In fact, I heard report that when a group of archeologists excavated a finding in the Jalisco Highlands that they discovered a recent body of a young boy who had been thieving the tomb and suffocated when the shaft collapsed. The *banditos* using him to do their dirty work fled, leaving him to die."

Cipriana shuddered. "What a horrible way to die and at such a young age!"

"If there is one thing that I've learned from this horrible war it is that many men consider life to be inexpensive and expendable."

Anthony's dusky face betrayed no emotion other than deep concern. "Mr. Eisler, do you mind taking us up to your dig to see if we can learn more of these *banditos*?"

Mr. Eisler seemed surprised. "Why, of course I would welcome your help! But surely you didn't travel to Mexico to help a part-time archeologist hunt down a band of local *ladrones*?"

"No, Mr. Eisler," agreed Anthony without overmuch elucidation. "But we fear they may be involved in a larger issue."

Dust billowed from beneath the balding tires of the rusting pick-up truck as it jounced up the rutted and pot-holed road that wound along the precipitous edges of jungle-covered hills north of *Santiago Ixcuintla*. Jim Anthony and Tom Gentry sat alongside Eisler, all three crammed into the cab of the truck. To Gentry's great perturbation, the Austrian was a poor driver who paid little attention to the road in front of him and more to the conversation at hand. For a man who was accustomed to being in control behind the yoke of a plane or helicopter or even the wheel of a car, it was all he could do to restrain himself from wrenching away control of the vehicle and relegating Eisler to the bed of the pick-up truck with his pair of aides, Rudiger and Friedhelm—short, stolid men with dirt-stained hands and a vague aroma of diesel fuel.

"How long have you been digging here?" inquired Anthony.

"I'm afraid I've lost track of time since I've been here," Eisler replied as he squinted through the dirt-caked, and cracked windshield. "Time doesn't accrue the same way in Mexico, and I've nothing left anywhere else—so I just take it one sunny day at a time."

"Surely you must have some inkling of how long you've been here," grunted Gentry as Eisler ran the truck over a pot-hole the size of Missouri.

"It was shortly before *Seniorita* Morales gave birth to her boy," said Eisler. "So perhaps four months I've been digging. Prior to that, I'd been exiled to Brazil where I have a few holdings—the remnants of my shipping empire, so to speak; a warehouse full of cotton textiles and a small tile-roofed *casa* that I stocked with pretty, young Brazilian housekeepers, but I still couldn't seem to forget my Korrina."

Jim Anthony stared out the side window at the passing greenery, suddenly disinterested in the details of Eisler's life. Gentry suspected that the news that Maria had been less than virtuous in his absence had hit him hard. Heaven knows that Jim had been exposed to plenty of temptation during his time away from Maria—and it hadn't been until their arrival at the Morales sugar cane plantation that Gentry understood why a red-blooded man like Anthony had been ignoring the attentions of some very beautiful women over the past year—his heart had been elsewhere. Why, Julien Le Grande's daughter, Marcelline, had practically thrown herself at Anthony and he had scarcely acknowledged the gorgeous girl's existence. "We were told that General Morales had adopted the boy from a village girl without a husband."

"Eh?" Eisler wrenched the vehicle back onto the dirt track after it nearly veered off the road. "You'll have to excuse me. Perhaps I've said too much. I was told that Maria was broken-hearted over some man and rebounded with a fellow that left her high and dry when he found she was in a family way. This sort of thing happened all the time in Austria, and I didn't suppose it was any different in Mexico."

A fleeting expression of remorse crossed Gentry's face. "I suppose it could have happened to anyone."

The rest of the trip passed in an uneasy silence punctuated by Friedhelm's harsh bray which was prompted by some rude jest, thankfully drowned out by the roar of the motor and the rattle of the dilapidated truck. Anthony was lost in his own dark thoughts, and Gentry seemed to be ruminating on the dilemma of some past misdeed. By contrast, Eisler was quite cheery as wrestled with the wheel of the truck, swinging the vehicle back and forth across the road as if it were a wild bronco, and he were barely able to rein it in.

They came to a rude clearing hacked out of the dense jungle, and the crumbling remains of several ancient buildings thrust up from the debris of the dying vegetation.

"The ancient inhabitants used to build their tombs beneath their dwellings," explained Eisler. "The poorer segments of their society don't seem to have rated a burial tomb of any sort, but the wealthier were often buried with their possessions. The only way to keep the tombs safe from enterprising grave robbers was for the family of the deceased to live right on top of it. We were fortunate enough to find two tombs that had never been disturbed before by man."

"What about beasts?" asked Anthony.

"The mummy in the tomb that was discovered before I arrived was eaten to the bones by scavengers of some sort. Fortunately, the other two shaft tombs were not pilfered by carrion-eaters. I'd be happy to give you a tour of the best tomb. We're still uncovering some fabulous artifacts."

Anthony still seemed distracted. "Yes," he agreed. "That would be most helpful."

They gratefully climbed from the cramped confines of the truck's cab and stretched their limbs, while Rudiger and Friedhelm unpacked a generator from the bed of the truck and hauled it across the crumbling walls of the structure. They made repeated pulls on the starting rope and finally were rewarded as the old diesel generator coughed to life.

"Ha, ha," laughed Rudiger. "I told you I had the touch!"

Friedhelm scowled. "Perhaps with machines you are the master, but when it comes to women I am the one that has all the luck."

"I'm just pickier than you," protested Rudiger. "That woman you took up with in Brasil was uglier than a hound's tail end."

In a moment they were hurtling German epithets at each other, and were about to come to blows when Eisler interjected by barking a couple of sharp orders in his native tongue. Rudiger and Friedhelm ceased their altercation, and kept their eyes to the ground as they removed a piece of plywood that covered a pit, and lowered a wooden ladder down into the hole. Rudiger plugged an electrical line into the generator, and as Jim Anthony stood at the edge of the shaft he could see a long wire hanging with bare bulbs, that descended alongside the ladder, illuminating the dirt walls that were braced with still-green timbers.

Eisler put a foot atop of the ladder and tested it to make sure it was set sturdily at the bottom of the shaft. Once he was satisfied he began to descend. "Come on down," he called to his guests.

Anthony absently examined the press of overlapping footprints and he involuntarily hissed as he noticed a peculiarity in one of the footprints. "The jeep driver who was devoured has been here. There's the mark of a crooked hobnail here in the left heel."

"Which of the shaft tombs has he been in?" asked Eisler, his head momentarily appearing above the surface of the pit.

"Probably this one, though it's a little difficult to tell. His prints have been wiped out by the foot traffic of you and your cohorts. I also see burro tracks entering the site from the south."

"So what, exactly, is your interest in these tomb thieves, Mr. Anthony?"

Again Jim Anthony side-stepped the question. "I'm beginning to wonder if I'm on the right track at all. Perhaps you can show us the tomb, now?"

"One grand tour coming up," said Mr. Eisler with an agreeable smile and a wave. He once again descended into the shaft and was followed, shortly thereafter, by Anthony and Gentry. The ladder was constructed of lashed poles, and it creaked beneath their weight, groaning again as Friedhelm descended with a reckless dexterity that reminded Gentry of a monkey swinging through a jungle canopy.

The scent of parched earth and decay was strong in the room into which they descended. The tomb was originally constructed by lining the earth with stones, but Eisler had replaced the rotted ceiling supports with fresh timbers, which Anthony was required to duck beneath. Gentry was just short enough that he could walk beneath the supports without hitting his head, but he was broad enough that both he and his boss had difficulty passing through the narrow corridor into the next chamber, which held two ancient sarcophagi, that Eisler and his crew had been painstakingly excavated.

"This is where we made our most magnificent discovery," informed Eisler with a gesture toward the stone coffins. "Two well-preserved mummies of the ancient indigenous people, as well as a number of artifacts with which they were..."

Eisler ceased speaking as the wan light of the overhead light bulb flickered and died, plunging the room into blackness. "Ach! That generator has been nothing but problems, but it would take me six months to bring in a new one by freighter, so I'm stuck with it."

A beam of light sprang into existence from the battery-powered flashlight in the Austrian's hand. The shaft of illumination cut through the dusty motes and shone upon a squinting Friedhelm, then Eisler swung the beam around when he realized that neither of the Americans were in the same positions they had been when the overhead bulb had been extinguished. Anthony was rising from behind one of the stone sarcophagi with one hand on his belt, and Gentry had a .45 pistol in his hand.

"No need to be jumpy, gentleman," chuckled Eisler. "It's merely an electrical outage." He handed the flashlight to Gentry. "I'll make my way up top and see what the problem is. In the meantime, make yourself at home." He gave a dry chortle at his jest, and disappeared into the dim corridor, with hands outstretched.

"The two of you are like little babies, afraid of the dark," mocked Friedhelm when his boss had left the room, and the creaking of the ladder could be heard under Eisler's weight.

Gentry holstered his pistol and flexed his right hand into a fist. "I'll show you what it's like to be afraid, you little Austrian puke."

Jim Anthony had half a mind to let Gentry teach Friedhelm a lesson in manners, but there was little to be gained by a rumble in the tomb, so he spoke up. "We're a bit jumpy, Friedhelm. Once we were in a bar in Bangkok and the lights went out just before a Chinese Warlord opened up with a Thompson machine gun."

"Ah," said Friedhelm. "Well, if that is the case I would be nervous when the lights go out, also."

"I'm going to check on Eisler," said Anthony as he headed into the corridor. "If bandits or thieves were the cause of our power disruption, then Eisler could be in trouble. I'll give you a whistle if there's danger."

Anthony left short pilot with the flashlight and his sharp eyes pierced the dimness of the corridor until he emerged in the first burial chamber, a shaft of the overhead sun illuminating a myriad of motes that danced and drifted in languorous peace-- a peace that was shattered by Eisler's scream.

"Watch out, Jim. *Banditos*!" The cry of warning was followed by the crack of pistol shots, and then a stick sparked and whirled down the shaft. The moment that Jim Anthony saw the spitting stick of dynamite falling down the shaft his muscles galvanized into action and, ducking low, he retreated at headlong speed through the narrow shaft, his broad shoulders scraping dirt off the walls as he barreled headlong into burial chamber, where he knocked over a startled Friedhelm.

At that moment a deafening explosion rocked the tomb shaft, a gust of super-heated air rolling across Anthony's back, just before the narrow corridor collapsed in on itself, and dry choking dust billowed into the surviving chamber. After long moments and ringing ears, Tom Gentry retrieved his fallen flashlight and perched himself upon a sarcophagi, the beam of light casting long shadows on an already morose features.

"At least our burial plot is already picked out," he intoned.

Anthony stood and hauled a still-shocked Friedhelm to his feet. "I recognized the sound of the pistol shots. They belonged to a Luger."

"So our Mexican *banditos* have an affinity for German weaponry?" asked Gentry.

"Perhaps, but something's not fitting."

"It may be a mystery we never solve," Gentry pointed out. "Tough to do much detective work from the inside of a tomb."

"On the contrary," said Anthony. "All the keys to solving the mystery may be right here, and with isolation from the outside distractions that have been clouding my mind, I may even be able to deduce the solution to the questions of grave robbers, German guns, ancient artifacts and Nazi sightings that have been plaguing us."

"And a fat lot of good it will do us if we suffocate down here," snapped Gentry. "I'd give my left arm for a shovel."

Friedhelm sat in glum silence upon a stone the size of sailor's chest. He seemed to be considering some weighty matter, and he spoke, finally, with a quiet deliberation most unlike his usual attitude. "That may not be necessary. Scrape away the earth from that mound to your left and you'll find a canvas sheet wrapped with picks and shovels. If you don't hide them well, tools have a way of disappearing from the Mexican jungle. In a mineshaft or no..."

With the dust still settling, Gentry set the flashlight on the leftmost sarcophagi and pushed away a thin layer of earth, momentarily uncovering the stash of earth-clotted tools, which the Austrian had described. "Friedhelm, if you were a woman, I'd give you a big kiss, right now."

"Don't get any ideas."

"Don't worry, you're not my type," Gentry chuckled and he hefted a sturdy shovel and tossed it to the Austrian. "But if we get out of here alive, the drinks are on me."

Anthony took up a long pry bar and jammed it in the seam between the second sarcophagi and its heavy lid.

Friedhelm gave a cry. "Don't disturb the sarcophagi, if we're not careful the contents may be ruined."

"Why are you wasting time with a mummy?" Gentry argued. "Our efforts should go into digging out of this tomb, the mummy isn't going anywhere."

"Call it professional curiosity," said Anthony, and he heaved aside the heavy stone lid with such force that it split asunder as it toppled. Tightly nestled inside were rows of filled muslin bags.

Tom Gentry's jaw dropped when he saw the contents, and he turned his flashlight upon the Austrian's begrimed and sweating face. "What's going on here, Friedhelm?"

"I swear, I don't know," babbled Friedhlem. "*Banditos* must have stolen the mummy and used the coffin to hide those bags."

"What's in them?" asked Gentry.

Anthony thrust a knife blade into one of the bags and a rusty brown powder spilled out. "Heroin. It seems that our friend, Friedhelm, is involved in a drug smuggling operation."

"I swear, I don't know what you're talking about," Friedhelm proclaimed.

"Tom, Friedhelm is breathing our very limited supply of air. Put a bullet in his head, so that we don't have to share it."

Gentry pulled his pistol and leveled it at the Austrian. No sooner had he done this and Friedhelm went to his knees his tongue begging to spill out secrets. "Don't kill me, I beg you! I'll tell you the truth. All of it!"

"Be careful that you speak only the truth," warned Jim Anthony. "The cave-in gave my mind a jolt out of dark thoughts that were distracting me and keeping me from seeing things clearly. But now that I am thinking with some clarity I see a number of things that have been concealed from me. For example, Friedhelm, your accent is not the Upper German of Austria, but the Low Saxon German of the northern regions."

"You mean that Friedhelm is a blasted German!" exclaimed Gentry.

"Not only that," continued Anthony, "but a German kriegsmarine—a U-boat navy man accustomed to taking orders from a superior officer—namely: Mr. Eisler."

Friedhelm looked devastated at this revelation and his fingers clawed at the earth. "How, how did you know?"

"Eisler barked his order to you and Rudiger with the same tone and words of other Nazi Officers, which I've had the displeasure of encountering. Also, since the cave-in, I've had a few moments to reflect upon Eisler's comment about trading in Finland during the early 1930s with the Papenburg Shipping Concern. This was a slip of the tongue on Herr Eisler's part. Among SSA intelligence officers it has been known for some time that Germany embarked on covert minesweeping training of its Kriegsmarine Officers in Finland during the period of 1928 to 1935—and did so under the direction of three guiding officers of Brautigam, Papenburg and Freiwald.

"Eisler was under pressure to come up with a plausible alibi, shored up by bits of detail to make it seem factual. In doing so he inadvertently used a name that had a significance I eventually remembered. And you, Friedhelm, seem to have spent some time aboard a U-boat yourself, judging by the way that you so handily descended the ladder. Sure, your ease on the ladder could have been attributed to any number of things, but the lingering smell of diesel fuel was also a clue that was pushed into place when I heard Herr Eisler bark out his orders to you and Rudiger."

Friedhelm trembled, either in awe of Anthony's marvelous string of deductions or in fear of what might happen to him now that his secret had been uncovered—but then he sighed, as if a great weight had been lifted from his shoulders.

"I don't suppose it matters anymore, since we're left to die in this tomb. What happens now in the land of the living—what is it to us now that bandits have killed Commandant Eisler and left us to suffocate?"

Anthony frowned, his face a brutal map of shadows in the tomb. "I don't want you to suffer under any illusions, Friedhelm. Eisler isn't dead, and he wasn't attacked by the *banditos* you've been buying heroin from. I didn't realize it at the time, but he instructed Rudiger to cut the power so that he'd have an excuse to return to the surface and fake his death.

"We would have heard an arrival of *banditos* via motor-powered vehicle. If they arrived by horse or burro I would have heard a nickering or whinnying, and even if they were on foot, the sounds of the birds' songs would have changed."

"You can't know this," said Friedhelm. "No one can tell what the birds are saying."

"That's true," agreed Anthony, "but the tones of their warbling alters, depending upon their circumstance. Think about this, Friedhelm, did you ever hear another voice besides that of Eisler and Rudiger during this supposed *bandito* attack?"

Friedhelm replayed the moments leading up to the explosion that had caved in the shaft tomb. "I guess not," he said, his voice grudging when making the admission. "But you can't possibly know all this from a minor detail—"

Anthony cut off the German. "I can and I do. Details can be misleading when considered one at a time, but if a person pays attention to their accretion then they tell the story as accurately as the accumulation of any other type of facts. For example, I could see from the grime beneath your fingernails and in the folds of your hands that you worked with your hands—this could have led me to believe that you were employed in digging these tomb shafts as Herr Eisler claimed or perhaps I might have paid closer attention to the fact that the grime was not consistent with the color of the earth in this area of Nayarit, and that it had an oily consistency which was in keeping with the texture of machine grime."

Friedhelm stared opened mouth, and even Gentry paid rapt attention. Though he had seen Jim Anthony's displays of deduction many times before, he rarely ceased to be amazed.

"Now if I were to pay attention to the aroma of diesel fuel that clings to your clothing," continued Anthony, "then I might conclude that rather than a digger of archeology, that you were actually a mechanic of some sort. It was your misidentified accent and Herr Eisler's inadvertent clues that were the final pieces to the puzzle."

"Is there anything that you don't know?" breathed Friedhelm.

"Certainly," said Anthony, "but I'm just as certain that you will want to fill me in on any details that I haven't yet discovered. You see, Herr Eisler has left you for dead—he sacrificed your life without a second thought, so that he could dispose of Tom and I. What loyalty could you possibly have left for him?"

"I'm still a German," retorted Friedhelm with a stubbornness that Gentry found both irritating and admirable.

"Let me kill him," pleaded Gentry. "You've already deduced everything we wanted to know. Even if we do manage to get out of here alive, we won't need him."

"True enough," agreed Anthony. "Put one between his eyes."

The exchange between Tom Gentry and Jim Anthony had the desired effect and Friedhelm threw up his hands in capitulation. "I'm dead to the German Navy, anyway—am I not? Ask me what you will."

"I'm presuming that the Kriegsmarine are trading in Mexican heroin for financing, unless I am mistaken and der Führer has developed a hefty drug habit?"

"We've been running our U-boat up to a small island off the coast of Baja and meeting American drug runners. Eisler takes enough for our expenses and sends the rest to der Führer to finance his war."

"An interesting use of a military vessel," commented Jim Anthony as he drew nearer to the German his dark eyes appraising the man with a shrewdness that made Friedhelm shudder. "However, if I am correct, there is another purpose to keeping the U-boat in Nayarit—one even more sinister than drug running. The presence of the U-Boat and the discovery of dead hunters bleeding from their ears is an unlikely coincidence.

Before we left the hacienda, I radioed some inquiries about the missing Dr. Archuleta. It seems he was not a medical practitioner at all, but rather a specialist in sonic amplification exploring the 'screaming' sounds that were sometimes heard in the jungle. This leads me to believe that he believed that the screaming was not a natural phenomenon at all, but rather one of man-made origin."

Anthony looked directly into Friedhelm's eyes, their faces illuminated on one side by the flashlight's beam and thrown into deep shadow upon the other. "Correct me if I get this next bit wrong, but I'm speculating that the reason the German U-boat is biding its time here in Nayarit is that Eisler is working on some sort of sonic weapon, and that those hunters found in the woods were guinea pigs for Eisler's weapon testing."

Friedhelm didn't respond, and so Anthony continued. "Further more, I think that Eisler has captured Dr. Archuleta and is using his expertise to fine tune this weapon until it is effective enough to be brought up the coast and used against the United States."

"You're a brilliant man," conceded Friedhelm in sullen tones. "And everything you say is correct. Eisler told me that Dr. Archuleta is only a few days away from completing the sonic cannon. If you can get us out of here alive, I will show you the location of the U-boat—if you promise not to kill me or have me thrown into a Mexican jail."

Jim Anthony picked up a shovel and tossed it to the German. "Agreed, now let's start digging."

The two-way radio in the hacienda crackled insistently and again *Ministro* Morales urgent voice repeated his plea. "Maria, pick up the handset!"

Outside the stucco walls of the hacienda, Maria pushed a cart of loose hay to feed the oxen. She dropped the handles and wiped her hands on her dusty trousers. "Coming, Papa," she replied, under her breath, and she mounted the veranda, the dark fringe of her braided hair swinging across the hourglass of her waist and hips.

She kicked off her shoes and her bare feet padded across the cool tile floor of the vestibule and down the hall to the radio room in the right wing of the hacienda. When she entered the room, she drew up short and gasped. "Senior Eisler, what are you doing in here?"

Eisler discreetly dropped the pulled power cord. "I heard your father calling over the radio and came to respond. Sadly, it seems that I arrived a little too late to speak with him."

"I hope he is alright," said Maria. "I worry about him traipsing through the jungles tracking down opium growers. Perhaps I should take Jim and go find him."

"That's what I came here to talk to you about, *Seniorita*. It doesn't appear that Mr. Anthony will not be back anytime soon."

Maria's eyes narrowed into dark-lashed slits. "What are talking about? Jim is going to ask my father for my hand in marriage!"

"I'm so sorry," said Eisler. "I had no idea that he had proposed marriage. No wonder he was so upset!"

"Upset about what?"

"Well, it seems that he somehow got the idea that your adopted brother, Arturo, was actually your child—and that your virtue had been compromised in his absence. I tried to disabuse him of such a foolish notion, but he was so angry that he would hear none of it. He said that he didn't want to see your face again and demanded that I drive him to Tepic so that he might catch a flight back to the United States."

"What about his plane sitting out on the runway?" said Maria with a gesture out the window.

"Tom Gentry told me that he would be back for it in a few days. After he had seen Mr. Anthony off."

Maria felt tears welling in her eyes even as her heart seemed to rend within her, but she did not so easily give in to despair. "Senior Eisler, you must immediately take me to Tepic so I can explain to Jim the circumstances of Arturo's arrival."

Eisler nodded his head and then turned away so that Maria couldn't see the slight smile forming at the edges of his lips. "Yes, of course, Senorita Morales. I am at your service."

Unearthing the collapsed tunnel was slow and treacherous work, but they dug out a few of the fallen support timbers and used these to brace up their diggings. As they filled a couple of battered tin pails with earth, Friedhelm would haul them to the back of the burial chamber and dump the dry dirt on a growing pile.

Finally, Tom Gentry broke the somber silence. "What do you think our chances are of digging free?"

"Never question the odds when there is no way to change them," said Jim Anthony. "All we can do is our utmost, and pray that God will see fit to fill in where we are lacking."

"It seems," said the pilot, "that the only time I remember to pray is when I'm looking death in the eye."

"That's human nature." Anthony threw another spade of earth into the empty tin pail that Friedhelm had just returned.

"Speaking of human nature, have you given any thought to Maria and baby Arturo?"

"I've given them quite a bit of thought," admitted Anthony. "In fact, it was my jealousy and dark thoughts that kept me from seeing through Herr Eisler's charade earlier than I did. I realize now that Eisler's mention of Maria's motherhood was designed precisely for that purpose."

"Do you think there's any truth to it?"

"First, consider the source."

"A Nazi U-boat captain smuggling heroin on the side, while pretending to be an archeologist?"

"That's the one," agreed Anthony. "At first my jealousy kept me too close to view the facts with rational impartiality, but as I considered the details the truth became clear to me...and I think that perhaps you suspect the truth of the matter, yourself. Or that at least you feared that it might be the case."

"What do you mean?"

"I mean that the physiognomy of Maria doesn't match that of little Arturo. However, that fact wasn't entirely conclusive, because Arturo might have easily been born with his father's features—and in fact he was."

"So you're saying that Arturo is indeed Maria's child?"

"No, he's not. I noticed that Arturo is very light-skinned for a full-blooded Mexican, with a few freckles and even a tinge of red to his dark hair. It was only when I matched the physiognomy of you and Cipriana that the full story was revealed. The timing matches, too. Apparently those long walks with Cipriana weren't as innocent as we all supposed and you took advantage of her giving nature."

"Now wait a minute!" blustered the Irishman. "It takes two to tango, and..."

"And yet you failed to make her an honest woman," said Anthony. "And now, to avoid the shame of being an unwed mother she feels it necessary to pretend that Arturo is a child adopted by *Ministro* Morales. What other way is there when there is no father present to provide?"

"What are our chances of digging free?"

Gentry slammed a spade full of earth into the tin bucket. "You've certainly got a way of making a fellow feel lower than a worm's belly."

"That wasn't my intention, Tom. The two of us have been through more predicaments together than I can count, and you're like the brother I never had—but if we get out of here, you need to do right by Cipriana."

Tom Gentry blanched at the thought of giving up his life of adventure to be a married man, but at least he wouldn't be alone in his unexpected marital status. Jim Anthony was quite pleased to be leading the way with his proposal to Maria. They kept digging through the claustrophobic press of the dark earth, and at times Gentry wondered if it might be easier should the ceiling collapse and swallow him up, then to face the consequences of his rash passion.

With no sky to mark the passage of the sun, moments and hours crawled into oblivion and the passage of time became mired in their constant efforts to extricate themselves from the collapsed tomb shaft. The three of them took turns sleeping, but for how long they slept no one knew. They kept track of time only by the mountain of earth that steadily grew at the back of the burial chamber.

The batteries of the flashlight began to fade, and for a long time they worked in the dusty, fading light—until that was gone, and they dug in Stygian darkness, groping their way to and fro. When Anthony scooped out a shovelful of earth and a glimmer of illumination broke through, he shielded his light-starved eyes and then breathed in a feeble draft of oxygen rich air that was a heady reprieve from the carbon dioxide laden atmosphere of the tomb.

Then with excited cries and renewed efforts they dug their way into a pit of shattered timbers and caved walls. They emerged from their dusty grave, covered in dirt and grime and thankfully breathed in the night air—for the glimmer of light that had shown the way had been cast by the overhead moon, and glittering panoply of stars that spread above them in a dazzling sheet.

The ladder that they had descended was gone, blown into a thousand pieces by Eisler's dynamite, but a broken timber jutted from the edge of the pit ten feet over Jim Anthony's head. He removed his belt and flipped a switch on his bulbous buckle, so that the thick cord of his belt extracted even further. Then using the buckle as a weight, he slung it up and over the timber, while holding on to the other end of the belt. Once the buckle wrapped around the timber, Anthony tested the belt and, finding it firmly ensconced, pulled himself up the makeshift rope and to the top of the pit.

Friedhelm followed without too much difficulty and then Tom Gentry pulled his hulking form over the lip of the pit and gazed down into the dark recesses below. Even as he watched their tunnel caved inward, the shoring timbers collapsing under the weight of the earth above, and a plume of dust arose in testament to how narrow their escape had been.

"I guess I wouldn't make much of miner," Gentry confessed. "My handiwork leaves something to be desired."

"Working in the dark with broken timbers, what more can be expected?" excused Friedhelm. "It was enough to get us out alive and I'm overjoyed with that."

Jim Anthony surveyed the camp and found it completely empty; even the generator had been removed. "Gentlemen, we've got a long walk ahead of us—but I think we can shorten it to seven or eight miles if we can find a bridge across the *Rio Grande de Santiago*. If I recall there was an empty jeep that we might be able to borrow."

"Four miles down the road," pointed Friedhelm, "there is an intersection which leads east to a broken bridge over the *Santiago* River. It won't support a vehicle, but the locals use it."

By the light of the moon they stretched their legs down the long, rutted roadway flanked by overhanging masses of jungle made impenetrable by the dense shadows that shifted with the moon. Overhead, large bats flittered through the night sky with raucous cries guiding their way. The trio made good progress, though when they reached the split in the road, the German's steps became more tentative, his attentions drawn into the deep of the shadows where he imagined he saw movement and heard the sinister rasp of scaled coils as they slithered through the underbrush of the jungle.

Perspiration not entirely from the exertions of the hike gathered on his forehead. "Don't you hear that?"

"I hear the screeching of the bats," said Gentry. "Hard to miss...or to hear anything else."

"No, it's a snake I hear," said Friedhelm. "It's the *serpiente del monstruo* that hot little Mexican maid keeps babbling about."

"Her name's Cipriana," snapped Gentry, his words sharp like a knife. "Watch what you say about her!"

Friedhelm glanced at Gentry, but even his surprise at Gentry's cutting words couldn't long distract him from the idea that a giant serpent was tracking them through the jungle at the roadside. "It's hungry again. It hasn't fed since it devoured Gottfried."

"Was it Gottfried's remains that we found on the rocky plateau near the abandoned jeep?"

Friedhelm nodded. "We can't have escaped being buried alive, only to be eaten alive. Perhaps we're marked for death, and there is no escape—no matter how hard we fight against it."

Gentry turned to friend. "Jim, do you hear this snake? Because I don't hear a dad-blasted thing."

Jim Anthony did not directly answer, but his response shot a dread chill through the pilot, just the same. "Pick up the pace. We're almost to the bridge."

The bridge was a rickety construction strung on fraying cables that were loosening from their posts, and as Friedhelm climbed onto it he snatched the rope rail while the entire structure swayed over the black ribbon of the roaring *Rio Grande de Santiago*.

Anthony looked back to the road and saw a large shadow detach itself from the darkness of the overhanging jungle. Moonlight gleamed against scale and coil. "Hurry it up, Friedhelm. We don't have much time!"

The German felt the spray of water on his skin and swallowed back his fear of slipping and plunging into the teeth of the raging river below. He let the fear of the *serpiente de monstruo* urge him onto the swaying suspension as quick as his legs would carry him.

For a long moment the two Americans stood transfixed at the mouth of the bridge, staring into the darkness—hoping to penetrate its veil and obtain a glimpse of the fiend that pursued them through the thick of night's fog. Gentry raised his pistol and the lines of his broad face lit up as he fired a staccato of hot lead into the shadows. There was no response from the darkness, and his smoking revolver emptied, Gentry opened up the cylinder and fumbled for fresh cartridges in the pouch at his belt.

"Don't waste your lead on something you can't see," said Anthony. "Get across the bridge before Friedhelm reconsiders his promise and decides to cut the suspension cables and leave us stranded on this side of the river."

Gentry snapped his pistol closed and forged onto the wobbling bridge. "You coming?"

Jim Anthony kept twin .45 colts semi-automatics tucked into holsters at the small of his back and he unsheathed one of these, his sharp eyes peering into the tenebre. There! A glimpse of a monstrous slitted snout, flickering tongue and fangs as long as a man's forearm. Before he could fire, the glimpse was gone, again obscured in shadow, and then Jim Anthony stepped onto the bridge, his sure feet carrying him across the thundering torrents of the *Santiago*.

When he reached the other side, he found Friedhelm screaming for Gentry to fire his revolver so as to sever the cables.

"Don't bother," said Anthony, and he pointed toward the river and a gigantic form that slipped down the river banks, sinuous coils carrying it into the torrents of the river. "Something that size doesn't use a bridge. The jeep should be about a half mile from here. If we don't hurry..."

"We're going to get eaten," finished Freidhelm.

Jim Anthony took the lead, his long strides jarring him over the uneven terrain of the field as they plowed through the long grasses. He tempered his pace so as not to leave his companions behind, but kept his stride just faster than theirs so as to urge them on to greater speed.

Their lungs labored and the taste on their tongues became coppery with each desperate intake of breath, and Anthony realized that the thickness of the grass was both an impediment to their speed and to their vision. For all he knew the *serpiente de monstruo* might be slithering through the grass at their side or might even have overtaken them and be waiting for them to run headlong into its gaping jaws.

Anthony slackened his pace as he saw Friedhelm stumble in a hole, then scramble back to his feet, his leg swarming with ants that attacked the intruder with vicious bites. The German cried out in pain and slapped at the nasty insects, and Anthony paused to call out to him.

"Ignore the bites and keep running! The ants won't kill you, but the serpent—"

Friedhelm began to respond but his words were suddenly cut off as great jaws rose up from the high grasses to the left of him, then lashed out and clamped down, the saber-like fangs punching through his torso. The German gave out a great cry, but was transfixed by the fangs unable to move. In the blink of an eye, the *serpiente de monstruo* heaved convulsively and swallowed the hapless Friedhelm in his entirety. Then the beast heaved its coils into the darkness and was gone, only the blood-spattered sward and the swaying of the grasses marking its passing.

Jim Anthony and Tom Gentry marked the whispering grasses and sent a torrent of hot lead as a farewell. Their bullets were ineffective against the beast and neither had any inclination to chase after the fiendish creature.

The gunsmoke from Gentry's revolver curled up his arm. "Let's get to the jeep before that thing gets a hankering for desert."

Anthony pushed a fresh clip of ammunition into the handle of his Colt. "Agreed. I don't think we've got the firepower to stop it. Our bullets seem to glance off its scales."

They turned and beat their way through the hindering grasses, and finally they saw moonlight reflecting from the rusty carapace of the abandoned jeep that they sought. Gentry was an expert hand at hot-wiring vehicles, a product of his misspent youth, but the darkness made it difficult for him to locate the proper wires and so he spent long minutes beneath the steering column of the jeep fumbling for the proper connection, even while listening to the rustling of the grass, and fearing that the *serpiente de monstruo* might be returning to finish its repast.

Finally the ignition growled and the engine coughed to life, and Gentry eagerly crawled into the driver's seat. He pushed the vehicle into gear and gave it some gas, but the vehicle lurched forward only a few inches before its momentum was halted.

"Now we know why the driver got out of the Jeep," grumbled Gentry. "He got stuck in the soft soil."

Jim Anthony was already behind the jeep, his thick arms bent against the steel plating of the bumper. "We've got one more set of hands and legs than the driver had at his disposal. Rock the vehicle back and forth, and we'll see if we can't get this Jeep out of the mire."

Gentry gunned the engine, rolling the jeep forward, the rear tires throwing clots of earth and grass behind. He hit the clutch and let the vehicle roll back, and then accelerated again. They repeated this process a half dozen times, and Anthony found enough purchase to give a mighty thrust with his legs. That final bit of momentum gave the jeep just enough combined propulsion to get it out of its rut and back onto firmer ground.

With a grin on his face Gentry turned to congratulate Anthony—the grin melting to trepidation and fear when he saw a dark furrow forming in the grass behind them, the rustling of the grass and the slithering of scaled coils concealed by the sound of the rattling engine. "Get in the Jeep!"

Jim Anthony saw the horror on his friend's face, and he leaped over the rutted mire, stepped on the rear bumper and rolled into the back of the jeep even as the *serpiente de monstruo* rose from the dark field, its jaws snapping shut inches behind him—close enough that he could feel the charnel breath of the reptile upon him.

As soon as Anthony dropped into the back of the jeep, Gentry accelerated—the jeep headlights reflecting from the thick grasses through which they recklessly plowed, jouncing and careening and praying that they would not collide with some unseen tree or have their tire sink into an anthill, like the one that had proven Friedhelm's undoing.

For long moments the serpent pursued, as if hoping to pluck either of them from the metal beast it chased. Anthony unlimbered one of his pistols and while hanging on tightly to the bucking jeep with his left hand, fired off a flurry of rounds. The bullets ricocheted off the scaled snout of the fiend, and whined futilely into the night. Despite the lack of meaningful damage, they must have inflicted enough pain for the monstrous reptile to become discouraged, and the *serpiente de monstruo* veered off suddenly, disappearing into the surrounding grasses.

"Slow up," called Jim Anthony as they hit a rut that jarred his intestines up into his chest cavity. "Or we'll kill ourselves as surely as that monster means to kill us."

Gentry complied, but still kept the jeep moving forward at a gait that bordered on the reckless, his eyes doing their best to pierce the curtain of night that enveloped them—in case the fiendish reptile returned to take another crack at them. Eventually they were able to find a rutted track that took them to the northwest, and finally after putting miles between them and the field by the *Rio Grande de Santiago*, they began to breathe more easily.

Dawn broke, a surly gray that melted into roseate fingers of brilliant light that streaked the painted sky. It was in this dusky illumination that Jim Anthony and Tom Gentry met a procession of decamping infantry wearing the grayish brown colors of the Mexican military uniform with the stand and fall collars. A few wore French style Adrian helmets, but most of the others had doffed their headgear even before the sweltering heat of the day begin to arise.

One soldier barked a sharp order at the Jeep and waved a Mondragon seven millimeter rifle in a gesture that could not be mistaken and Gentry laid into the squeaking brakes to bring the vehicle up short.

"Get out of the vehicle and lay on the ground," barked the soldier in a rapid-fire Spanish.

The occupants of the Jeep reluctantly complied, but as Anthony stepped out of the vehicle he spoke to the man in fluent Spanish, hoping to find out why their arrival had been so unwelcome. *"Cuál es el problema?"*

"Consiga en la tierra, el bandido, o el I' lanzamiento del ll usted por completo de agujeros."

Anthony sighed and got down on his knees in the dirt as two more infantrymen rushed forward with Mondragons pointed in the newcomer's direction.

"What did he say?" demanded Gentry.

"He said," translated Anthony, "that if we don't get down in the dirt he's going to fill us full of holes. I'd get down before he starts shooting."

Gentry put his hands on the back of his head and kneeled as another soldier rushed forward and relieved him of his revolver."

The soldier brandished the pistol and made a loud proclamation. "*Son bandidos del gringo!*"

"Even I understood that," grumbled Gentry. "Tell them that we are friends of Minister Morales."

"*No somos bandidos. Somos americanos aquí en la invitación de Morales del ministro,*" explained Anthony.

There was some movement, the infantryman and a stern man in an impeccable uniform came forward. His eyes were dark and incisive, and he wore a gray mustache that matched the gray hair that protruded from beneath his cap. "So a couple of dirt-covered gringos claim to be here at my invitation? I've never seen them before in my life. Haul them off to the jail with the drug runners until we can figure out what they are doing here."

Ministro Morales paused for one last look, and his eyes narrowed with surprise. "Mr. Jim Anthony and Mr. Tom Gentry?"

"Yes, Senior," said Anthony.

Ministro Morales gestured at the soldiers and gave an order. Immediately they lowered their weapons. "These men are my friends!" said *Ministro* Morales.

As Jim Anthony stood, *Ministro* Morales embraced him and clapped him on the back, a cloud of dust arising. "It seems that you've collected half of the jungle floor."

"Your house guest, Herr Eisler, was giving us tour of a tomb shaft when he made an excuse to leave and caved it in with a stick of dynamite."

Ministro Morales frowned, but he did not appear to be surprised. "I'm afraid that Senior Eisler completely deceived all of us." He led them forward through the press of infantrymen to a group of raggedly-dressed men whose hands were bound behind their backs and who were guarded by a pair of zealous riflemen. "I didn't realize it until we managed to capture this group of drug-running *banditos.* When we started to question them, several were quite willing to spill their secrets if it meant a little leniency in the punishment of their crimes. They reported to me that they've been passing heroin to a German fellow that they meet at the tomb shafts. Eisler told me that he was an Austrian, and I believed him; he had a wealth of detail to back up his stories..."

"I believed him, too. At first," said Anthony. "He has a skill at diverting one's attention so as to spoil clear thinking."

"I tried radioing Maria to warn her, but there was no response. I'm worried that Senior Eisler may have done something to her. Unfortunately, I travel slowly on foot and especially with fifty soldiers and eight prisoners to bog me down even further."

Anthony smacked his fist into his palm. "If you are able to leave command with another man, we can take the Jeep back to the plantation. Tom can drive about as fast as anyone, I wager. And with you directing us, we won't get lost on the wrong roads."

"*Si*, let us waste no further time," agreed *Ministro* Morales and he called to a stolid man with a crooked nose and quick eyes. "Captain Alvarez, you are in charge of escorting the prisoners to the jails. I have pressing business, elsewhere."

"With these gringos?" asked Captain Alvarez, with distaste or suspicion—Anthony could not tell which.

"These gringos are like family to me," said *Ministro* Morales. "So any insult or slight to them will be taken personally by me."

Captain Alvarez saluted. "*Ministro*, I assure you there was no insult intended. I will carry out my orders."

With light in the sky and *Ministro* Morales pointing the way, Tom Gentry sent the Jeep barreling over the rutted and pot-holed back reaches of the jungle-shrouded roads.

"*Ministro* Morales," said Anthony, "There's been something I've been hoping to talk to you about."

Ministro Morales sighed. "I had an idea that this might be coming. Your letter exchanges with Maria have not gone unnoticed."

"Am I the only one who didn't realize what was going on?" interjected Gentry.

Anthony ignored his friend's interruption and forged on. "I would like your permission and blessing to marry Maria."

"You're a good man, Jim Anthony, but I've had some time to think upon this," answered *Ministro* Morales, "and I have three objections: Number one is that you are not Mexican. You have dark enough skin to be native born, but my objection is not so much one of race, but that you're a citizen of the United States and will reasonably have a desire to live there—meaning I will see very little of my daughter."

"And your second objection?"

"Is one of religion," responded *Ministro* Morales. "Maria has been raised a good Catholic girl, and I expect my grandchildren to be raised up as such."

"I have no protest against that," said Anthony. "What is your third objection?"

"You are a good man, but you live a life of danger. You've been both skilled and lucky, but that luck won't hold out forever—and I fear that Maria may become a young widow."

Anthony considered this for a moment. "To the first objection I can only promise that we'll visit frequently, and to the third objection I can make no concession. While good people suffer it is my obligation to use my skills and resources to help them, and it seems inevitable that those efforts bring me into conflict with the evil causing that suffering."

Ministro Morales face tightened, and from the language of his face Anthony anticipated that his answer was not well received. But in this case, he found that he had misread Morales expression.

"Well put, my friend. I'm pleased that my new son-in-law is a man of such moral integrity. Such a thing is worth more than all the wealth, power, or fame that this world has to offer."

A broad grin broke across Jim Anthony's face and it didn't slacken until they reached the cane fields of *Ministro* Morales' plantation. The workers had begun harvesting some of the outlying fields and everything appeared to be normal, except when they approached the hacienda Cipriana bounded from the veranda clutching little Arturo in her arms. She was followed by a handsome young man—a field foreman that *Ministro* Morales had recently hired.

"Maria's been kidnapped," wailed Cipriana. "Ignacio found this note pinned to the door of the hacienda with a kitchen knife."

The dust still roiling from beneath the tires of the Jeep, Ignacio handed the crumpled note to *Ministro* Morales.

Dear Ministro Morales,

I thank you for your hospitality during my stay in Nayarit. However, events have made it necessary for me take an early departure. I have temporarily made your daughter my guest to ensure that you do not further interfere with my plans. If you cooperate Maria will remain unmolested and be released three days from now in Puerto Vallarta. Cross me and I'll feed her to the sharks.

With great respect,
Herr Eisler.

As *Ministro* Morales read the message his face turned a dark shade of scarlet. "The fiend has the temerity to eat my bread and then violate my trust by stealing my daughter!"

"He's lying about setting Maria free in Puerto Vallarta," warned Jim Anthony. "Eisler has a U-boat tucked away in near Laguna Agua Brava. He has enlisted the help of the kidnapped Dr. Archuleta and has been working on developing a sonic weapon, which is nearing completion."

"How do you know all this?"

"Tom and I had the opportunity to speak with Heinrich at length while we were digging our way out of the collapsed tomb shaft. He was most informative once we exposed his identity as a German kriegsmarine."

Ministro Morales slammed a fist into his palm. "He was here for months and I did not realize."

"I regret that I did not realize earlier that his accent was not Austrian at all. But my point is that, despite what Herr Eisler claims, has no plans to release Maria in Puerto Vallarta. The sonic weapon is intended for use against the coastal cities of California and the U-boat will be heading northward—not south past Puerto Vallarta."

"He'll kill her," muttered Gentry. "Or worse..."

Anthony shot his pilot a dark look that indicated he should shut his mouth.

"I fear that I cannot risk going after him," anguished *Ministro* Morales. "If there is but a small chance that he is telling the truth and will release Maria unharmed, then I have to hope and pray for the best." Then he turned his sharp eyes upon Jim Anthony. "But you can go after her. Eisler thinks that you and Tom are dead and has no idea that you know of his whereabouts. Perhaps, with that element of surprise you might be able to bring Maria safely away."

Anthony clasped *Ministro* Morales hand. "I'll do my best."

They wasted little time departing the sugar plantation, heading North for Laguna Agua Brava. Gentry waved at Cipriana, but she apparently did not see his farewell and turned toward the hacienda with the field foreman. Anthony's thoughts were on Maria and the danger she was in, but Irishman's thoughts were elsewhere.

"Who is that Ignacio clown that's following Cipriana around?"

"Eh? Perhaps she's become romantically involved in your absence. You couldn't blame her. After you had your way, you left Nayarit and had no further contact with her. She had no indication that you might still have an interest. You effectively abandoned her."

Gentry grunted an imprecation that was directed more at himself than anyone else. "But Arturo's my boy. I took a close look at him when

Ministro Morales was reading the note from Eisler. The boy has the Gentry family nose."

"There's nothing that can be resolved until we return to *Ministro* Morales' plantation," said Anthony. "In the meantime try to focus on the matter at hand. I nearly got us killed earlier; because of my distraction I didn't realize what was going on."

The sun rose high in the sky, and the wind buffeting through the open top Jeep was a welcome relief from the scorching rays, as was the shade of the sheltering mangroves that towered over the roadways, which were little more than goat trails winding through thick wilderness. Soon they topped a plateau and glimpsed the glistening waters of the Laguna Agua Brava through the tree tops—a vast inland lagoon thick with egrets and surrounded by towering mangroves strung with nets of trailing, flowered vines. Heinrich had divulged that Eisler had captained the U-Boat through an ocean inlet, and through the treacherous river way so that they could carry out their sonic experiments in the isolation of the Agua Brava.

The path took them lower toward the lagoon and finally Gentry pulled the Jeep into a pull-off at the side of the road and the two of them bailed out and began cutting foliage to conceal the location of the jeep. Soon they had the vehicle covered so that it was no longer visible from the road.

As they proceeded on foot down the rugged incline a stench rose above the salty scent of the lagoon, and everywhere they cast their eyes they saw the rotting cadavers of birds and animals littering the ground.

Jim Anthony paused near the carcass of a sea-turtle and saw crusted blood around the ears of the animal. "It's the sonic weapon. They've been testing it on the jungle wildlife."

"Just imagine them using that weapon on San Francisco or Los Angeles," said Gentry. "It looks like Friedhelm wasn't blowing smoke. We're on the right track, but the lagoon is immense. I don't know how we're going to locate a u-boat—especially if it's submerged."

"The tire tracks along the path match the tracks of Eisler's truck. He's used this road many times. If he's got a crew of kriegsmarines back here then he's got to feed them somehow. They've let all the meat of these animals go to waste, so Eisler must be provisioning his crew from Tepic."

They crept down to the edge of the lagoon, and from the forest's edge they, indeed, found the battered hulk of Eisler's truck parked at the water's edge. A tarp was thrown aside from the truck, and the bed was overloaded with crates of food provisions, which were being loaded into a small boat and being ferried out into the lagoon, where they saw the conning tower of a U-boat emblazoned with the German swastika. In addition, the entire length of the craft was about two feet above the waterline. German kriegsmarines made themselves busy on its deck, in the final stages of constructing an apparatus unlike any that either Gentry or Anthony had ever seen.

The base of the weapon tower was affixed to the deck of the U-boat on hinged hydraulic rods, which would raise up the tower and the great sonic drums, which were affixed to it. There was a metal shell, currently retracted, which looked as though it was meant to slide over the entire apparatus, to protect it from the sea water when the U-boat was submerged.

"I wonder how long it takes for them to raise the weapon and make it active," muttered Gentry from his concealment. Anthony continued to work his way forward, settling behind the bole of a tree where he could get a better view.

"I'm guessing four of five minutes for the kriegsmarines to manually pump the hydraulics, and raise the speaker drums," he replied. "Even if we managed to hijack the rowboat it would take at least that long to cross. It would be best if we could wait until after dark. I can swim the distance at night and disable the weapon before they know I'm aboard."

"And Maria?"

"My duty to the United States is to destroy that weapon. Once the weapon is disabled, I'll find and rescue her. I just wish I had some evidence to show whether or not she is onboard. If I could examine the tracks along the shoreline I might be able to spot her footprint."

Gentry chuckled softly. "I've sometimes been able to recognize a women by the color of her hair, the shape of her figure, or even her legs—but never her..."

A meaty thud interrupted Gentry's musings and the pilot groaned. Anthony turned and found a statuesque blonde woman in high leather boots and a German uniform standing over his friend's slumped form. In her right hand she held a bloody pipe wrench and in her left hand she held a Mauser pistol which she pointed at the fallen pilot.

"Please don't let me interrupt your planning," laughed the woman, her English carrying a thick German accent. "I believe you were telling how you planned to disable the sonic weapon aboard the U-boat and rescue your beloved."

"You are Korrina Eisler," said Anthony. "I recognize you from the photograph. Though it appears that Herr Eisler did not tell the truth about your untimely demise."

"*Kapitän* Eisler has been known to manipulate the truth to suit his audience. I'm not dead, nor am I his wife. Though we have been known to pretend so when convenient. It seems to me that *Kapitän* Eisler also stretched the truth a bit when he told me that the two of you were dead. It was a good thing I was out watching the perimeter or you two might have waltzed in and caused all kinds of trouble."

"Will you allow me to tend to my friend? It appears he's got a nasty gash over his ear."

"Not until I'm thoroughly satisfied that you are no longer armed." Korrina continued to point her pistol at the unconscious Gentry. "I just gave him a tap, but you are going to do exactly what I tell you or your friend will earn a few extra holes. Now take off your shirt."

Anthony loosened his belt and removed his shirt and the blonde clucked appreciatively as the rippling musculature beneath was revealed. "Now I understand what that Mexican peasant girl sees in you, half-breed. Put your hands on your head and turn around slowly."

He complied, heard the crunch of twigs underneath Korrina's booted feet as she drew nearer and felt the tug at his belt as she plucked away the first of his Colt Automatics that were holstered at the small of his back. He felt the cold barrel of the Mauser press up against the back of his neck, and now that Gentry was not in danger Anthony decided to make his move.

It was always a mistake to press the barrel of a gun directly against the target that was being held captive. It gave the captive the first move, and the gun-wielder just a moment of time to react. Anthony shifted aside, spinning and driving an elbow into the side of Korinna's head. She staggered, stunned by the sudden blow, and the Mauser fell into the dark loam.

In the next moment Anthony tore off his loosened belt and wrapped it around Korrina's neck as he bore her to the ground from behind. His left knee rested on the back of her gun arm, keeping it pinned, even while he tightened the belt around Korrina's throat. Her red lips parted as she gasped for air that would not come, and finally her tongue lolled out, and she fell slack upon the ground. Anthony kept the pressure on her neck for a few moments more in case she was feigning unconsciousness and then loosened the belt. His father had taught him a chivalry toward women, and he could not bring himself to kill the Nazi, despite the fact that was what she clearly had intended that fate for them.

Anthony plucked unconscious woman's Mauser from the loam and tossed it into the lagoon. One of the Nazi Seamen, ferrying a couple crates of provisions, turned from his oars at the sound of the splash, but he saw nothing but the spreading ripple and figured it had been a jumping fish.

"She staggered, stunned by the sudden blow..."

The seaman returned his attention to his oar, and bent his back toward the U-boat.

Seeing that he was momentarily safe from discovery, Anthony replaced his belt and went to Gentry's side. The wound was a nasty gash over Gentry's ear but the pilot was starting to come out of it. His eyes were still unfocused and his words were groggy and disoriented. "Yes, the legs. It's the legs that I like."

"You got clocked, but good," explained Jim Anthony. "Are you able to sit up?"

"Darn right, I can sit up." Gentry began to push himself into a sitting position, and then immediately toppled over. He waved Anthony off when he attempted to help. "I can do this. Just give me a minute."

Anthony heard the crackle of a radio, and turned to find that Korrina had regained consciousness, and though she still lay among the foliage, she held a two-way radio in her hand and barked out a few words in German—words that Anthony well understood. "The two Americans are here! Tell Eisler to blast the jungle!"

Realizing that his sense of chivalry had just cost him the element of surprise, Anthony bounded over to Korrina and brought his foot down on the German's arm. She gave a short curse and Anthony tore the radio away. His German was good enough to communicate and he depressed the button to speak to the radio operator on the U-boat. "This is Jim Anthony. Tell Eisler that Korrina is my prisoner. If he wants to see her again he should send Maria Morales to shore in the rowboat. If the sonic weapon is deployed, then the deal is off."

"Wait a moment," replied the radio operator. There was a few moments of dead air, and then the voice of the operator returned. "*Kapitan* Eisler agrees to your proposition. He will be on deck shortly to oversee the exchange."

There was some commotion on the deck and the pair of Nazis, oblivious to what was going on, continued to plow the heavy-prowed rowboat through the waters of the lagoon. As they reached the side of the U-boat, the Nazi kriegsmarines on deck threw over straps and they began to hoist the crates onboard.

Korrina spat out a mouthful of leaves and spoke from beneath Anthony's foot. "Are you going to let me up?"

"No. For the time being you stay on the ground where I can keep an eye on you."

"Eisler will never trade Maria for me."

"Why not?" asked Anthony.

"Because he cares nothing for anyone but himself. He fools many, but I am closer to him than any—and I can see the truth."

When Maria awoke, the scent of chloroform and diesel lingered in her nostrils and a headache raged inside her skull. She was hanging by her arms in a dark room, not much larger than a closet. Her hands were bound with a rope, and the rope was strung over a pipe that ran above her head. How long she had been hanging by her arms she didn't know, but they ached fiercely, and her wrists were swollen and chafed. Somewhere she heard the thrumming of an engine, the vibrations carrying through the metal floors and walls.

She remembered that it had been Eisler who had forced the chloroformed rag over her mouth. She had fought, but the drug had sapped her strength and robbed her of consciousness. In the dim light that seeped through the corners of the doorway, Maria moved to a coupling in the overhead pipe. Here she began sawing the rope back and forth against the protuberance.

At first she saw little progress, but since she had nothing else to do she continued her efforts and finally she was rewarded when she saw that the fibers begun to fray. For how long she continued the sawing motion, she did not know. Her hands were numb and her arms were in constant pain, but she continued and eventually the last strand parted. She gave a gasp as fell to her knees, arms dropping to her side, and her wrists trailing the broken cords.

Outside the door of the closet she heard booted feet ringing on the walkway, and the guttural sounds of the German language. She heard the rasp of chain against the door handle and heard the hasp of the lock release. Maria leaned forward on her haunches, and just as the door began to open she launched herself outward—pushing it open so that it slammed into one of the Nazi seamen outside.

The kriegsmarine staggered back, clutching at a broken nose and Maria ran headlong into the body of the second sailor. He clawed at her back, trying to get a grip on her but in the frantic seconds that followed she managed to pull loose the Luger pistol from the leather holster at his belt and she pulled the trigger twice. The body of the kriegsmarine jerked as the bullets plowed through him, and he staggered back against the metal wall of the narrow corridor. As he slid to the floor with a groan, leaving a trail of crimson on the wall, Maria turned and fired three shots past the gap between the open door, and into the seaman with a broken nose. He dropped like a rag doll, the shots still ringing in Maria's ears.

Maria breathed heavily—her exertions, the fear and adrenaline making her tremble. She knew that she must be on a ship of some sort, but where she did not know. Cries filtered down the corridor and she knew that her escape attempt had been too loud to go unnoticed. She was unfamiliar with the pistol and didn't know how many rounds she still carried, nor did she know how many foes might be lurking around the corner.

On the shore the faint pop of gunshots came to Jim Anthony's ear, and for a moment he diverted his attention from the buxom blonde officer beneath his heel. It was a moment too much, and with surprising strength, Korrina heaved to her feet. Throwing Anthony off balance. Maybe it was Anthony's chivalry that caused him to hold the fire of his pistol for a moment, or perhaps he didn't have a clean shot, but Korrina lunged at him. She must have had a switchblade hidden among her clothing, because now it was in her hand—the tip of the wicked blade cutting a furrow across Anthony's torso as dodged the worst of the blow.

The ground gave beneath his feet and he fell hard on his back. In an instant the German hellcat was astride him, the switchblade pressed against his carotid artery. "Love makes you weak," she snapped. "You're too worried about your peasant girl to keep an eye on the threat under your own feet."

Korrina pressed down the blade and Jim Anthony felt a sharp jab of pain, but the artery was never sliced. Anthony heard the double report of a .45 revolver, and two vermillion blossoms erupted on the blouse of Korrina's uniform. She coughed, and blood as crimson as her lips trickled from her mouth. Her eyes became glazed and she toppled as Anthony pushed her aside.

He rose to his feet and found Tom Gentry still aiming the smoking revolver that had killed Korrina.

"That chivalry garbage is going to be the death of you, yet," he croaked. "It's a good thing you've got me around to watch your back."

"Yes, it is, Tom. Can you walk?"

"I think so, but I'm not going to be particularly steady on my feet."

"Get back to the Jeep and hightail it out of here. Tell *Ministro* Morales where we found the U-boat."

"What about you?"

"I'm going to get Maria back, or die trying."

A German kriegsmarine peeked around the corner of the corridor and Maria fired off a shot that ricocheted down the metal hallway. The German promptly pulled his head back and Maria leaned over the corpse of the broken-nosed sailor at her feet and recovered his pistol. Then she scuttled back into the closet where they had confined her, considering that it would be much better cover than if she stood exposed in the middle of the corridor.

She was holed up in the closet, peeking out the metal rim of the portal when she heard a voice that she recognized, the deep and accented tones of Senior Eisler.

"Maria, you are proving to be far more resourceful than I gave you credit for! However, I have a moral dilemma and if you'll stop firing for a few moments perhaps you'll be able to help me decide the best course of action."

"I have no time for any more of your lies," shouted Maria.

"No lies, no tricks," said Herr Eisler. "In fact, you may keep your gun and make me your hostage until I've explained my dilemma. Then, if you decide I've dealt unfairly with you, you are free to shoot me."

Maria licked her lips, long strands of her dark hair hanging across her face. "Come out then, and tell me of this dilemma."

Eisler appeared from around the corner at the end of the corridor. He wore a German Captain's uniform and held his hands in front of him with his palms open and empty. For a moment Maria was tempted to shoot him, but she was no cold-blooded killer—and even now, though she had acted purely in self defense, she shook with terror at the death she had inflicted on the German seamen who had come to take her from her imprisonment.

"Before you make any decisions," said Eisler, "I want you to come up to the conning tower and see with your own eyes what I have seen."

"Conning tower? Where have you brought me?"

"You're on a submarine," Eisler answered. "A German U-boat of which I am the commander."

"You're a German? You've deceived me and my father since the beginning, why should I now believe anything you say?"

"Precisely why I want you to see this with your own eyes. It seems that Senior Anthony was so disappointed by your infidelity that he has taken up with a European tramp that he discovered in Tepic."

"I wasn't unfaithful," snarled Maria. "It was more of your lies!"

Eisler shrugged. "A mere misunderstanding—a faulty conclusion to which Senior Anthony jumped, perhaps. But don't let my words sway you. Come see the evidence of your own eyes. It is ironic that he should bring her sight-seeing in the very lagoon where we have secreted my U-boat, so imagine my shock when..."

"Enough!" Maria cried out. "Let me see for myself."

"Very well," Eisler said turning. "I will lead the way, but mind you watch the trigger to that gun. I see you've a very lethal temperament—it's no wonder that Anthony gave you up with so little effort. He must have been aware of your flaws of character."

"I'm the one holding the gun, Nazi. You best watch your tongue."

"Consider me duly reminded of my peril." A slight smile played at the edge of Eisler's lips as he led the way through a maze of diesel-scented corridors and to a ladder that mounted the interior of the conning tower.

Maria managed to climb the ladder with one hand, keeping her pistol trained on Eisler's posterior as he climbed ahead of her. The plethora of armed kriegsmarine below and above made her very nervous, but as long as her gun remained aimed at their commander they kept a respectful distance and made no move toward their weapons.

The fragrance of the water and the lush vegetation that grew thick around the edges of the lagoon carried away the scent of diesel, and Maria felt the warmth of the sun against her skin as they emerged from the portal atop the conning tower. Only one other kriegsmarine shared the top of the conning tower, holding a machine gun and wearing a bandolier of grenades. A number of other German seamen worked on the deck below, hauling in goods from a small rowboat.

Maria kept the muzzle of her weapon trained on Herr Eisler. "Where is Jim?"

Eisler motioned in the direction of the south shore and handed her a pair of binoculars.

Maria accepted them and motioned with her head. "Stand against the rail so that I can see you even as I look through the binoculars."

She put the glasses to her eyes and her heart leaped within her when she saw Jim's face. He stood bare-chested among the foliage, and then her heart rent in twain when she saw him kneel and lean over the form of a voluptuous blonde woman that lay in the tall grass next to him. She gasped and would have continued to view the scene that was playing out, except that Eisler pushed the binoculars away.

"Such a thing is not for the eyes of one with delicate sensibilities," advised Eisler. "He is so blinded with passion that he is not yet aware that we have emerged and that there are observers to his sordid affair."

Maria dropped the binoculars and they clanked against the metal plates of the tower, the right lens shattering. Her vision swam before her and she lowered the pistol.

Eisler pried it from her fingertips and spoke into her ear. "I have the means to rectify Mr. Anthony's sleight against you, Maria. One of you I will let live and the other must die. Say the word, and it will be Jim Anthony that dies."

"And how will he die?"

"Oh, most horribly; I assure you, Senorita. It will not be a pleasant death. Blood will pour from his ears and his eyes will burst from their sockets."

Maria's face was impassive. "Perhaps you have confused me with another vengeful woman you may have known. Even if Jim Anthony is not the man that I was sure he was, I will not become worse than he out of spite."

Herr Eisler's calm visage twisted into a mask of anger when he saw that all his subtle lies had not marred Maria's virtue. He produced a small metal vial from within the breast pocket of his uniform. "Maybe, you don't understand the other option, Senorita Morales. If you do not drink this flask of poison and sacrifice your oh-so-virtuous life for that of the unfaithful rogue, Anthony, I will surely unleash the powers of this submarine upon him."

Maria's dark fingers suddenly snatched the flask from Eisler's grasp. "If you do not understand my words, then let my actions speak." She threw back her raven hair and guzzled the dark poison so that it burned down her gullet. She felt the effects immediately; black spots appeared in her vision and her knees buckled beneath her so that she stayed on her feet only by clinging to the rail.

Herr Eisler's dark form blocked her view. "I thought I could break you as easily as Dr. Archuleta, but you've proven yourself as virtuous as you claimed. That poison was developed by some friends of mine who run the Jew camps in Germany. You've only a couple of minutes left Senorita Morales."

Maria turned and all she could see between her blots of blackening vision was the grinning kriegsmarine clutching his machine gun. "I go to a better place," she gasped. "One without cruel men and vicious tyrants."

Eisler laughed and called to the deck below. "Dr. Archuleta, one last test of the *Schreihammer* before we embark for the shores of California!"

Dr. Archuleta frowned, but then nodded his acquiescence. He called to the German sailors. "Prime the hydraulic lifts for the Scream Hammer!"

While the hydraulic arms began to lift the sonic drum and sailors scrambled to hook the power cables into the U-boat's engines Eisler turned toward the shore, ignoring Maria as she sagged against the rail. He saw Korrina's body still laying in the grasses, but there was no sign of Anthony.

Eisler knew that on full power the *Schreihammer* was capable of penetrating six miles inland, but that was only five or six minutes if that pesky pilot was driving, and Eisler didn't want to take the chance that the two Americans might escape and warn *Ministro* Morales of the U-boat's location. There was only a very narrow outlet back to the sea and if *Ministro* Morales were to drop a few mortar shells into the inlet while the U-boat passed they would never make it back to the Pacific Ocean. "Quickly! I'll shoot any man I see lagging!"

The sailors redoubled their efforts to at least appear as though they were frantically busy, but there wasn't much they could do to speed the hydraulic arms. They lifted at their own languorous pace, pushing the sonic drums aloft and trailing thick power cables.

Then the machine gunner in the conning tower shouted to Eisler. "There's something in the water!"

Eisler glanced to the clear water of the lagoon and saw a muscular form gliding below the surface, pulling himself toward the U-boat with powerful strokes. "It's Anthony. Shoot you fool!"

The machine-gunner took aim, but as he placed his finger on the trigger he felt something tug at his shoulder. He glanced back and found Maria holding a pin-less grenade that she had plucked from his bandolier.

Eisler dove from the conning tower, his foot catching on the rail so that he spun awkwardly to the deck below—his ankle snapping when he hit. The machine-gunner was less fortunate; he spun and back-pedaled in fear, then fell through the open hatch in the conning tower. Maria tossed the live grenade in after him and covered her head with her arms.

A series of deafening explosions rocked the U-boat, drowning out the screams of the kriegsmarines within, and flame gouted from the open hatch followed by black, billowing smoke. The *Schreihammer* was erect now and the sonic drum ready for deployment, but Dr. Archuleta was shaken and unsure whether he should command its firing and at what target.

At this moment of panic and confusion, Jim Anthony pulled himself from the water and onto the rowboat next to the U-boat. He ducked under the blow of the first Nazi, taking the hit on his shoulder, and then his mauling fists laid out the two oarsmen—one plunging into the water, and the other falling unconscious across the spine of the boat.

Anthony grabbed hold of a hoist line and scaled the rope with a remarkable alacrity for such a large man. Within a few moments he swung onto the deck of the U-boat and found himself amidst a profusion of confused Nazis. When they saw a half-naked man, drop, dripping wet, among them, they were momentarily taken aback. Anthony used this split second of indecision to plow in amongst them.

In a few moments of surprise that were afforded him, Anthony dropped two sailors to the deck, unconscious. He was a very strong man, but he knew that he couldn't hold out long against the numbers that now assailed him. In his zeal to rescue Maria he had acted rashly, and now he was in the thick of things with little hope of reprieve. He had retrieved his .45 automatics from Korrina while she lay dying and before the press of fists and bodies became overwhelming he drew them and began to fire into the crowd. Bodies fell away from him like wheat before a scythe, and then his guns were empty and their barrels smoking.

"Fire the *schriehammer!*" shouted Archuleta.

A German technician flicked the switch and a sonic scream shredded the sky. Birds plummeted from the air and shallow-swimming fish floated to the surface. Even though Anthony and the kriegsmarines were below and behind the cone of deadly sound, the high-pitched shriek was nearly unbearable. Sailors went down on their knees, clutching at their ears while Anthony staggered to the *schriehammer* apparatus. With face wracked in agony he grabbed hold of the rubber-coated power cable and exerted all his strength. The muscles stood out taut in his body and then he tore the sparking cable free and tossed the end over the side of the U-boat.

The scream of the *schriehammer* died and a great pop sounded from within the hull of submarine as the electrical system shorted out and went dead. Anthony spotted Maria on her knees atop the conning tower, her head leaning against a bottom rail, black hair draped like a funerary curtain.

With ringing ears, Anthony moved to the conning tower and the stunned German sailors made no move to stop him. He mounted the ladder and gathered Maria's limp form in his blood-spattered arms. Her breath came in shallow gasps, and her eyes could scarcely focus upon his face as he cradled her near.

"Jim," she gasped. "Tell me that you've always been true."

"How could you doubt my love for you?" he asked gently.

"Just tell me," she said. "And know that I've been true to you."

Then Jim Anthony told her of his undying love and loyalty, but his words fell on the ears of the dead, for she gave her last gasp. Her body shuddered and her soul departed. With the terrible anguish upon him, Anthony muttered a vow—for he knew that to love another woman could only bring death and misery.

When he finally stood, he screamed out his rage. The Germans cowered, not daring to further incur his wrath. The fight had gone out of them. Some sat despondently on the deck and others abandoned the smoking U-boat, hoping to swim to shore and lose themselves in the jungle.

Anthony noticed the row-boat crossing the lagoon and nearing shore. Herr Eisler leaned into the oars, driving the boat across the carcass strewn waters as fast as he could push the craft. Then, unbeknownst to Herr Eisler, trees and vegetation wavered along the shoreline, moving as if before a massive bulk pushing its way through.

Anthony saw the shuddering leaves and Dr. Archuleta spotted the movement, too. Anthony could hear the doctor's whispered words rising from the deck below. "The *serpiente monstruo!* The schriehammer has again disturbed its slumber..."

Herr Eisler drove his boat onto the shore and then dragged himself onto the bank. Standing, he hopped on his right leg to avoid putting weight on his broken ankle. He turned and took one last look at his U-boat and the smoking column that rose into the sky. Then the vegetation parted and fanged jaws unhinged and swallowed him up. The sun gleamed against scaled coils as they undulated through the jungle growth, and then the serpent was gone, with Eisler slowly digesting in its belly.

The noonday sun beat mercilessly on the square in Tepic, and Dr. Archuleta and eleven Nazi sailors swung from the gibbets. Jim Anthony turned away from the grim sight as Tom Gentry pulled the Jeep next to him.

"Time's a-wasting," said Gentry. "I need to put some wind beneath me."

"In a minute," said Anthony. "I need to pay my respects to *Ministro* Morales."

The *Ministro* came up aside of Anthony and laid his hand on the American's shoulder. "That's not necessary. You've done good work here and I still believe you're a good man. I wish you the best, but I pray that our paths don't cross again. Seeing you will only remind me of the daughter that I no longer have."

"And seeing you will only remind me of the love that I have lost," said Anthony. "Fare thee well." He climbed into the open Jeep and they left behind the city and the outskirts before either of them spoke a word.

Gentry broke the long silence. "I talked to Cipriana. Apparently her family isn't too keen on their daughter marrying a gringo—and she's taken up with Ignacio, the field foreman. They'll be getting married next month, it seems."

"What do you think of Ignacio?"

Gentry shrugged. "Not much at first, but I have to admit it was just jealousy. He's a great guy and a hard worker and he obviously loves Cipriana. He's agreed to adopt Arturo as his own son."

"And how do you feel about that?"

"I have mixed feelings, but it's probably best for Arturo that he has the chance to grow up with a mother and father in the same home."

"Yes," agreed Jim Anthony, and his thoughts turned back to Maria—the ghost of her face, figure and scent haunting him in the light of day, even as it would in the lonely nights for many years to come.

The End

From Jim's Early Days

When Airship 27 offered me the chance to take a crack at writing a Jim Anthony story I decided I'd better do my research on the character. So I decided to read a couple of the original tales and see what inspiration might strike me. I purposely avoided reading any of the later 'pastiche' stories, because I wanted my own pastiche to be based on my impressions of the real Jim Anthony—and not someone else's perception of Jim Anthony.

The pair of novels I read were Legion of Robots and Murder's Migrants—the former being an early Jim Anthony book and the latter being a story from late in his career. I quickly found that there was quite a dichotomy between the two. Legion of Robots was more fantastic in content and presented Jim Anthony as a Doc Savage style of hero with extraordinary strength and abilities and Murders Migrants dealt with less fantastic themes and, in hardboiled style, left Anthony framed for murders he did not commit.

For my story I opted to take a route somewhere in between, allowing Jim Anthony his great deductive abilities and strength, but grounding him in the real world with World War II raging in Europe. However, I didn't entirely abandon the fantastic—and introduced a sonic weapon and a giant serpent.

The inspiration for The Scream Hammer struck me when I was reading Legion of Robots and Tom Gentry has fallen head over heels for Jim's new secretary, the leggy Linda Tabor. Unfortunately, for Tom, Linda Tabor has eyes only for Jim Anthony, but Tom plans to change her mind by telling her about a Spanish woman named Maria Flores who killed herself over Anthony. However, Linda will believe nothing bad about about Jim Anthony and so in a fit of pique Tom decides to quit his job as Anthony's pilot and right-hand man.

This intrigued me and I wondered about the story behind this brief mention of the unfortunate Maria Flores. Apparently, at one time, Jim Anthony had sworn never to love a woman (presumably because of the danger his occupation) but later on he seems to have amended this vow in favor of engagement with the lovely Dolores Colquitt, the daughter of Senator Colquitt and a trained psychiatrist. (By the way, Linda Tabor knew all about this engagement and despite the fact that Anthony showed no interest in her, other than professional, she still set her sights on him).

I wondered if perhaps this Maria Flores might have been the reason that a red-blooded man like Anthony might have made the drastic vow to never love a woman, and then I set out to tell that tragic tale.

Somewhere along the line I decided that Flores was Maria's middle name and Morales was her last, and I decided that Spanish meant that she was of Spanish descent and placed The Scream Hammer in Mexico. By the end of the tale I quite liked Maria and I hated to see her die, but her fate was already cast and the tragedy was inevitable.

JOEL JENKINS, his lovely wife, and his clan of troublemakers live in the heron-haunted hills of the Great Northwest. A former lead singer for such bands as Red Dye #5 and Static Condition, he now gets his creative fix by telling tall tales. His books include the sword and sci-fi Dire Planet series, the guns and guitars thriller The Nuclear Suitcase, the supernatural detective novel Devil Take the Hindmost, two City of Bathos dark fantasy novels and a children's book called The Pirates of Mirror Land.

For more information and disjointed ramblings about his latest projects visit Jenkins' blog at JoelJenkins.com.

UNDER A COMANCHE MOON

by Frank Byrns

Jim Anthony's eyes snapped open, instantly awake.

He had always been a light sleeper, going back to his boyhood. His subsequent globetrotting adventures as an international man of action had only deepened this trait. Fully alert, he listened carefully, training his ears towards the hallway outside his bedroom, towards the movement there that had awakened him.

Anthony's "sixth sense" was turning backflips in the pit of his stomach. Some would say that this extra something was nothing more than pure instinct, but Anthony knew it was more than that. Whatever it was called, Anthony had an unerring ability to detect when things were about to take a turn for the worse. And the way he felt right now, things were about to head south quickly.

A soft rap at the bedroom door sent Anthony's right hand creeping across the sheets towards the bedside table, where a small Derringer lay hidden in the top drawer. No, he thought, that won't be necessary—if someone had broken into Penthouse A intent on doing him harm, they certainly wouldn't be knocking at the door. But he unlocked the drawer anyway. Just in case.

"Excuse me, Sir?"

Anthony withdrew his hand from the gun drawer, recognizing the voice in the hall. "Yes, Dawkins?" he called.

The door cracked open, and Anthony's long-standing manservant stuck his head into the room. "I hate to disturb you, Sir," Dawkins said, "But there is a pair of local constables waiting in the parlor that wish to speak with you."

Anthony noted the time on the tall grandfather clock in the corner of his room: just past four o'clock. "Clearly an urgent matter," he said, stifling a yawn.

"Clearly indeed, Sir." Despite the hour, Dawkins was dressed in his usual working attire. Dark suit, tails, tie perfectly in place. Not for the first time, Anthony wondered if his man slept in that suit.

Anthony swung his powerful, tree-trunk legs over the side of the bed, sliding a bathrobe on over the strap t-shirt and shorts he slept in. He ran a meaty paw through his thick mane of dark hair in an effort to clear the final remnants of sleep from his brain. "I'll put on some coffee, Sir," Dawkins said before retreating silently towards the kitchen.

Anthony completed his late night ensemble by sliding on a pair of hard-soled slippers, then followed Dawkins down the hall towards the parlor. He entered the room and saw that there were indeed two policemen waiting for him, watching the nearly-empty streets some forty-four stories below through a large bay window.

One of the detectives was unfamiliar; an earnest, clean-cut, fresh-faced boy, really, one Anthony quickly pegged as a Midwesterner. His partner, though, needed no introduction to Anthony. Short, a little round, a pair of steel-rimmed spectacles resting atop a bulbous gin blossom of a nose. His rumpled jacket and wrinkled trousers led Anthony to wonder if he, too, had slept in his suit. Both men turned as Anthony entered the room; the more familiar of the two spoke. "Well, well, if it isn't the world-famous Jim Anthony, Super-Detective," Detective Reynolds Pearce said.

Many of New York's Finest appreciated the help that Anthony had afforded them on many cases over the years; in fact, several members of the force were card-carrying members of the Anthony Legion, a loosely-organized network of men from all walks of life, ready and willing to provide Anthony information and other resources to crack a case whenever he sounded the Anthony Call. Others, though, were not as thankful; they felt Anthony was a dangerous, reckless vigilante, someone who would be better served to leave crimefighting work to the 'trained professionals'. Detective Pearce stood squarely in the latter camp. Anthony had clashed with him over the course of several investigations in the last few months.

"Detective Pearce," Anthony said cheerfully. "Not exactly the face I was hoping to wake up to."

Pearce squatted down towards the parlor's large fireplace, lighting a cigarette on the dying embers from the previous night's flame. "Believe me, Anthony, the feeling's mutual. You're a poor substitute for my old lady any day of the week."

"I should hope so," Anthony said. "Well, now that we're all awake, maybe you'll tell me what I can do for you fellows this evening. . . or should I say morning."

Puffing on his cigarette, Pearce rose to his feet. He shrugged. "I was going to wait until your man brought in the coffee, but if you insist—I believe you know Miss Argentina Devine?"

Anthony ran a hand along his granite jaw—clearly, this was not a question he was expecting. "I know Miss Devine, yes."

Anthony knew a lot of the women on the Gotham social scene. As the publisher of The Daily Star, one of New York's numerous dailies, he spent many evenings at one charity benefit or another, Broadway premieres and the like. Easy access to the most eligible—and most beautiful—maidens in town was definitely one of the more enjoyable perks of the job.

Pearce nodded. "And when was the last time you saw the lady?"

Anthony's sixth sense did a triple-gainer, landing even deeper in the pit of his stomach. "I had dinner with her last night, as a matter of fact. And judging by the smug look on your face, I'd wager you already knew that— You mind telling me what this is all about?"

Pearce nodded again, clearly enjoying himself. "What time would you say you last saw Miss Devine?"

"Well, let's see—I'd say I dropped her at her building a little before midnight, maybe? Again, I have to ask you—What is this is all about?"

"And that was the last time you saw her? No. . . nightcap for a legendary playboy like yourself?"

"Miss Devine is hardly that kind of woman, Detective—has something happened to her?"

"Yeah, you could say that." Pearce squared his shoulders, and found himself looking up into the eyes of the much larger Anthony. "Miss Devine is dead."

❋ ❋ ❋

"Dead?" Anthony sank into the nearest chair, its fine leather groaning under his massive frame. "How can that be—I just saw her last night."

Argentina Devine was the daughter of a South American beauty queen and the United States' former ambassador to Argentina, hence her rather exotic name—and rather exotic good looks. Dusky-hued with long, raven tresses, Argentina had moved to the Big Apple a few months prior, and had caught Anthony's eye long before a mutual acquaintance—The Clarion's publisher Frank Havens—had set them up on a date. As a rule, Anthony hated to be set up socially like that, but had made an exception for the stunning young beauty.

And now she was dead.

"Dead?" he said again, to no one in particular. Anthony looked up suddenly, directing his next statement at Pearce. "You can't think I had anything to do with this."

"You tell me, Super-Detective. As best we can tell, you were the last person to see Miss Devine alive."

"That is preposterous," Dawkins said as he entered the parlor carrying a tray with three fresh mugs of coffee. Pearce's young partner, who had yet to as much as introduce himself, helped himself to a cup. The other two sat steaming on the tray, untouched.

Pearce shrugged again, blowing smoke towards the parlor's high, vaulted ceiling. "Maybe so. We're just covering all our bases here."

"And just what kind of motive would you attribute to me, supposing that I were your killer?" Anthony asked, finally finding his voice again.

"Oh, I don't know. You said it yourself—Miss Devine wasn't that kind of girl. Maybe you thought she was, before your date, and then you get up to her place, find out firsthand that she wasn't. And that didn't sit well with you—shelling out all that money for dinner, dancing. . . Famous playboy like you—big guy like you—I can see you losing your temper."

"To suggest that Mr. Anthony is even capable of something like—"

"Spend a couple days with me, Jeeves," Pearce said, cutting off Dawkins' protestations. "Won't be long until you believe that anybody is capable of anything." Pearce turned, blew a smoke ring in Anthony's direction. "Even a Super-Detective."

"I can assure you that Mr. Anthony returned here to the Penthouse no later than 12:15 last night—what's your estimated time of death?"

Pearce smirked. "Your very livelihood depends on Anthony's generosity—hardly a credible alibi."

Anthony finally stood, unfolding his full frame to tower over Pearce. To his credit, the detective didn't flinch. "Are you asking me for an alibi?"

"I don't know—do you need one?"

Anthony held Pearce's stare for a long, uncomfortable silence. Finally, Anthony broke the standoff with a smile. "Look, it's late," he said. "Or early, I suppose. I know you're not here to charge me with anything, or you would have already done so. Why don't I come down to the station later this morning and we can sit down and sort this whole thing out." Anthony reached down for one of the coffee mugs, downing it in three quick gulps. "What's important here is that we focus on Miss Devine, and spend our energies towards finding whoever is responsible for this tragedy."

"I am focused on Miss Devine, Anthony, and I don't want you spending your energies anywhere near this case. Is that clear?" Pearce turned to his partner. "Let's go. We'll reconvene with Mr. Anthony in a few hours."

Anthony nodded. "Let's say nine? Your place, this time?"

Pearce headed for the door without responding, his partner trailing behind. Dawkins was there ahead of them to hold the door open, ever proper. Pearce nodded at Dawkins as he passed out into the hall. His partner, however, stopped in the doorframe, then turned back to Anthony.

"One last thing, Mr. Anthony," he said, pulling a small notebook from the inner pocket of his jacket.

"Certainly, Detective. . . I don't believe I caught your name."

"You didn't." The farmboy flipped through his notebook. "Now, admittedly, you are one of the smartest, if not *the* smartest, men in this city."

"I don't know that I would say—"

"False modesty aside, I was hoping you could help me out. I found this at the crime scene, and I was stumped. I asked everyone there, and nobody could tell me what it was. But then I thought, you know what? We're going to see Jim Anthony. If anybody knows, he's the one. So." He held the notebook towards Anthony, sharing with him a single word written across the page. "Think you could help me out?"

Anthony read the word—there was no mistaking its meaning. His sixth sense bounced off every wall of his stomach, up into his throat, and back again. "Where did you find this word?"

"It was written on Miss Devine's carpet—in her blood. You know it?"

"It's Comanche."

The young detective raised an eyebrow. "Yeah?"

"It means 'I'm sorry.'"

❊ ❊ ❊

At precisely 6:10 every morning, Dawkins took the private Penthouse A elevator down the forty-four stories to the lobby of the Waldorf-Anthony Hotel. From there, he exited the building and hustled across the street and up the block to Dickie's newsstand, nestled in the shadow of Mollari's Steakhouse. He said his morning greetings to Dickie, an old friend who had returned home from The Great War nearly twenty years ago with enough of the Kaiser's shrapnel in his leg to open a junkyard and enough money in his pocket to open this newsstand. Dawkins then picked up one copy of each of New York City's myriad daily newspapers: The Herald, The Times, The American, The World, even The Daily Mirror. And, of course, Jim Anthony's own Daily Star.

Dawkins paid Dickie an even dollar for the bundle, then hustled back across the street, into the elevator, and back up to Penthouse A, where he spread the newspapers across the dining room table for Anthony's 6:30 breakfast. If he had time, he glanced through the headlines, placing the ones he thought Anthony would find most interesting towards the top of the pile.

The early morning police visit had already ruined today's schedule, so Dawkins didn't mind (too much) that he was a couple of minutes late, laying the papers on the table at 6:32. Anthony was still in his laboratory, where he had retreated as soon as the detectives had left a few hours prior.

Dawkins quickly scanned the headlines as he arranged the newspapers, humming softly to himself. He stopped his show tune mid-note when he saw the forty-eight point headline screaming above the fold in The Daily Mirror:

GOTHAM SOCIALITE MURDERED

And just below it, in even larger type:

JIM ANTHONY PRIME SUSPECT

Jim Anthony's laboratory was a testament to futurism. From this room, by far the largest in Penthouse A, Anthony had conceptualized and devised numerous devices that had helped him crack untold numbers of previously unsolvable cases. In addition to every piece of bleeding edge technology imaginable, the lab also housed one of the most impressive scientific libraries on the planet. Biology, ecology, psychology—the inventory of –ology texts alone was staggering. Mix in the philosophy, history, linguistics, and everything else? A truly remarkable collection. Even more remarkable, Anthony had read them all. More remarkable still? He remembered them all—every page.

Hunched over his desk, Anthony's back was to Dawkins as the faithful valet silently entered the lab, clutching The Daily Mirror's front page to his chest. Since entering the lab, Anthony had traded his robe for more familiar garb consisting of a sweatshirt and a pair of yellow swim trunks. A large tome was spread open on the desk in front of Anthony, and he pored over it intently.

"My grandfather believes that the Numunuu tongue is dying, Dawkins," Anthony said without looking up from his book. "With each generation that passes, fewer and fewer speak it—and even less Comanche than that can read and write the old words."

"And how many of them were in New York last night?" Dawkins added.

Anthony spun his chair around to face Dawkins. "Only one that I know—my grandfather is up at The Teepee."

"A linguistics professor at Columbia, perhaps? NYU?"

Anthony shook his head. "Maybe. But I just can't shake this feeling that that word was meant for me."

"I've certainly learned to trust your instincts over the years, Sir—you think someone's trying to frame you?"

"No, I don't think so. I think it was a message."

"From who?"

Anthony stood up from the chair, stretching his impossibly-wide back. "Well, that's the question now, isn't it?"

"Indeed, Sir." Remembering the newspaper in his hands, Dawkins clutched it to his chest even tighter, suddenly unwilling to bear even more bad news to his employer.

"What do you have there that you're not showing me?"Anthony asked, forcing the issue. "Is that The Daily Mirror I see? What kind of garbage is Hearst foisting upon our fair city this morning?"

Dawkins sighed, then spun the paper around slowly, giving Anthony a good view. The large headline was clearly visible despite the cavernous size of the laboratory. The article itself was barely longer than the headline; not surprising, given the immediacy of the story and the lack of solid fact. Not that that ever stopped William Randolph Hearst's Daily Mirror.

"Hearst," Anthony said, shaking his head. "They must have pulped the first run, then gone back to press when news of Miss Devine's murder broke."

"It's unconscionable, is what it is. Lumping you in with Daddy Browning and the like."

"Well," Anthony said, smiling thinly. "You know what they say about the Mirror. Ninety percent entertainment, ten percent news."

"If that. I wonder if this won't backfire on The Mirror? Surely none of the millions of Anthony true believers would spend a penny on this rag after this?"

"I would hope not, Dawkins—why don't you go wrap some fish with that?"

"Certainly, sir—your breakfast?"

"Oh, I'm sorry, I already ate—I sampled some of the Anthony Rations I've been working on. They're almost right—couple more tweaks and they'll be ready for the military boys. Has Tom returned from the Teepee yet?"

"No, sir—he and your grandfather should be here any minute now. I'm sure Mr. Gentry is racing across town as we speak, poor Mephito scared to death in the passenger seat beside him."

"Good. Let me know as soon as they arrive."

"Certainly."

Dawkins began folding the paper underneath his arm—then Anthony changed his mind. "On second thought, I'd like to hang on to that," Anthony said, reaching for the tabloid.

Dawkins nodded—he had learned to trust Anthony's second thoughts as much as his instincts. "As you wish, sir."

Anthony unfolded the paper once more, looking at the photograph below the headline. It was a shot of himself and Argentina Devine dancing, hand in hand at The Butterfly Club, taken two nights before. It had run in the afternoon edition society page of every paper in town yesterday. "Don't worry, sweetheart," he said to the smiling beauty in the picture. "Someone will answer for your murder."

Jim Anthony believed in punctuality. As such, he walked into the precinct at exactly three minutes 'til nine.

"I can't believe you're even doing this, Big Jim," Tom Gentry, his long-time right-hand man, said as they entered the station. Gentry had arrived at Penthouse A a little after seven, with Anthony's grandfather Mephito in tow. He and Anthony had left the ancient Comanche shaman behind in the parlor of the Penthouse, where he was currently burning spirit sticks in the fireplace, much to Dawkins' dismay. "After everything they accused you of—"

"—They haven't accused me of anything, Tom."

"Not yet. Fine, so after what they all but accused you of—"

"—Tom. They're just trying to do their jobs."

Before the freckled aviator could respond, they were interrupted by a familiar, booming voice. "Yes, we are, Jim—and I apologize for my detectives' overzealousness. This all could have waited until normal business hours." Without turning around, Anthony knew that the voice behind them belonged to Police Commissioner Carothers. Anthony had known Carothers a long time, and though they had butted heads from time to time over the course of various investigations, he considered the man a friend.

Anthony nodded. "Hello, Commissioner. Just happy to come down and do my part."

Gentry grumbled inaudibly. Anthony elbowed the smaller man softly in the ribs.

Carothers motioned for Anthony and Gentry to follow him. "Come on—we'll do this in my office."

The three men made their way through the detectives' bullpen inside the squad room, drawing stares and whispers from more than one officer. "Nasty business in the Mirror this morning," Carothers said as they walked. "I just want you to know that in no way are you considered a suspect."

"Yet," Gentry said under his breath. Anthony elbowed him again.

"Thank you, Commissioner," Anthony said. "That's good to hear."

"Detective Brock is waiting for us inside," Carothers said as they reached his office door. "Pearce was called away for a moment—he'll join us as soon as he is able."

Anthony shot Gentry a knowing look. "Tom, why don't you—"

"I think I'll just hang back out here," Gentry said, taking the cue. He wet his fingertips, than ran them through his thick red hair in a futile attempt to tame it. "Maybe see what kind of trouble I can get into over in the typing pool."

"Stay safe," Carothers said with a wink.

The farmboy detective—Brock—stood as his boss and Anthony entered the room. "Mister Anthony, so nice to see you again," Brock said with a false cheerfulness that clearly took a lot of effort. "I do have some good news for you—we tracked down the night watchman for Miss Devine's building, and he did report seeing a man leaving the building two nights ago. His description of the guy wasn't much of a match for you."

Anthony and Carothers joined Brock at a small conference table. "That is good news," Anthony said as the trio took their seats.

Brock shrugged. "Of course, a world-renowned master of disguise as yourself—can't say as that counts for much."

"Where are you from, Brock?" Anthony asked, throwing the big kid off-guard.

"Nebraska."

"Lovely people out that way. Comanche country, in fact."

"Not anymore."

Anthony's sixth sense was buzzing—there was a real air of hostility about Brock, something more deeply-seated than the usual macho police posturing.

"So, Detective," Anthony said, choosing to let it lie for now. "You talked to the night watchman—any more developments in the last few hours?"

"...master of disguise as yourself –
can't say that counts for much."

Brock didn't answer, so Anthony continued, directing his words towards Commissioner Carothers. "I think the Comanche word on the carpet will prove to be the tipping point on this one. I spent some time this morning researching—"

The office door flew open, interrupting Anthony. Detective Pearce entered the room, wiping his glasses clean with the end of his necktie. "Sorry I'm late," he said directly to Carothers. "My old lady phoned, wanting to know what I'd like for dinner tonight."

"And?" Brock asked.

"I told her that I probably wouldn't be home for dinner tonight, because the call before hers was from the dispatcher—seems as though we've got another dead socialite on our hands."

Anthony's sixth sense didn't like this news at all. Neither did his other five. "Charity O'Brien," Pearce said. "Another friend of yours, Anthony?"

"I know her," Anthony said in a measured tone.

"I figured you might," Pearce said.

An uncomfortable silence filled the room. Pearce lit a cigarette.

"Mind if I come along?" Anthony asked finally.

Carothers nodded. "I think you'd better."

Charity O'Brien lived in a small one bedroom apartment in a building a few blocks up from Central Park.

"This just gets better and better, don't it?" Gentry asked as he parked Anthony's towncar against the curb, just outside the cordoned-off crime scene. "I remember Miss O'Brien, Boss—you coulda done a lot worse for yourself than that one."

Anthony remembered Charity O'Brien, too—they had attended the Broadway premiere of Porgy and Bess together just a week ago. It had been a fine evening, and Anthony had promised to call on the fiery redhead again, but had yet to get around to it. Now, it appeared, it was too late.

Anthony and Gentry took the stairs up to Charity's third floor apartment, where they were greeted at the door by Detective Pearce. "I don't want either one of you out of my sight," Pearce said. "Super-Detectives or no."

"This is your show, Detective," Anthony said. "I wouldn't dream of getting in the way—just here to observe."

The first thing Anthony noticed as he entered the apartment was the smell. It was clear to anyone with a nose that several days had passed between Charity's death and the discovery of her body. Gentry grimaced. Pearce noticed. "We figure she's been dead a week or so," he said.

Pearce reached down towards a small end table just inside the apartment door and picked up a copy of the previous Friday's Daily Mirror. Someone had folded the paper open to the Society page, then folded it in half again so that a large photograph of Anthony and Charity seated together at the play was plainly visible. Pearce waved the picture at Anthony. "Say, last Thursday night or so?"

"You people are unbelievable," Gentry said, taking a step towards Pearce. "Tom," Anthony cautioned, steadying his longtime friend by placing a broad hand across his chest.

Pearce seemed eager for the confrontation. "And where were you last Thursday night, Gentry?" he asked. "If you can even remember where you were—probably soaking yourself in some run-down gin mill across town."

Before Tom could respond, they were interrupted by the booming voice of Commissioner Carothers. "Excuse me, gentlemen," he said, poking his head out of Charity's bedroom into the hallway. "Would you be so kind as to join me in here for a moment?"

Gentry gave Pearce his best 'This isn't over' look; Pearce lit a cigarette and returned the glare. Both men followed Anthony down the hall and into the bedroom. The stench was even stronger in this room; Charity's sheet-covered body lay half in the room, half in the adjoining bathroom. One bare foot poked out from under the sheet.

"Over here, gentlemen." A disembodied voice floated up from the other side of Charity's unmade, four post bed. Anthony moved towards it and found Detective Brock squatting down, poking at the carpet with a penknife. "Care to translate for us, Mr. Anthony?"

It was more Comanche, again written in blood, a full sentence this time, rather than the single word found at Argentina Devine's place. Anthony frowned, his sixth sense all over the place. "It's another apology," he said.

Brock stood without taking his eyes off the words. Carothers and Pearce joined them, looking down and around either side of Anthony's wide shoulders. "A good bit longer than the last one," Carothers said.

"This one's more specific," Anthony said. "It says, roughly, 'I'm sorry I could never be who you wanted me to be.'"

Pearce blew a smoke ring towards the bedroom's low ceiling. "What the hell's that supposed to mean?"

Anthony shook his head. "I wish I knew."

❋ ❋ ❋

The stifling silence turned the forty-four story elevator ride up to Penthouse A interminable, as far as Gentry was concerned. He had been Anthony's driver and pilot for years now, and their relationship had long ago moved beyond simple employment and into the realm of friendship. Somewhere around the thirtieth floor, Gentry could take it no longer. "Dammit, Jim, why are you letting them do this to you?"

"I told you, Tom, they're just doing their jobs."

"No, what they're doing is railroading you into these murder charges! If you don't do something, you're going to ride the lightning for sure."

"Now, Tom, I'm sure that—"

"And another thing—how can you be so cold, so, so clinical about the whole thing? This isn't one of your lab experiments—this is your life we're talking about here."

The elevator chimed, indicating that they had reached Penthouse A. The door opened, and Anthony stalked ahead without a word. "Jim!" Gentry called after him. "What's the matter with you?" Anthony did not turn around. He opened the door to his lab, then closed it behind him softly.

"Welcome home, Master Gentry," Dawkins said as he joined Gentry in the foyer. "I trust that your business at the precinct did not go well?"

Gentry exhaled deeply. "You don't know the half of it, Dawkins. I've never seen the big guy like this. He seems. . . lost."

"Perhaps he feels somehow responsible for the death of Miss Devine?" Dawkins asked.

"There's been another murder, Dawkins—Charity O'Brien was found dead in her apartment this morning."

"Another bloody message?"

"Give the man a prize."

"My word." Dawkins frowned. "You don't think—"

"Dawkins! Of course not! How could you even say that?"

Dawkins pursed his lips, waiting for Gentry to cool off. "I was going to ask if you don't think that this is all coincidence, and that someone could be trying to frame Mr. Anthony." Dawkins looked down, smoothed a non-existent wrinkle out of his vest. "I would never suggest otherwise."

"Sorry, Dawkins, of course you wouldn't." Gentry's mood brightened suddenly. "Howsabout I fix the both of us a drink?"

Anthony spent the afternoon alone in his lab, seeking answers. In times of great crisis, he always turned to science. It was the one place where the rules still applied; the one place where things still made sense.

The news didn't get any better at lunch, when Rob Roberts, the archives editor for The Daily Star, telephoned. Anthony had spoken with Roberts earlier in the morning, and asked him to try and dig up any possible connection between Argentina Devine and Charity O'Brien.

"Sorry, Boss, nothing doing," Roberts said. "The only connection these two girls had was you."

Near sunset, Anthony emerged from the lab, bleary-eyed from hour after hour of poring through one textbook after another: linguistics, forensics, anything he could think of to make sense of the morning's crime scene that had been etched into his mind by his legendarily photographic memory. He made his way into the parlor, where his grandfather sat on the brick hearth surrounding Anthony's large fireplace. Mephito turned to Anthony, smiling grimly. "Trying times, Grandson," he said.

Anthony nodded his agreement. To his eyes, Mephito had not aged a day in the last quarter century. Of course, twenty-five years ago his grandfather was already impossibly ancient. No one was sure just how old the wizened old shaman really was; then again, no one was sure they even wanted to know.

"I have had a vision you might like me to share," Mephito said, stirring the embers of the fire with an iron poker. Anthony nodded again. He was a man of science, to be sure, but he was also a man of deep faith. He put as much stock, if not more, in Mephito's Comanche mysticism than he did in any knowledge he could glean from a science text or laboratory.

"Our people," Mephito began, "and not just Comanche, but many of the people. They all share the legend of the Buffalo Without Color."

"A white buffalo," Anthony offered.

"No," his grandfather said. "One so pale as to be without color."

Anthony nodded, frowning. "I see."

"The legend holds that the birth of such an animal will signal the beginning of the end of days. He would return to purify the world, bringing back the spiritual balance and harmony of the ancients. As such, this buffalo must be protected at all costs.

"And not just the buffalo—my grandfathers taught that one who harmed even a squirrel without color would be rewarded with the loss of his hunting ability. One who harmed a deer without color would lose his life, in an accident at the hands of his own hunting ability. And one who harmed a buffalo without color. . ."

Mephito poked at the fire again, sending a plume of white smoke up into the flue. "You are a great hunter, Grandson," he said. "A hunter of men. It would pain me deeply to see you lose that ability."

"I'm not sure I follow."

"It is our duty to protect those without color, Jim, because they cannot protect themselves. They are easy prey, too visible, unable to hide. To hunt them, we would only destroy ourselves."

Anthony watched as a lone ember hopped from the fire out onto the hearth. It burned brightly for a moment, then faded. "Your vision," he said, his eyes on the hearth. "There is one of these buffalo that needs protecting? One that needs my protection?"

Mephito turned from the fire to stare deep into Anthony's eyes, his voice low and distant. "No, Grandson. In my vision, you are killing such a beast. Strangling him with your own bare hands."

The coffee was always terrible.

Joseph could count on that, no matter the dive. The diners, the pancake houses, the little mom and pop restaurants that dot the highway all the way from Oklahoma to Pennsylvania back to Nebraska and New York again.

Bitter, flavorless—the coffee here in the lobby of the Waldorf-Anthony was no better than the rest. At least it was wet, which helped to wash away the God-awful apple crumble he had just choked down, the pie's stale crust like an old shoe box.

Joseph's waitress stopped by his booth again—Violet, according to the brass nametag pinned to the upper left-hand side of her white apron. "Anything else I can get you, honey?" she asked. "Some cream for that coffee, maybe?"

Joseph looked up, made eye contact with the waitress for the first time. She was short, a little thick, her ample hips straining the seams of her knee-length white dress. Cream for his coffee—"That some kind of joke?" he asked. "You think you're funny?" He held her gaze a little longer than was socially acceptable.

Violet backed away from the table slowly, the pencil tucked behind her ear falling to the ground as she did so. She squatted down to pick it up, her eyes never leaving Joseph's. "I, uh. . . Just didn't look like you were enjoying the coffee, is all," she stammered, clearly unnerved by Joseph's un-natural red eyes. "I thought a little cream might help with the taste."

Violet stood up, smoothing a wrinkle from her apron as she did so. "Didn't mean nothing by it, honest."

Joseph held her gaze a moment longer, then nodded, satisfied, return-ing his attention to The Daily Star in front of him. Her offer hadn't been a crack about his appearance, after all.

Violet moved to walk away, then stopped. She stood quietly at the booth, waiting for Joseph to notice her. He took another long sip of coffee, then looked up. He said nothing.

"I, uh, I couldn't help but notice your paper there," Violet said. "We have a few copies of yesterday's Star left up front, if you're interested. . . "

Joseph looked back down at the newspaper spread on the formica ta-bletop in front of him, open to the Society page where billionaire publisher Jim Anthony danced the night away with yet another starlet, this one a petite blonde named Anastasia Vollmerhausen.

Violet backed away, the look on Joseph's pale face not exactly inviting more conversation. She pointed at the dateline atop Joseph's paper. "News a little more recent than three weeks ago, anyway," she said. "It's a real shame what they're doing to Mr. Anthony, isn't it? After everything he's done—how can anybody believe he's a killer?"

Joseph grabbed the newspaper off the table with his thick, meaty hands. He folded the paper in half, then halved it again so that Anthony's picture was all that was visible. "No, this'll do just fine," he said finally. "It might be old news, but I have a lot of catching up to do."

Mephito's vision of a bloodthirsty, murderous Anthony had rocked the Super-Detective to his core; it was no surprise to any of his entourage when he immediately returned to his laboratory. It was also no surprise to any of them when Anthony worked straight through dinner. Dawkins threw together a quick supper of beef, potatoes, and corn; Mephito, Gentry, and the faithful butler ate silently in the kitchen. The table's empty fourth chair went a long way to discourage conversation.

At 9:30, the Penthouse A doorbell rang. Impossibly loud in the eve-ning's dour silence, the chime startled Gentry out of his seat and on to the floor, flat on his back. "What now?" he grumbled, to no one in particular, from his prone position.

Dawkins answered his question by leading Detectives Pearce and Brock into the kitchen. "I meant that rhetorically," Gentry said.

The detectives had not come alone. They were accompanied by a trio of the burliest uniformed beat cops New York City had to offer. Pearce looked towards the floor, sneering. "Don't get up on our account, Gentry."

"Wouldn't dream of it, Detective—you look better from this angle, anyway."

"I'll fetch Mr. Anthony," Dawkins said.

Two of the uniforms took up sentry positions near the front door of the Penthouse; the third stayed close to Brock.

Pearce had a seat in Anthony's empty chair, reaching across the table to pick at Gentry's plate with his fork. "This late at night, Gentry, I'm surprised you're even capable of standing," Pearce said, watching Mephito help Gentry to his feet.

"Keep talking and you'll be incapable of standing," Gentry said.

"Is that a threat? You hear that, boys?" Pearce said, looking towards the other cops. "I believe Mister Gentry just threatened an officer of the peace."

"Gentlemen, it's awfully late." As usual, Anthony's booming voice preceded him as he entered the kitchen, Dawkins trailing behind him. "Don't you ever sleep?"

"Well, I was at home," Brock said, speaking for the first time. "But I made a special trip back out for this."

"We're honored," Gentry said, not quite under his breath.

Brock ignored him, never so much as taking his eyes off Anthony. "A superman is, on account of certain superior qualities inherent in him, exempted from the ordinary laws which govern men." Brock paused here, reaching into his jacket pocket for a pair of handcuffs. "He is not liable for anything he may do."

"Nathan Leopold," Anthony said, nodding.

"Very good, Detective—I may even have read that quote in your paper."

"Publishing business aside—what does Mr. Leopold have to do with me?"

Brock stepped forward, holding the handcuffs towards Anthony. "I just wanted you to know, Mister Anthony. Before I arrested you, I wanted you to know that a superman is most definitely liable for everything he does in my city."

"Arrested?" Gentry said.

"Jim Anthony, you are under arrest for the murders of Argentina Devine, Charity O'Brien, and Anastasia Vollmerhausen."

Anthony's brow narrowed. "Wait—Anastasia, too?"

"That's right, big guy," Pearce said. "They found her body tonight—and this time, the doorman was paying attention. Described a guy just like you—a 'big Indian', he said—leaving the building some time after lunch." Pearce looked around the room. "Any of you care to alibi your boss this afternoon?"

"I was in my lab all day." Anthony shook his head. "Alone."

"There's a surprise," Pearce said, as Brock placed the bracelets on Anthony's wrists. The two officers at the door stepped forward and took Anthony by the elbows. "This way, bigshot," the surlier of the two said.

"I must say, Detectives, this is preposterous," Dawkins said.

"Maybe so," Pearce said. "Either way, I'd polish up my resume—not a lot of work for butlers in Sing Sing."

The blonde had been the easiest. She was smaller than the others, unable to fight back quite as much. From what Joseph could tell from the papers, Anthony preferred the leggier types—the blonde must have been a blind date, something set up by a mutual acquaintance.

"Hey, buddy—can I get ya anything else?"

Joseph looked up from his coffee, snapped out of his introspection by the diner's grill jockey. "Gonna be closing up in a few," the cook said from his position behind the counter. Joseph didn't answer. The cook shook his head, grumbling something under his breath as he turned back to his grill brick.

Despite the poor coffee earlier in the day, Joseph had returned to the Waldorf-Anthony a little after 8 PM. He chose a booth inside the diner that provided an excellent view of the hotel's lobby, so that he could easily keep track of the comings and goings inside. When the two detectives entered a few minutes ago, trailed by three of the largest beat cops he had ever seen, Joseph knew that everything was about to come to a head.

Joseph dug a nickel out of his pocket and dropped it on the table for the coffee, then stood and headed out of the diner into the lobby. He wanted an even better vantage point for what was coming next. Out in the lobby, the elevator bank to his left chimed. He turned to see the same two detectives from a few minutes ago leading a handcuffed Jim Anthony out towards the street. A pair of hotel dicks lingering near the front desk sprang to their feet at the sight of their boss in chains, but Anthony stayed them with a simple wave of his hands.

The three beat cops led the way, clearing a path for Anthony and the detectives. One of the cops gave Joseph the stinkeye as he passed. The look was familiar: Curiosity, mixed with revulsion. It was all Joseph could do to stand there and do nothing; every inch of his being wanted to rush the man from behind and slit his throat.

But he controlled the urge. He had to; he had come too far to ruin things now with a base impulse. His plan had worked to perfection at every step along the way, and the endgame was near.

He was used to that look. The white kids in school had worn the same face since the first day he set foot in Pennsylvania. Palehorse, they called him, first behind his back, soon after to his face, their fear and cruelty out in the open. They thought they were clever, taking his given name—Nighthorse—and twisting it, mocking his heritage and his appearance at the same time.

They knew that it was hateful, cruel. But what they didn't know was that Joseph liked it. His own grandmother had told of a colorless buffalo, one whose birth would mark the beginning of the end of the world. She died when Joseph was nine, afraid of her own grandson. At Carlisle, Joseph learned that the white man had his own version of this legend, only it was a pale horse. And it's rider was death.

He smiled at the memory. They had no idea.

Anthony himself was passing now, flanked by the two detectives. Anthony locked eyes with Joseph, turning his head as they passed to keep his eyes on Joseph. "What's the matter, Anthony?" the younger detective asked as they made their way through the lobby's revolving door out into the street. "You look like you've seen a ghost."

"Clarence Darrow? Really? Why don't you just paint a big 'guilty' sign across your forehead?"

Dawkins had been instructed earlier in the day that if the situation turned dire he was to contact Darrow immediately. Anthony had met the famed attorney a few years prior at a fundraising event in Chicago. They had hit it off famously, and before the night was through Darrow had promised to consider coming out of retirement one more time should Anthony ever need representation.

Judging from Detective Brock's loud reaction, Dawkins had succeeded. And, more to the point, Darrow had agreed.

Anthony heard Brock long before he ever saw him, the detective's voice booming far ahead of him as he stormed down the concrete corridor towards Anthony's cell. Given Anthony's celebrity, Police Commissioner

"The three cops led the way..."

Carothers had ordered him placed in his own private cell in the precinct's basement, which meant that Anthony had spent the twelve hours since being booked devoid of human contact. He passed the time by doing several sets of push-ups, two hundred at a time, and losing himself in a Comanche meditative trance he had learned at his grandfather's knee many years before as a boy.

Anthony listened as Brock's heavy footsteps drew closer. He waited until the detective turned the corner and stood in front of his cell before responding. "Just what are you implying, Detective?"

Brock shook his head, his words dripping with disgust. "Clarence Darrow. Last refuge of a guilty man. Well, a guilty rich man, I guess."

"Still don't follow."

Brock jabbed a beefy finger through the bars of the cell towards Anthony. "I'll put it another way. Leopold and Loeb. Ossian Sweet. Thomas Massie. Darrow's the guy you call when you know you killed somebody, and you know you're not getting away with it."

"Is that right?"

Brock nodded. "That's right. Practically an admission of guilt. All Darrow's gonna do for you is keep you from riding the lightning."

Anthony exhaled deeply and took a seat on the cell's thin metal cot, calming himself. "I am not a murderer, Detective Brock."

Brock's upper lip curled, barely able to contain his contempt. "No, you're a Super-Detective." Brock fiddled with the cuffs of his starched white shirt, rolling up the sleeves. The lack of air flow in the basement left it stifling. "Let me ask you something, Anthony. In all your adventures, you never once killed a man?"

Anthony started to answer, then changed his mind. "I didn't kill those women, Detective," he said instead.

Brock grinned, savoring his small victory. "Of course you didn't."

"Let me ask you something, Detective," Anthony said, getting to his feet. "What did I ever do to you to make you hate me so much?"

"You think this is personal?"

"It's not?"

Brock looked down at his shoes for a moment, gathering his thoughts. "My father," he said finally, without looking up. "When he was a boy back in Nebraska, he watched his own father murdered right in front of him."

Anthony's eyes narrowed, not sure where this conversation was going. "Sorry to hear that."

Brock shoved his hands deep into his pants pockets, then looked up at Anthony. "His mother—my grandmother—disappeared. They took her. Never found her."

"I'm s—"

"No," Brock said, cutting him off. "You don't get to be sorry. They were slaughtered. Massacred."

"What does—"

"It was your people, Anthony."

"Comanche."

"Yeah, goddamn Comanche. And not just my family—families all across this country. And to see you, living a life like the one you lead, barely fifty years later?" Brock's lip curled into a sneer again. "The newspapers, the fancy penthouse, the beautiful women—I can barely stomach it.

"Your. . .ancestors ruined my father." Brock leaned on the honorific, turning it into a slur. He stared at Anthony, murderous intent clear in his eyes. "He was a broken man by the time he was twelve years old."

Anthony held Brock's eyes for a long while. "I didn't kill your family, Detective," he said evenly.

Brock looked away, back to his shoes. Anthony took no solace from his small victory. "And I didn't kill those women, either," he said softly.

Brock absorbed himself in a small piece of litter on the jailhouse floor, poking at it with the toe of one shoe. He slid it across the floor a few inches, then gave up. When he looked up again, the dark intent in his eyes had returned. "What you're saying's all well and good, but tell me this, Super-Detective—If you didn't, then who did?"

Anthony shook his head. "I wish I knew."

When Joseph was eight years old, the white men came for him. They came to Broken Arrow under the cover of God, promising that they could provide every Indian child on the reservation with the kind of decent Christian education that was the natural birthright of all children. Joseph's mother bought what they were selling, thanks in part to some urgent persuasion from her own mother, who lived in constant fear of her colorless grandson. Ten days later, Joseph and nine other Comanche boys boarded a train headed towards Pennsylvania.

The two men that accompanied the boys east were nearly as pale as Joseph himself, their tongue and dress strange and foreign. They were the first white men any of the boys had ever seen. Joseph would learn later that the white man had as many tribes as his own people had, with as many different dialects and customs, as well. The two men that changed his life forever were British white men, their own home even further from Carlisle than Joseph's own. Joseph thought of them again now as he watched Jim Anthony's manservant busy himself through his morning routine at the newsstand across the street from the hotel. From what he had overheard of the man's voice over the last few weeks, Anthony's man was British, as well, though his dialect differed slightly from Joseph's old schoolmasters.

"Thank you, Dickie," he heard Dawkins say as he casually handed the vendor a dollar bill for his bundle of newspapers, as if the sum meant nothing to him at all. It probably didn't—the money belonged to Anthony, anyway.

"Let your boss know I haven't had one customer yet who believes what they're saying about him," Dickie said. "I'm about to let Hearst know just what he can do with that fish wrap of his." Dickie jabbed his finger on the newsstand's counter for emphasis, pointing out the Mirror's headline:

JIM ANTHONY, SUPER-KILLER!

"That will certainly lift his spirits," Dawkins.

"Well, I just want him to know we're all behind him."

"Indeed we are, Sir."

Tucked away in the shadow of a walk-up's flight of stairs just down the street, Joseph's blood boiled. He bit back the urge to leave his vantage point and break both men's necks with his bare hands. The Anthony Legion were fools, then, if they still believed in such a man. The evidence clearly painted the man guilty—what more would it take?

Dawkins said his goodbyes to the crippled veteran behind the counter, then began the short walk back to the Waldorf-Anthony. Glad to be on the move again, Joseph followed, closing distance with each step. He felt Dickie's eyes burning through his back as he passed the newsstand, but he would not allow himself to stop. Not this close to the end.

Dawkins passed through the revolving glass door into the hotel's lobby, Joseph right behind him. He moved quickly through the lobby, still relatively quiet in the early morning hour. He could smell the cheap coffee brewing in the diner as he passed, could smell the morning's first bacon sizzling on the skillet.

Joseph caught up to Dawkins just the butler pressed the penthouse el-

evator call button. Using his bulk to shield his actions from the house detective flirting with the night clerk not thirty feet away at the registration
desk, Joseph grabbed Dawkins' elbow firmly with his left hand, steering
the much smaller man into the elevator. "Not a sound, old man," he hissed.
"Not if you have any hope of ever finding out anything about your boss's
dead girls."

Dawkins complied without so much as a glance back in Joseph's direction. He fished his elevator key from his jacket pocket and turned the slot
towards 'P', his hand as steady as if he were the sole passenger in the car.
He even smiled and nodded in the direction of the Anthony employees at
the front desk as the elevator's gate came down, betraying nothing. His
seeming casualness put Joseph on edge—he would have figured the butler
to have soiled himself by now.

Breathing deeply as the elevator climbed, Joseph calmed himself.
Dawkins had been Anthony's butler for years now, he reasoned. Clearly,
the man had found himself in some tight spots. His calm demeanor now
did not necessarily mean he had something up his sleeve—it was probably just a byproduct of the man's utter and complete faith in his employer.
Such fealty was disgusting. Joseph leaned over towards Dawkins' ear. "The
big man's not around to save you this time, pal," he said.

"Your doing, no doubt," Dawkins replied matter-of-factly. He smiled
thinly at Joseph, watching his reaction in the polished brass of the elevator's door. "You cannot possibly hope to get away with whatever it is you
think you're getting away with."

There was no mistaking the butler's tone—at least not to Joseph's ears.
He had heard it for years as a child, from one teacher after another at the
Carlisle school. "Don't tell me what I cannot do," he said quietly, before
grabbing Dawkins by the hair and driving his face into the cold metal of
the elevator door. "I've already done it."

Tom Gentry had not taken his boss' arrest well. By the time Pearce
and Brock escorted Anthony through the hotel's lobby, the aviator had
helped himself to a second drink. And by the time they made it back to
the station, his bottle was empty and he was headed out into the Gotham
night looking for more. He tried to get Mephito or Dawkins to join him
on his bender, but that was a non-starter—both men had more important
things to do. Dawkins spent the night on the phone with Clarence flip-

pin' Darrow—a mistake, Gentry thought. If that didn't scream "guilty as charged", he didn't know what did. And Mephito passed the night in front of the fireplace with those godawful spirit sticks.

So, alone and already well-lubricated, Gentry made his way out into the sticky summer night. He didn't get very far before deciding to darken the first door he came upon. He ended up a few blocks away at Mollari's, where he weighted down a barstool and knocked back whiskey neat until well after closing time.

He argued politics with the restaurant's tuxedoed piano player—Chopin thought FDR was doing a helluva job pulling the country out of the mess it was in, but Gentry wasn't so sure. Then, tiring of that, he argued baseball with the bartender—Hollis didn't want to see a Jew break the Bambino's homer record but Gentry thought that Greenberg had a real shot. Gentry didn't care much for Ruth, anyway, not since the Babe had drunk him under the table on seven consecutive legendary nights at this very restaurant in the summer of 1931—and then left with Gentry's girl, to boot. "Don't get me wrong, I ain't no Tigers fan either," he explained to Hollis. "I just want to see that fat bastard get his."

"Look, Tommy, it's four in the morning," Hollis said, pleading with Gentry as he guided him by the elbow towards the door. "I gotta get home or the wife's gonna think I'm making time with the hatcheck girl."

"I thought you were making time with the hatcheck girl."

"I was. Moved on to the cigarette girl—you seen the cans on that one?"

Gentry shook his head slowly—but not slowly enough. "You're too much, Hollis," he said once the room stopped spinning. "I guess that's my cue, then."

"G'night, Tommy."

Gentry pushed himself up and away from the bar, then found his way clumsily to the door. He stumbled back up the block and into the lobby of the Waldorf-Anthony, where the lone house dick on duty barely looked up in his direction, his eyes focused solely on the green-eyed college girl working the registration desk. "Night, Mr. G," the detective called as Gentry passed.

Gentry didn't reply; he threw up a hand in a half-hearted attempt at a wave as he all but fell into the open penthouse elevator car. His trembling hands had some trouble pulling the key from his front pants pocket; once they succeeded, he inserted the middle key into the middle hole and turned it to the right, sending himself up towards the top floor.

Penthouse A was dark and quiet—funereal, even—as he stepped off the elevator, and Gentry banged his shin on an unseen coffee table as he made his way towards the guest bedroom in which he sometimes slept. He bit back a profanity-laced scream as he toppled onto a plush nearby couch. Hey, he thought as he sat himself upright. This is pretty comf --

Gentry awoke with a start nearly two hours later, still seated in the same position on the couch. He had a deep, sharp kink in his neck from sleeping upright, his head hanging over the back of the couch, eyes directed towards the ceiling. He blinked twice in an effort to clear the black spots of pain from his eyes, then closed his eyes to gather himself. When he opened them again, he found himself staring at Dawkins' back. The butler was lying facedown on the carpet in front of him. Standing over Dawkins' body was the largest Indian Gentry had ever seen—the man was even bigger than Jim Anthony. And while his size was impressive enough, it wasn't his most striking feature; the man was ghostly pale, his skin so white as to be nearly translucent, his hair the color of nothing. Gentry hoped frantically that this was another one of his drunken fever dreams, but somehow he knew that it wasn't. He knew instantly who this man was; he had read about him many times before, as a child, in the Bible. This man was Death.

This is too easy, Joseph thought as he delivered a heavy right hand that caught Tom Gentry square in the nose. He followed that up with a quick left to the cheekbone that felt solid enough to blacken the eye of Anthony's little yes-man. Joseph watched as Gentry slipped back into unconsciousness, then turned and quickly scanned the rest of the penthouse. He had an uneasy feeling that he was being somehow set up by Anthony. He knew that this was a foolish thought. Anthony was locked away at the police station; he had seen the man taken away with his own two eyes. His plan had worked to perfection. But still. . . He had read accounts of enough of Anthony's escapades over the years to know that nothing was ever as it seemed. And right now, this all seemed too easy.

Joseph made his way through the sitting room towards the parlor, his nose suddenly crinkling in recognition of an odor he had last encountered a lifetime ago. It was the smell of Comanche spirit sticks, ones that had burned for hours and were just now dying out. Joseph stepped through the open doorway into the parlor, where the oldest Comanche he had ever seen sat cross-legged on the floor in front of the fireplace. His eyes were closed, his palms upturned in what Joseph immediately recognized as an ancient meditative trance.

Joseph stood motionless for a long while, watching; clearly, the man was Anthony's Comanche grandfather, although he looked old enough to be the grandfather of even the old shamans Joseph had known back on the Broken Arrow reservation. Joseph considered his next move carefully; this man clearly intended on living forever, and, as such, was not to be underestimated.

Mephito's shoulders rose and fell as he sighed deeply, his mind returning to his body from whatever faraway place it had traveled. His deep eyes opened slowly, betraying nothing as they widened to focus on Joseph. The only recognition that he had even noticed Joseph in the room came from his upper lip, which quivered with a nearly-imperceptible curl. Then, just as quickly, his face returned to stone. Most men would have never even noticed the movement.

But Joseph was not most men. He noticed. Morever, he recognized the look that had passed across Mephito's face, however briefly. It was a look he had seen many, many times before as a child.

It was the look his grandmother had given every single time she had ever looked his way. Joseph recognized the apprehension, the fear, in the old man's eyes, if only for a moment. Joseph's face burned with shame, even while Mephito's remained impassive.

The old man held his stare for a long while, then looked away. He muttered gutturally under his breath.

"What's that?" Joseph asked, taking a step towards the ancient mystic.

The man looked back up silently, his chin held high, impossibly still. Joseph took another step towards him. "Say that again, old man," he said.

When Mephito spoke again, it was much more distinct—this time, it was clear that he was speaking Numunuu. And even though the teachers at Carlisle had used lye to scrub the Comanche language from Joseph's tongue every time he spoke, he understood without reservation what the old man was saying. He had heard those words his whole life. His grandmother's words: Tasiwoo tosaabitu.

The buffalo without color.

Joseph nodded. "And hell followed with him," he whispered as he drove his heavy fist into Mephito's face.

Three weeks into his studies at Carlisle, Joseph ran away.

It was the first attempt of many.

He did not get very far, that first attempt. He spent the night in the woods near the campus, then made it all the way to the train station in town before being caught by school officials. He spent a week in solitary confinement upon his return to the school, as punishment for his escape attempt. He was eight years old.

The time alone did nothing but harden his resolve. Eight hours after being allowed to rejoin his classmates, he ran again. This time he spent the night in the cemetery, sleeping fitfully among the hundreds of headstones belonging to other, less fortunate Indian children. They caught him before the sun rose.

The headmaster tried a different tact this time—humiliation. He strapped Joseph to a chair and proceeded to take a pair of scissors to his shoulder-length white hair. "We must curb that fierce warrior spirit, son," he said as Joseph watched his flowing locks fall limply to the floor with eyes damp and warm from tears of anger. The headmaster stepped back to admire his own work, placing a possessive hand on Joseph's shoulder. "There now, isn't that better? Kill the Indian, save the man—do you understand now, son?"

Joseph bolted again the next night—his warrior spirit anything but broken.

He thought about all of this as he surveyed the carnage he had wrought inside Jim Anthony's famed Penthouse A. The butler, the pilot, the shaman—all three men lay at his feet, felled by his own hands. Yes, his warrior spirit burned as brightly as it ever had. He would never be what they wanted him to be.

For the first time in weeks, Joseph relaxed. His shoulders dropped as he exhaled deeply, the weight and pressure of the last month slipping away. His plan had worked to near-perfection. Jim Anthony was in jail, and, perhaps more importantly, publicly discredited.

An ornately-carved Swiss cuckoo clock sounded out in the foyer: 6:30. On the couch, Gentry stirred, but did not rise. His left eye had already swollen shut—he couldn't open that one even if he wanted to. Satisfied that no one would be moving for a while, Joseph walked the halls of Anthony's home. The size of it, the opulence, the greed—it turned his stomach. For all of this to be owned by one man was too much, but to be owned by an Indian—and it was; half-breed or not, Anthony was still Numunuu, down to his bones—that was beyond the pale.

Joseph turned his attention to the framed artwork in the long corridor that connected the front of the home with the bedrooms. Was that a Picasso? Joseph knew a little about art; as a homeless teenager bouncing from one city to the next, he always made a point to find the local art museum, as there were far worse ways to spend a bitterly cold winter morning. A security guard at the Met here in Manhattan had been especially kind to him, sometimes allowing him to enter the hall early, before it opened to the public. The man even invited Joseph to his home for one of his wife's casseroles; Joseph had arrived to find that in actuality, there was no wife, and things got worse from there. Joseph said his goodbyes, then capped the evening by leaving the man a gurgling, dying mess on his own kitchen floor. Was this the life the white men wanted for me? he wondered then. He thought the same thing now as he wandered through Anthony's home.

The door closest to the parlor was locked; it wouldn't budge even as Joseph leaned a shoulder into it. Clearly, it had been reinforced far beyond a typical bedroom door. This must have been the fabled Anthony Laboratory.

Suddenly, Joseph was consumed by an overwhelming desire to get inside that room. The plan that had been complete just moments ago now rang hollow. He had destroyed Anthony's women; he had destroyed his public persona. In the last few minutes, he had destroyed the man's family. But now, standing outside the most famous scientific laboratory in the world, Joseph knew the job would not be complete until he destroyed the man's work.

He quickly returned to the parlor, grabbing a long iron poker from a basket next to the fireplace. Back in the hallway, he attempted to pry the lab door open. That idea failed miserably as he bent the poker out of shape before the door even thought about moving. His frustration mounting, he used the poker to try and pry the doorknob off the door. No luck there, either; the poker snapped in half under the strain.

Joseph picked up the heavier end of the poker and fired it down the hall, gaining a moment's satisfaction when the tool's sharp edge left a small hole in the penthouse wall. He cursed his luck softly, under his breath, a guttural Comanche phrase. He was pleasantly surprised that he still remembered the words; he hadn't as much as thought them in years. Kill the Indian, save the man. . .

His spirits temporarily buoyed, Joseph moved into the kitchen in search of something—anything, really—to help him get into that room. The pickings were slim, and after rifling through several drawers finally settled on a thick wooden rolling pin. He returned to the reinforced door and began pounding on the knob with the rolling pin.

Once again, the door did not so much as budge, and after five minutes of repeated hammering, Joseph was ready to try a different tact. He dropped the pin on the floor with a loud crash, then stepped away from the door to regroup.

Joseph moved back into the parlor to check on his victims; none of the three had moved an inch, despite the racket he had created in his attack on the laboratory door. Satisfied with their condition, he steepled his hands in front of his mouth and exhaled softly into them, a calming gesture that always helped him think. It was clear that brute force was not going to get him into that room, but there had to be another way.

A soft click on the other side of the door snapped him out of his thoughts—he rushed down the hall towards the lab for a closer listen in an effort to make sure he hadn't imagined the sound. He stood motionless at the door until a second click confirmed that he wasn't hearing things. On the third click, the door fell open, moving slowly inward to reveal the interior of Anthony's lab.

Joseph stepped into the open doorway, filling the entire frame. He was eager to access Anthony's sanctum sanctorum—but stopped cold at the sight of what waited inside for him. No, Joseph thought. This can't be happening.

The man inside the lab was broad-shouldered, nearly as large as Joseph, clad in a familiar outfit of sweatshirt and yellow swim trunks. "Hello there," he said to Joseph. "I'm afraid I've been a terrible host. I don't believe I caught your name—I'm Jim Anthony. Welcome to my home."

Joseph's immediate reaction was to look for Mephito—clearly the old shaman was up to something, some sort of spirit illusion. Anthony couldn't be standing here in front of him—he was locked up downtown. Joseph had seen him escorted out of the hotel with his own two eyes not twelve hours ago. But the old man was right where Joseph had left him, flat on his back in the Penthouse parlor.

For the first time in the last few days, Joseph felt a pang of worry—this was not part of the plan. "Were you out there long?" 'Anthony' was saying, his voice full of a mock pleasantness. "I guess I didn't hear you knocking— I can get so wrapped up in my projects in here. Sometimes I don't even come out to eat."

Joseph took a step backwards, towards the parlor, his eyes never leav-

"I'm Jim Anthony. Welcome to my home."

ing the Anthony doppleganger. Whatever black magic was involved here, he wanted no part of it. He needed to get out of here, go to ground, regroup before he lost complete control over everything.

'Anthony' followed him out into the hallway, wiping his hands on a oily rag in a vaguely menacing way. His eyes roamed over Joseph in a similar fashion, like a wolf sizing up a small child. The man's dark eyes grew darker still as his gaze fell over Joseph's shoulder, where Mephito, Dawkins, and Gentry all lay immobilized on the parlor floor.

"What have you done?" he asked quietly, all pretense of good cheer now lost. His eyes returned to Joseph's now, a murderous rage creeping across his face. For Joseph, it was like looking into a mirror.

The man lashed out with a hard right cross, catching Joseph flush on the jaw. Definitely not an illusion, then, thought Joseph as he stumbled backwards from the blow. The pain radiated out from the point of impact until nearly his entire skull was numb. Joseph hadn't been hit like that in a long time. He bared his teeth, a feral grin as he wiped the spittle from his chin.

This was going to be fun.

As he often did, Anthony had lost himself in his labwork the night before, and had not even realized the sun had risen until he heard the terrible banging on the locked laboratory door. It couldn't have been Gentry or Dawkins knocking, looking for him. For all they—and the rest of the world—knew, he was locked up down at the police station, awaiting arraignment in the morning. Even as one who was never easy to surprise, the last thing Anthony expected to find on the other side of the door when he opened it was this pale tank of a man.

The sight of his uncle and friends in such distress had sent Anthony spiraling into a black rage. Before he even blinked again he caught the intruder with a big right hand, sending him sprawling. As the man straightened back up to his full height, Anthony gave him a quick once-over. Tall, thick, broad-shouldered—rare was the man who was a physical match for Anthony, but this one clearly was. The man's eyes glowed red with anger, set deep in a face that was a white so pale it appeared blue. Is this the buffalo of Mephito's vision?Anthony wondered, the sudden violence as the punch connected doing much to clear his rage-clouded mind. And is he smiling?

"I don't know who you're supposed to be," the man said, wiping a rough thumb across his rapidly-swelling jaw. "Jim Anthony's in jail."

Anthony threw another right hand, but this time his opponent was ready, and ducked under it. Joseph fired back with an off-balance upper-cut of his own, which Anthony sidestepped easily. "Yeah?" Anthony said. "Don't believe everything you read in the papers, son."

Joseph tilted his head quizzically, and Anthony took the opportunity to throw another punch. The albino was quick, avoiding most of the blow with a sideways jerk of his head, but there was enough strength left behind the blow to move him back a step. Anthony stepped into the gap quickly, following up with a quick left, another right, and a final left, each punch connecting more squarely than the last. Joseph was reeling, and Anthony used the advantage to take him all the way to the floor with a football tackle that would make Jim Thorpe proud.

"I saw them cart Anthony away myself," Joseph wheezed. Anthony had him pinned down, the detective's full weight driving his ribs right into his lungs. "Two detectives and three big beat cops."

Anthony's eyes widened at this rather accurate description of the previous night's events. How long has this man been in the Waldorf-Anthony?

The momentary distraction was all Joseph needed to raise up his right leg to knee Anthony right in the groin. Anthony groaned and reflexively shifted to his left, allowing Joseph to roll free and scramble back up to his feet.

"This is impossible," Joseph said, hands on his knees, speaking between gasps of air. "I worked too hard for this—planned all of this for too long."

He flailed wildly at Anthony, who easily sidestepped the clumsy attempt. "Jim Anthony is in ruins, dammit."

Anthony stood motionless, his eyes and mind clouding over darkly once more. "All of this?" he asked slowly. "Did you—That was you?" His anger boiling over, Anthony's words spat out in an ugly shout. "You killed those girls?"

Anthony lowered his head and charged at Joseph a second time, this tackle violent enough to drive him through the open doorway into the laboratory. Perched atop Joseph's shoulders, Anthony began raining down one fist after another. Anthony's power coupled with his rage proved to be too much for Joseph, and his face was quickly and bloodily pulped. Anthony's final blow broke Joseph's nose with a sickening crack.

His rage subsiding, Anthony looked down at Joseph, flat on his back on the floor. "That's right," Joseph said, his mouth thick with blood and broken teeth. "I killed your whores."

Impossibly, Joseph rolled over, then got up on all fours. "Want to know why?" he asked.

"No."

Joseph pushed himself up with his hands, rising on unsteady feet. "No, you're going to listen to what I have to say," he said. He coughed once, then spit up a mouthful of blood and another tooth. "I hate you for what you've become. Your adventures, your money, your influence. For how easily you move in their world."

Joseph's hands dropped to his sides, almost pleading. "I could never be who they wanted me to be. How could this all be so easy for you?"

Anthony reached out with his left hand and grabbed Joseph's shirt collar, steadying him, readying him for a killing blow. "Time to say good-bye, friend."

✳ ✳ ✳

"Grandson, don't!"

Anthony's right fist dropped to his side as he whirled towards the hall, where Mephito leaned in the open doorway, holding his forehead, still feeling the effects of Joseph's attack. Anthony watched as Mephito shook his head. "Don't," Mephito repeated.

Anthony's grandfather could not have arrived at a better time for Joseph; with the very last of his strength he took advantage of the distraction and twisted free of Anthony's grasp. He ran towards the other end of the laboratory, and the window in the wall there. He accelerated as he neared, ducked his shoulder—and then launched himself into and through the window, glass shattering, wooden sashes splintering as he tasted the morning air for a brief, glorious moment before plummeting to the street forty-four stories below.

Anthony and Mephito rushed to the now-open window, peering down at the street, looking for Joseph's body—and finding nothing but empty pavement. The murderer was nowhere to be found.

"What—where is he?" Anthony asked. "He couldn't have survived that fall."

"It would appear, Grandson, that you are not the only one with a surprise or two up his sleeve this morning," Mephito said. "Our tasiwoo is as resourceful as he is deadly."

Out in the parlor, Gentry moaned as he came to, shaking loose the cobwebs. "Somebody tell me I was dreaming," he said. "Wait—Jim? Why aren't you in jail?"

"All those girls," Anthony said to Mephito, ignoring his friend for now.

"All three of them dead. This man—whoever he is—he has to pay for that. We have to find him."

"I fear that will not be a problem—I have a strong feeling that he has yet to finish with you. Right now, though—you have a court date to prepare for."

Detective Brock slipped into the back of the courtroom just as the arraignment began. Anthony was being charged with three counts of capital murder, and as expected, the room was full of reporters. District Attorney Dodge was before the judge now, laying out the case against Anthony in exacting detail. No A.D.A.'s on this one; a chance to lock horns with Clarence Darrow in a case as high-profile as this one proved too much to resist for the boss, especially with reelection now less than a year away.

Darrow sat quietly at the defense table, watching the proceedings alongside Anthony, leaning down occasionally to scribble a note. Brock wasn't impressed in the least by the legendary barrister; celebrity had little effect on him lately, and the circumstances by which he finally met the world's most famous detective had not done much to change his mind.

Anthony sat silently at the table, shoulders hunched over, staring at his hands, looking as uncomfortable as a grizzly bear stuffed into a three piece suit. It appeared that the gravity of the situation had finally begun to wear him down. Brock smiled, glad to see it. He glanced down at his watch; Pearce was late. Probably another fight with the wife.

Anthony's entourage sat in the front row of seating, just behind the railing. The three of them—the butler, the shaman, the pilot—all looked the worse for wear. A lot more sleepless nights in their future, Brock reckoned, wondering where their next paycheck would come from, once their meal ticket rode the lightning at Sing Sing.

"The people request that bail be denied in this case, Your Honor." Dodge stood before the bench, wrapping up. "Given the defendant's extraordinary resources and even more extraordinary penchant for exotic travel."

"Your Honor, my client is one of the most-recognized men in the free world," Darrow interjected, speaking for the first time since Brock's arrival. "How the prosecution would expect him to elude detection and simply disappear is a mystery not even the Super-Detective himself could solve."

This drew a chuckle from the large crowd in the chamber; Brock assumed it would play even better in the afternoon editions, which was surely Darrow's intention. Judge Ahearn banged everyone back into silence with his gavel. "Councilor, please save your one-liners for Hearst's boys on the courthouse steps," Judge Ahearn said. "Not my courtroom."

"My apologies, Your Honor."

"Bail is denied." Ahearn slammed his gavel again, punctuating his decision.

"Your Honor, if I may—"

But Darrow never got the chance to register his objection. He was interrupted mid-rebuttal by the unmistakable sound of gunfire. The gunshot echoed throughout the cavernous courtroom, the reverb quickly mixing with the screams of terror from the gallery. Brock moved as quickly as he could, fighting the fleeing crowd, towards the side door that led to the judge's chambers, as best he could tell the direction from which the shot originated.

The bleeding bailiff by the chamber door confirmed this, as did the hulking albino standing over him, pistol in hand. The gunman was battered and bruised beyond anything Brock had ever seen, his body racked with fresh cuts and bruises and wounds. Brock reached into his jacket for the service revolver nestled there in a shoulder holster, but the wounded gunman was quicker. He raised his pistol and fired again, this time towards the defendant's table. The bullet had the same deadly accuracy as his first shot, and caught Jim Anthony square in the chest. Brock watched helplessly as Anthony pitched forward headfirst onto the table, still seated in his chair—and then exploded.

The smoke and sparks rising from Anthony's chest only added to the confusion in the courtroom. Brock could hear his fellow officers across the courtroom, trying to fight their way through the crowd to his position. Given the chaos in the room, it would be another few seconds before they made it. Brock didn't need his police training to know that this situation needed to be contained, and it needed to be contained two minutes ago. There would be time enough to figure out the smoking mechanical—or whatever it was—Anthony later. Right now, he needed to take care of the giant armed maniac who was at this very moment turning a pistol in his direction.

It was obvious that the gunman was seriously wounded, unsteady on his feet. He wobbled as he turned towards Brock, and the shot he fired was well off the mark, the bullet lodging in the carved wooden seal of the great state of New York hanging on the wall above Judge Ahearn's bench. Brock ducked the second shot just as easily, and when he straightened up, he had a clean shot at the gunman's head.

But before he could pull the trigger, a large hand flashed out of nowhere, folding itself over his own hand and gun. "Brock. Don't."

Keeping his gun hand steady, Brock turned his head to see yet another Jim Anthony. This one's chest was intact, and using a slow, easy pressure, forced Brock's gun down to his side. "You are an excellent manhunter, Detective Brock," he said in the same kind of slow, easy voice. "I would hate to see you lose that."

Brock nodded, then looked back at Joseph, who had lowered his own gun, the look on his face one of a man who has just seen a ghost.

A trio of uniformed policemen burst through the crowd; two of them tackled Joseph to the floor, high-low style, while the third kept his gun trained on the whole scene. Joseph offered no resistance.

Brock looked over to the defense table, where Anthony sat, a smoking, sparking hole in his chest. Then he looked back to his right, where Anthony stood, arms crossed, watching as the gunman was handcuffed by the police. "C'mon, Detective," the standing Anthony said. "You're a smart guy. Figure it out."

"A what?"

"A robot."

Anthony and Gentry sat in the dining room back at Penthouse A. Following the events at the courthouse earlier that morning, Anthony had been released on his own recognizance, advised only to not leave town for a couple of days while everything sorted itself out. The courthouse gunman had given his name as Joseph Nighthorse, and then proceeded to give an unsolicited cursory confession in the deaths of Argentina Devine, Charity O'Brien, and Anastasia Vollmerhausen. He also confessed to the unsolved murder of a Metropolitan Museum security guard some years ago, then told the police where to find the body of a coffee shop waitress who had just been reported missing a few hours before. The cloud of suspicion now lifted from Anthony's head, the city moved quickly to avoid any further embarrassment by sending him home, hoping to quickly put the whole sordid affair behind them.

Anthony took another bite of the thick porterhouse Dawkins had prepared upon their return to the Waldorf-Anthony. He chewed slowly, thoughtfully, savoring the taste. "That play we saw in Norway a few years back. Remember?"

Gentry shook his head. "I musta been asleep or something," he said, mouth full of steak.

"You almost made it to the opening curtain. A personal best for you."

"Hey, the house lights go out, so do I. It was a play about robots?"

Anthony nodded. "Rossum's Universal Robots. I've been working on some schematics in the lab, off and on, ever since. A mechanical man?" Anthony dropped his fork, growing excited at the possibilities. "Body doubles for the president to foil assassination attempts. Tireless, abundant labor. Motherless soldiers. The applications are endless."

Gentry shrugged. "Once you fix the whole smoking and sparking thing—your guy sure didn't take a bullet well."

"I've got some ideas on that already. Given the press this is sure to get, I've got to tighten this up fast. The War Department will certainly be calling for a new prototype."

Gentry reached across the table, helped himself to another spoonful of Dawkins' mashed potatoes. "I wish you had told us—you had me fooled completely. When'd you make the switch?"

"I knew that once I was arrested on those charges, the police would stop looking. They'd have their killer, end of story. But if I could have an Anthony Duplicate serve the jail time, then I could continue searching for the true killer. And then we got lucky—the killer came to us."

Gentry scowled and rubbed the purple knot on his jaw. "Lucky for you."

Anthony reached over with a bear paw and pounded his friend on the back. "You've been in tougher scrapes than this one, Red."

"I guess you're right. As usual," Gentry smirked. "I'm sure Pearce and Brock are happy to know they locked up a robot—and I'd sure like to be there when they explain that to their boss."

"Ahem."

Anthony and Gentry turned towards the doorway where Dawkins stood, none-too-subtly clearing his throat. "If I may interrupt, gentlemen—Speaking of Detective Brock, he's in the parlor to see you, Sir."

Gentry slammed his fork down on his plate in disgust. "I've had about enough of those guys today—"

Anthony reached a hand out to calm his friend. "Easy with the good China, Tom. The man's just doing his job."

Gentry shook his head. "You keep saying that."

Anthony took one final bite of his steak, washed it down with the last of his milk, then pushed away from the table. He found Brock standing at the parlor window, watching the traffic start and stop at the busy intersection down below. "Nighthorse gave a full confession," Brock said. He didn't turn around, choosing instead to watch Anthony in the window's reflection. "Signed, notarized, the whole bit."

"Good."

"In light of your. . . status, Mayor La Guardia wants as public an apology as possible. Press conference tomorrow, noon, front steps of City Hall."

"That's hardly necessary—"

"I agree. But the mayor's the mayor, you know?"

Anthony nodded slowly. The mayor was the mayor, that was for sure. He'd be there. "I'll be there," he said. "On one condition—give me a few minutes to speak with Nighthorse afterwards. I've got a lot of questions he needs to answer."

Brock finally turned around, looked Anthony square in the eye. "I don't think I can make that happen, Anthony."

Anthony shrugged. "Maybe the mayor could, then. We'll speak about it tomorrow before the press conference."

Brock shook his head. "Not even the mayor's that good—Nighthorse hung himself in his cell this afternoon."

The news rocked Anthony; he took a step backwards to balance himself, regain his composure. "The end of days. . ." he said softly.

"What's that?"

Anthony shifted his weight from one foot to the other, gave his head a tiny shake. "Nothing."

Brock reached into the inner pocket of his sports coat, producing a piece of paper that had been folded in half, then halved again. He held it out towards Anthony. "He left a note—I think it's for you."

Anthony took the note from the detective, but did not unfold it. "You think it's for me?"

"Yeah, you or Grandpa—it's written in Comanche."

Anthony unfolded the note, then read it. Then he read it again.

"Well? Am I right? It's for you?"

"If the Great Spirit had desired me to be a white man, he would have made me so in the first place," Anthony said, translating aloud. "He put in your heart certain wishes and plans; in my heart he put other and different desires.

"Each man is good in the sight of the Great Spirit." Anthony looked up at Brock for a moment, then finished the note without looking back down. "It is not necessary that eagles should be crows."

Brock nodded. "Impressive," he said, the word dripping with sarcasm. "A poet and a killer."

Anthony folded the note, handed it back to Brock. "These are not Nighthorse's words, Detective."

"Yeah? Who wrote it, then? Another robot, maybe?"

"You misunderstand. Nighthorse wrote these words—but he was quoting. This is Sitting Bull."

"Well, it certainly is beautiful." Brock returned the note to his jacket pocket. "Speaking of crow, I best be getting home. I've got a lot of it to eat tomorrow—gonna be a long day."

"Look, I know you're just doing your job," Anthony said. He extended his right hand towards Brock. "I want you to know there's no hard feelings here, Detective."

Brock looked down at Anthony's hand for a long while, but didn't take it. "I'll go ahead and let myself out," he said instead.

Anthony watched as the police detective turned on his heels and walked across the parlor. The front door closed behind him with a soft click. Anthony stood there a moment longer, then turned and walked back into the dining room, where his family and friends awaited.

The common schools
are the stomach of the country
in which all people that come to us
are assimilated within a generation.
When a lion eats an ox,
the lion does not become an ox
but the ox becomes a lion.

-- Henry Ward Beecher

The End

Writing Pulp Fiction

Pulp fiction?!?
Aren't those the old, over-mannered stories where people talked like this! And THIS! No, scratch that. People in pulp stories never talked. They spat. They growled. They glowered.

Pulp fiction, with its over-caffeinated, hyper-macho, purple prose?!?

No, thank you.

At least, that was my initial response when I was first approached by Ron Fortier to try my hand at a pulp tale for Airship27. I had come across a Call For Writers-type thing that Ron had posted on one writer's board or another, looking for the next generation of pulp purveyors. My mind immediately moved to a few guys I had come across in my time as editor and publisher of A Thousand Faces, the Quarterly Journal of Superhuman Fiction (PLUG!) who I felt would be exactly what he was looking for. So I dropped him a quick line, including links to pertinent examples of these writers within the pages of my magazine, as well as their contact information, figuring that would be that.

So Ron replied back quickly (as he always does), thanking me for my suggestions and promising to contact those guys post haste. He also posed a question to me: when was I going to take a shot at writing a pulp story of my own?

I laughed; all the thoughts I opened with ran through my head. Pulp fiction just wasn't for me; I was a superhero writer. (And yes, I knew how ridiculous that sounded, even then.) Why would I want to write about larger-than-life figures who donned ridiculous costumes to battle street-level crime and/or international conspiracies? Many of whom did so under the cover of night, with just as many doing it at odds with the local authorities? Arch-villains with amazingly-convulted plots to conquer the world, comic relief sidekicks, beautiful damsels in distress....

Wait a minute.

So I told Ron I might give it a shot. In person, it probably would have been a sheepish response, but through the anonymity the internet provides... He sent me the character bible of any and all public domain characters that Airship27 was or might possibly in the future be working on. Some of them were pretty cool; and some of them, since we're being honest here, were pretty lame. (There's a heretic in the temple!)

I don't know if it was me that requested a Jim Anthony tale, or something that Ron suggested. But once again, my initial take was skeptical. Genius scientist, millionaire businessman, unparalleled athlete, globetrotting adventurer... Check. I can work with all of those. Throw in the womanizing, the dark temper... there's a few interesting elements you don't see in a typical superhero story.

But that sweatshirt and swim trunk outfit. That hideous caricature of a grandfather. The whole backstory—half-Comanche, half-Irish in a time period where most of America—less than three generations removed from a time period where Native Americans and white settlers would massacre each other routinely—would call him a half-breed (to use the ugly parlance of the time) first, no matter the size of his heroics....

Wait a minute.

There's the hook.

I have long wanted to do a story that in some way dealt with the Carlisle Indian School, one of the most heinous movements (however well-intentioned) in American history, and one you don't learn much about in high school history class. Once I figured a way to incorporate the school into this story, I was off and running. Add in a little William Randolph Hearst yellow journalism (Did you know there were over thirty daily newspapers in NYC in the thirties? Of course Anthony owned one of his own.), a little Clarence Darrow (in many ways the Johnnie Cochrane of his time), a few Native American folk tales—what more do you need?

Robots.

Yeah. Now we're talking.

Or spitting.

Or growling.

Or glowering.

Take your pick.

FRANK BYRNS - lives and writes in suburban Washington, DC. His short fiction has appeared in such places as Strange Horizons, Cyber Age Adventures, Everyday Fiction, Powder Burn Flash magazine, and the WW Norton Anthology of Hint Fiction. His latest collection of superhero fiction, Things to Come, was released in 2009, joining Requiem (2006) and My Father's Son (2004); all three are available for order wherever fine books are sold. You can visit him online at www.frankbyrns.com

When he's not writing, he serves as the editor and publisher of A Thousand Faces, the Quarterly Journal of Superhuman Fiction. Visit the magazine at www.thousand-faces.com

As you've probably gathered from this essay, this is his first stab at pulp fiction. Hopefully it won't be his last.

NEIGHBORHOOD IN PERIL

by Erwin K. Roberts

The man in the floppy greatcoat seemed a bit disoriented. Or drunk. And maybe a bit dumb. After all, walking alone late at night in the High Street neighborhood seemed far from the smartest thing to do. The hunched over man also seemed to be looking for someone.

His sort of sideways crab walk led him into the vestibules of the buildings he passed. At least those that were open. He shambled up to the bank of mailboxes, or building directory in each place. His face seemed to be squinting as he almost touched the surfaces with his nose. If the words could not be read he pulled a large box of kitchen matches from a coat pocket. Hesitantly striking a Lucifer on the wall his head would bob from name to name. Then that same head would shake side to side before he shambled on. The man seemed not to notice that a crumpled two dollar bill fell to the ground the last time he pulled out the matchbox.

As the stooped man headed for the next building another man stepped out from behind a big mailbox bolted to the sidewalk. This man stepped into the vestibule just vacated. With a flexibility belying his fire plug like build, he deftly picked the crumpled bill from the floor. His humorless chuckle could not have been heard outside, even if the door had been open to the street.

Back out on the street, the second man stepped under the nearly useless streetlight. In that tiny amount of light he made hand signals. Three other shadowy figures detached themselves from various pools of blackness on the block. Following instructions they slipped to the front of the building just past where another match had just flared. The leader felt, more than heard; his fellows force the door open and enter. He slipped behind the stairs to a first floor flat as the searching man came out and moved toward the building where a surprise waited.

The man in the greatcoat stumbled a bit as he entered the new building. His recovery brought him to the center of the stairwell and lobby of the three story office building faster than the three men waiting for him expected.

Jerry Larson waited in a phone booth. Skids stood just around the corner of the stairs to the floor above. Thin as a rail George almost disappeared in the inset of a door frame. Both of them could see the phone booth door open. As one they quietly converged on the shambling man.

On gum soled shoes George glided up behind the target with one arm raised. Jerry smiled. Watching George work with that cosh he picked up in England was always a pleasure. One light tap and any danger from the victim would end. George's hand started down.

George's hand stopped. The imported blackjack flew across the lobby. A flurry of motion erupted from the greatcoat. Jerry's instincts overcame his astonishment. He charged forward, his arms open to catch the target in a bear hug. Jerry's open arms caught George's flying form instead.

As he landed in a heap with George, Jerry saw the hunched figure rip the greatcoat open. He heard flying buttons bounce off the walls. Skids' body came into view as he launched himself from the sixth stair.

Suddenly the shadowy figure of their target seemed to have grown near a foot as he swirled the huge coat toward the stairs like a matador taunting the bull with his cape. The greatcoat wrapped itself around Skids' head. Their target stepped to the side. As the shrouded attacker flashed by a large fist smashed down. Skids landed nose first with a loud thud.

Jerry struggled to his feet. The mark seemed to be running. But not far. He yanked open the street door to grab the boss before he could react. Snatching up two hands full of topcoat, the mark heaved backward. The boss weighed in at least two hundred and fifty pounds. He came through the door like he was on roller skates. The mark planted one foot in the boss's stomach and rolled backward. The boss rolled with him. Then the mark's leg straightened explosively. The boss landed on the far side of Skids.

Jerry bolted for the door trying to brush past the mark. The man convulsed, springing to his feet from his back without use of his hands. Jerry just had time to note the mark wore next to nothing before those unused hands sent him to oblivion with a one-two combination.

A moment later a flashlight's beam swept the lobby. Jim Anthony surveyed the group of figures unconscious on the light parquet wood floor. Glad to be out of the steamy greatcoat on this warm spring night, he stretched his muscles free of the knots built up by keeping that stooped posture. Then he pulled a coin from the waistband of his gold swimming suit.

A moment later he used the pay phone. At his penthouse in the Waldorf-Anthony hotel Dawkins, the butler answered. Jim gave the building's address, adding, "Send them."

Dawkins finished writing down the address, then stepped over to a shortwave radio transmitter. As the set warmed he transposed the numbers of the address and modified the street name in a manner similar to Pig Latin. Ready, he keyed the microphone. Using proper armature radio procedure, he initiated a call that ended with the coded street address.

✳ ✳ ✳

As he waited Jim Anthony's mind reviewed the facts leading up to the evening's masquerade. He had returned to New York three weeks ago after some time out west visiting his mother's people. Jim had participated in ceremonial hunts and fasted for three days before running cross country further than a marathon. Coming back on the train he expected to get lots of rest in his Pullman suite. Didn't happen. The guy in the connecting suite ended up dead in strange circumstances. With local police and Texas Rangers wanting to sidetrack the entire train indefinitely Jim stepped forward and solved the case. Once the county coroner understood Jim's death by misadventure theory the train departed.

But the word of his work sped ahead. It seemed that every time the train so much as slowed down a reporter, or two, or three, jumped aboard. Every last one assigned to get an exclusive interview with one Jim Anthony.

The train crew really tried to pay him back for them getting under way again. But the reporters seemed like a swarm of mosquitoes. The Conductor and the porters would swat one, but two more took his place. Two "journalists" got into a fistfight over picking the lock on the door of the now empty connecting suite. They were tossed off with the Railway Post Office mail sack as the train slowed at a wide spot in the road. At three o'clock in the morning one female reporter knocked on Jim's door wearing a bathrobe. And not much else. The Conductor left her at a whistle stop, without her luggage.

By the time Jim reached Manhattan he felt like he had walked back. The penthouse of the Waldorf-Anthony was empty. By being several hours late Jim had missed flying to the Catskills with Tom, Delores, and Dawkins the butler. Some of his fiancée's friends were rehearsing a play there that might end up on Broadway. Delores decided to lend moral support while trying to help the producers find a financial 'angel.' So Jim threw himself into bed. He would join them at the Tepee tomorrow or the next day. More tired than even he realized, he slept from dusk till noon.

On waking Jim's stomach rumbled. His body reverberated like a minor earthquake. Jim dived into the near scalding hot shower bent on finding food to his liking as soon as possible.

Not long after Jim Anthony, dressed in slacks, a sports coat, and fedora emerged from the subway on Canal Street near the edge of Chinatown.

Jim really enjoyed spending time in this part of Manhattan. Buildings old and new peaked his interest in architecture. And the food...

After way too much train food. After only filling his coffee cup half full to forestall spilling it from the train's motion, Jim wanted to eat. A lot. But what remained to be seen. A world of food lay within a few minutes walk for his long legs. A block away sat Chinatown. He would stride past the tourist area. No Chop Suey Parlor for Jim. He knew most of the Ma and Pa places where the residents went for a taste of the old country's different regions. Hunan, Szechuan, both hot enough to make most Mexicans melt. He could order and thank the staff in Cantonese, Mandarin, and even the Wu dialect. His mouth watered just thinking about the cuisines.

Just a bit further away stood Little Italy. Jim loved spaghetti, but he loved the Northern Italian style even more with its almost total lack of red sauces.

In Soho, and below Canal Street, cuisines most American's never heard of waited. Lebanese and Syrian food. Czech pastry delights. Borscht. Small bakeries and more.

Jim drifted along Canal Street. After the southwest his noise balked at the city smells. He ignored them. He waited for the tantalizing fragrance of some foreign kitchen to catch his attention. When he found the right scent he would track it to the door of the restaurant without hesitation.

His nostrils twitched. Something was being fried. Not in lard, but olive oil. Not chicken. Something a bit spicy. Falafel! Nabil's place two blocks over. His wife made magnificent stuffed grape leaves. Suddenly Jim realized that his feet had taken off before he decided to go in that direction.

Jim ducked down an alley. He jaywalked onto the block he wanted. Nabil's electric sign was broken Jim noticed as he passed the corner dry cleaners. He glanced at the drugstore window as he passed. He almost walked head on into a bull of a man who stepped out of the vestibule of a Five & Ten.

Jim's amazing reflexes allowed him to halt without running into the fellow with a huge cauliflower ear. For some reason this seemed to disappoint the roughly dressed man.

"Sorry," said Jim as he started to step around, "I didn't see you there."

"Where you headed in such a big hurry, pal," came the rumbled reply.

"Lunch," smiled Jim.

The huge man slid back into Jim's path. "You ain't goin' to that foreigner's place, are you?"

"What foreigner," replied Jim in a near monotone? Anybody who knew Jim Anthony at all would recognize that tone. It meant, clear the decks, action imminent.

"Th' bum on this block taking jobs away from real Americans. We going to see he goes back where he came from."

Jim pretended not to notice the two others slipping up behind him. Instead he gave the first man a puzzled look. "You want to send Nabil back to Queens?"

"What you mean? Queens?"

"I happen to know that Nabil and his wife were both born in Queens. Now get out of my way. I'm hungry."

Normally Jim avoided a fight when he could. He was not looking for trouble now. However, if a fight was requested, Jim's mood allowed for no turning of the other cheek.

He took half a step forward. The tough's hand impacted his chest with enough force to throw most men back into the arms of his waiting friends. Jim Anthony didn't move. Not an inch. The tough rebounded a bit. His hand did not.

A seemingly iron vise gripped his hand and twisted. Several joints popped as he went to his knees. What was keeping Lou and Pete?

Lou and Pete stood in shock for a moment. Big George bossed the group because he was tougher than both of them together. Instead of stumbling back where they could grab him, this mark put Big George on his knees in a heartbeat. His face looked like somebody did with a slug in the chest.

Pete threw off the shock first. He flicked his head forward at Lou. As he saw Lou begin to rush ahead Pete reached into his coat pocket. He saw the mark lean over. Pete never figured out what happened next.

Jim Anthony let all his recent frustrations vent themselves. He bent down as Lou charged ahead. In a move derived from the French La Savate his left heel impacted under Lou's jaw with tremendous force. Maintaining his right hand's grip on Big George's twisted arm, Jim grabbed a large handful of the thug's crotch with his left hand. With one mighty heave Jim turned completely around with Big George held at arm's length above his head. He took one step forward. Just like a pro wrestler he body slammed Big George. Pete absorbed much of that impact. His body folded like an accordion.

Quickly Jim pulled Big George off of Pete. Without seeming to he slammed the side of the man's head with his elbow. Now sure that the leader could not interfere he checked the other two. Pete's head had rebounded from the sidewalk. Out cold. Lou would be eating through a straw after they wired his jaw shut. End of fight.

Jim quickly went through the pockets of the three toughs. On Lou and Pete he found a blackjack, two knives, and a piece of broom handle just as wide as its owner's hand. The trio's spokesman yielded a much handled, carefully folded piece of paper with a bunch of numbers written on it. This he slid into a jacket pocket as he heard footsteps approach from behind him.

Jim pretended not to hear. He let a gravity knife blade lock itself open. The footsteps became louder. Intentionally, Jim decided. He snapped the blade off against the sidewalk. The approaching feet kicked something. He tossed the ordinary jack-knife, the stick, and the blackjack into a storm drain.

From behind him came a barely audible voice, "My stars, it was sweet what you did to those three, Mr. Anthony."

Jim rose and turned. One of New York's finest stood there, hands on hips with a big scowl on his wide face. Just as the Officer drew breath to speak, one eye scrunched up in a knowing wink. The astonished Jim Anthony then found himself being loudly berated for fighting in public. He was further admonished about searching the fallen men. Strangely no mention was made of his foes' weapons. In fact, as the Constable On Patrol spoke his feet deftly shoved the broken knife into the same storm drain. The tirade ended with an order to stay out of further trouble. Speech over the Officer calmly walked past Jim. His lips didn't move, but Jim clearly heard, "Meet me at the envelope factory in half an hour. Take the tour."

Forty-five minutes later Jim knew more than he ever wanted to about envelope production. He guessed that machinery in the sixty year old building once ran by steam power. His guide led him to a display and sales room, poured him a just perked cup of coffee, then departed.

"Now what?" thought Jim as he decided the coffee was excellent. Almost before he could swallow the first sip the beat cop entered by another door.

"Thank you for coming, Mr. Anthony," the man said with a smile. "Please keep this to yourself. I'm putting my badge at risk here."

"Officer, unless you confess to a serious crime, I'll keep anything you tell me off the record. Fair enough?"

"More than fair. I'll bet you have a few questions, by now."

Jim nodded, "Nabil tells me that he's had threats to himself and his family by phone and with messages left in various places. Also vandalism. His help's been run off. He has no idea why this started. That street thug claimed that Nabil took jobs away from "real" Americans. Usually a term like that is twisted to mean of Anglo-Saxon descent. That's exactly what Nabil's employees were. Now they are out of work. Further, I defend myself against a mugging and you give me a public lecture on good citizenship that can be heard a block away. You're darn right I have questions. You saw the whole fight, but you didn't rush in. Why?"

"Spalpeans like those three have been popping up on my beat, and some others, for about a month now. Bother all sorts of people they do. Thompson, two beats north of here, ran two of them in when he caught them threatening a Polish lady and pushing her kids around. The lugs got bailed out in well under an hour. Then Thompson, a good man, got transferred to a midnight shift in the Bowery.

"Word came down that we were to leave loiterers alone unless we could actually charge 'em with a felony. And no harassment, like keeping a close eye on them. Our Captain about choked on his temper getting that said at roll call. Nobody knows the how or the why of it, but the skids are greased way high up for this to go on. There it is, Mr. Anthony."

Jim said a couple of unpleasant words in the Comanche tongue. "So if you had walked up and told them to leave me alone, you would be in trouble?"

"Yes, sir! Probably riding the garbage scows as a guard. I even came here by the old steam tunnels. I don't dare be seen consorting with a full time good deed doer like you. Here's how it was. I caught a glimpse of you jaywalking onto the block. I didn't recognize you at first, but you looked to be a big strong man. That Big George always pushes the victim back for the other lugs to do the real dirty work. I got as close as I could out of their sight. I would have been on the other two before you got hurt. I'm good enough with the night stick to put 'em out before Big George could jump in. Anyway, that was the plan. I ain't proud of it, but I wanted to get those three off of my beat.

"Then, at the last second, I recognized you. And I said to myself, 'Self, this is going to be worth seeing.'"

Jim reflected for a moment before continuing, "So you figured that my working them over would cause less trouble?"

"Yes, sir! I've heard a lot about your fighting abilities. Figured even if your rep only turned out to be a fifth right you could take those three an' not break a sweat. Any of 'em managed to pull a knife or rod I'd shoot. And in the head if I could safely. As for the lecture, a couple of buddies and I compared notes on all this. We think these bums have spotters around the area. If I'd come over and congratulated you I might catch Hell for it. So I gave you some instead."

"In that case, a wise move on your part Officer Burland. Let's arrange some method of keeping in touch."

❋ ❋ ❋

Jim Anthony left the Tension Envelope factory carrying a large box of double envelope thank you cards. He walked a couple of blocks then caught a cab to his newspaper, The Daily Star.

The City Editor knew nothing of the situation, but promised to put all his available stringers on alert and to have the police blotter checked. Next Jim spoke with Gibbons, the Managing Editor. Here he found some disturbing pay dirt.

"We've lost two delivery route boys in that area this month. Both just called in and quit. Well, that happens now and again. And for no reason sometimes. But this morning I mentioned it to Gunigun at the Sentinel. He turned the air around us bluer than the sky. Seems one of his boys in the same area got hit by a truck yesterday!"

Gibbons read the tone of the words that came out of Jim Anthony's mouth. Suddenly he decided he was glad he didn't understand Comanche. Jim reigned in his temper, but his eyes blazed as he spoke. "Call Billy Barton. Tell him the situation. Tell him that I am personally paying for this. Have him dress up and report to Circulation for information on the first route we lost. Make sure he understands that this may be a more hazardous situation than our usual problems. Leave a message at the penthouse when he can start. Tonight, if possible. I'll be in the morgue."

Jim took the stairs all the way down to the newspaper's morgue to cool off. Starting a war hot headed just begged for unnecessary trouble. And a war this would be. For a long list of reasons Jim Anthony hated corruption in government. He hated bullies even more. And he would not tolerate anybody, but anybody, threatening those who worked for him.

Arriving in the basement Jim opened the morgue door and called out, "Robb, are you here?"

A bespectacled man's head appeared from behind a stack of packing cases. "Ahhh... Big Jim... Is it safe to come out? Gibbons called down that you were breathing fire and headed in my direction."

Jim could feel his tensions lessen as he laughed. "That's a fair picture, all right. Come on out. There's an area just east of Chinatown, north from the Civic Center to at least Canal Street. Teams of thugs seem to be trying to control the area through intimidation. They have damn good protection from somewhere. Gibbons just told me they're working on the newsboys, too. I want you to try to figure out why the area is that important to someone. And then there's this," Jim continued holding up Big George's folded paper.

"What is it," asked Robb, as he moved in for a close look.

"Some sort of coded diagram, I think," said Jim holding the paper carefully by one tiny corner. "Want to try dusting for fingerprints if you still have that kit."

"Bring it over to the copy camera while I grab some tweezers. Here, use these to spread it out on the centering marks while I get the photo-lights turned on. Move the camera down... Focus... Shoot... Please turn it over. Fine. Two shots of each side at slightly different exposures. Now let me find that kit. Here, dust away while I develop the film."

A few minutes later Robb inquired, "Find anything useful?"

"One set of prints that probably belong to Big George, plus a couple of partial prints from somebody else."

"Did you check for a watermark?"

"Yes," sighed Jim, "a fairly common maker of above average stationary. Not exclusive enough, according to your reference book, to try tracing. The photos come out?"

"Excellent, if I do say so. Got full size prints in the fixer bath now. If you don't mind I'll take a set to an editor I know over at Street and Smith. He's big on codes. Writes a regular column for their Shadow title."

Jim chuckled again, "Sure, if you trust him. Say, don't tell me you're peddling purple prose to that outfit."

"Of course, 'I' am not." said Robb with a broad wink. "But surely you've heard of that penny-a-word-smith R. Erwin Kennedy?"

"Can't say that I have," replied Jim. "The Star's parent company publishes fiction magazines, too. Are you appearing there, as well?"

"I can't crack the market. Seems I'm much better at action than innuendo. All your titles are 'snappy,' or 'spicy,' or whatever the current term may be. Besides Street and Smith has better rates."

✷ ✷ ✷

Just before five o'clock the next morning Jim Anthony watched from a deserted building vestibule as a truck with Daily Star markings dropped a large bundle of newspapers across the street in the one street light's cone of brightness. A small figure squatting against a building wall rose and stepped into the lighted area.

"Are you Jerry Smith?" came a voice from the back of the truck.

"Yes, sir," was the reedy response.

"I see your bag. You got your ties... Route listing... Phone numbers? Good kid! Lot of first timers get excited and forget stuff."

"I used ta' have a route up in Queens."

The unseen voice replied, "Good deal. That'll make it easier on both of us. Any problems you call Circulation. Fast. Let's roll, Mike!" With that the truck pulled away.

Jerry Smith sat on the curb to roll up his papers. Finished, he slung the heavy bag over his shoulder and began walking. As quiet as the shadow of a gliding bird Jim Anthony followed at a distance.

The boy left his papers in various places as requested by the customers. Finally he reached an unusual five story building marked Harpist's Bizarre. Jim was familiar with the place. Offices, shipping services, and light manufacturing on the upper floors with open air shop-stalls at street level. The night gate stood partly open as fish and produce vendors came in from their suppliers to set up for the new day's business.

As Jerry Smith entered the lobby to leave papers for the upper floors Jim found a large empty produce box. He reversed his all black jacket to the merely very dark fabric side that did not make its wearer as though he was trying to hide. Pretending the box was still full Jim put it on his shoulder and walked inside the market area.

Jerry finished with the lobby. He began to circulate among the maze of small storefronts. He left papers in the diamond shaped holes of the night gates as he passed. He turned down the row furthest from the food vendors. Here the high ceiling light was out. He looked around as if worried about something. Identifying a subscriber's booth, Jerry tossed a paper over the chicken wire gate and hurried on. Two big men stepped out of the next cross-aisle and turned to face him. One just stood there while the bigger one approached Jerry, his long arms effectively blocked the passageway.

"Paper, sir?" asked Jerry meekly.

A very unpleasant laugh came from the big man. "Kid, like I tol' the last brat, paper boys ain't welcome around here. Now git, an' don't come back. You understan' me? Not on this route. Nowhere!"

"But how can I explain..."

"I don't care, but you mention me an' I'll find you and break every bone in ya' body. You're mouthy with me, kid. I don't like that. I gonna teach you a little lesson."

Jim left the empty box near one of the produce stands and hurried to where he thought Jerry Smith would be. Then he followed the trail of delivered papers. Ahead he noticed one of the overhead lamps was out. No, broken. Jim hoped he was not too late as he rushed ahead. Right into two thugs rushing to meet him. From just around the corner came a high pitched scream!

"...Jim put it on his shoulder and walked inside..."

Already in a no mercy frame of mind Jim Anthony went through the two thugs like a charge of salts. Jim stepped to one side and pivoted ninety degrees while bracing himself. As the lead tough stumbled past him Jim grabbed the collars of his coat and shirt in a grip of spring steel with his left hand. Simultaneously his right hand flashed straight out. With the first two knuckles folded in that flying hand sank into the second man's throat at the Adam's apple. Before the second man could even begin to crumple Jim turned his entire attention back to the first. Those folded knuckles delivered a kidney punch of incredible force. Jim hurried onward. He leaped over the still falling form of the second thug.

The scene turned out to be as bad as he feared. Lots of blood on the floor, more dripping onto a pile of Dime Novels just inside one booth. And there squatted "Jerry Smith" rummaging in the bottom of his newspaper bag for something.

Jim sighed as he said, "Don't light that cigar, Billy. This is far from over."

Billy Barton looked up at Jim in disgust, "You're payin' the bill, pal. I just may add a box of Monte Christos to the tab if you keep me in character."

Jim nodded. At just under four feet tall, Billy Barton was a perfectly proportioned midget. With a little bit of makeup, a wig, and if he shaved at least twice a day, Billy could make anyone think he was the most innocent child. He had spent some years with a circus learning acrobatics and other skills. He even joined the midget wrestling circuit for a time. He loved knives. And if any man hated bullies more than Jim Anthony, it was Billy Barton.

One thug lay on the floor almost disemboweled. The aisle blocker leaned against the night gate of a stall with a small throwing knife sticking out of each arm and leg. Now that Jim Anthony had arrived Billy lowered the knife he held in ready position.

Footsteps approached from both sides. As Jim quickly frisked the dead man he said, "Stay in character, Billy. At least until we get done at the police station."

An hour and a half later Jim and "Jerry Smith" were ushered into the local Police Precinct Captain's office. Captain Steven O'Rorke rose saying, "You got my message, I take it, Mr. Anthony?"

Jim grasped the extended hand. "Your secretary whispered it in my ear. Don't call my lawyer until I saw you alone. Her manner and voice added a 'pretty please with sugar on it.' I imagine that's why you sent her."

"You bet. Myra is the only one in the building I could trust not to make it sound like a threat," replied O'Rorke.

"My lead attorney might show up anyway. He knew the area I'd be in. The Daily Star will have let him know about the event in the Bizarre. Therefore we may be short on time here."

"All right, Mr. Anthony. Fair enough. I'm going to cut you free as soon as I logically can without causing myself trouble. We're not supposed to take note of what those infernal hoodlums do. Far as I'm concerned that means we don't give a damn what happens to 'em. At least not much of one. All of the punks got long records. They did it to each other. This young man just got caught in the middle.

"Now I know you were trying to uncover why your newsboys were quitting. But I'm concerned that you let a child get into danger to do so."

Jim and Billy looked at each other. Billy's face formed a question. Jim nodded, "Okay, Billy."

Billy Barton stood to his full three feet eleven and five-eights inches. He pulled off his wig and let it drop. The metal plate under the hair made a gong like sound on the stone floor. His receding hairline revealed a different and rougher skin tone than his face. From a hidden pocket in his baggy pants he produced his Private Investigator identification which he placed in the open mouthed Captain's hand.

Captain O'Rorke broke out laughing. For a moment he had trouble reading the document. Finally words emerged from among the guffaws. "Billy... Barton....explains a lot... You fooled my best detectives... No wonder the Feds bring you in..."

Shortly Jim and Billy were quietly smuggled out of the police station in a repair truck.

For the next two weeks Jim Anthony prowled the problem area at all hours. At first he found groups of thugs on almost every trip. In six days he sent seventeen men to the hospital making sure to fracture a leg or foot bone on each one. During that time he collected four more of the strangely marked sheets of the fine quality paper. The editor at Street and Smith could not find any similar cyphers in his references. Robb mentioned having a theory, but needed at least one more sheet to prove or disprove it. On the eighth day a group ran once they identified him.

Jim made a point of never using any real disguise other than changes of clothing. Often he even wore no hat. In addition to keeping a close eye on his environment Jim counted on his in built sense of danger to warn him of people with guns. This gang seemed to have two unwritten rules. They did not use firearms as far as Jim could tell. And their written threats were never mailed. Breaking New York's strong handgun law might bring State Police involvement. The gang would not want the Postal Inspectors jumping in either. All this gave Jim the notion that the gang's protection stemmed from purely local influence. What came next shook him badly.

❄ ❄ ❄

Jim entered the Waldorf-Anthony by a side door. As he headed for elevators he noticed a rugged featured man rise from a chair in the lobby. Jim stepped into a waiting car. "Penthouse," he said to the operator.

Without seeming to hurry, the neatly dressed man entered just as the operator began to close the outer door. Jim braced himself for a possible fight. Then the image of a newspaper clipping popped into his head. Jim relaxed, as much as he ever would with an armed man standing next to him. Completely out of the operator's line of sight the man put the index finger of one very large hand to his lips. The other hand opened to reveal a badge. His slightly oversize mouth then smiled as he told the operator, "We're together."

Many floors later the two stepped off the elevator. The lanky man looked around. "Say, this isn't the penthouse."

"That elevator doesn't even serve the penthouse. The operator is calling security by now. I can cancel that if you will finish identifying yourself."

"Very slick, Mr. Anthony. Just let me put the badge back with the identification document. Now, take a look."

"Pleased to meet you, Mr. Fowler," said Jim extending his hand. Jim could feel the power that lay in Dan Fowler's big hand, but the man played no strength games.

Jim turned back to the elevator call panel. While he held both call buttons down he pulled open a section of the Art Deco wall plate. This revealed a tiny array of twelve unmarked buttons. Jim's fingers played over the buttons like an accountant with an adding machine. "That takes care of the interruptions," he continued. "Now, to what do I owe the honor of a visit from the F.B.I.'s roving trouble shooter?"

"Mr. Anthony, I have a message to relay to you. I don't think you are going to like it."

Inwardly, Jim Anthony sighed. He had been expecting something like this for the last week, but only on a local level. He kept his voice steady, "Let me guess. Somebody doesn't like my recent activities?"

Fowler's brief chuckle could not have been heard three feet away. "That's putting it mildly. I was ordered to inform you to cease and desist all actions in and around Chinatown."

"Chinatown? I've barely been in Chinatown proper except to grab a meal. Soho, and Little Italy, and below Canal Street sure. You're a lawyer, Mr. Fowler, surely you don't think this 'cease and desist' business carries any legal weight."

"I'm just the messenger here. I was headed out of town to look into some murders related to forest fires when my supervisor gave me this little errand. The message didn't originate with him, either."

Jim decided to try another tack. "I'll just bet your supervisor grabbed you because we are more than a little alike. We prefer the direct method, if possible. And, if your boss is based here in Gotham, he knows I'm unlikely to hole up at the Waldorf-Anthony on just a blanket request without knowing the source. Tell me, do you think this came from your organization?"

Fowler paused before replying, "Don't really think so. I can read my boss pretty well. What he said, and how he said it, gave no indication that this came from our higher ups."

"Thanks for being candid with me. I agree. More likely I'd have had a phone call from your Director waiting for me when I got upstairs. Here is my reply. Take notes, if you wish.

"Almost all the threats and actual crimes are against people whose names definitely are not found on the roster of those who came over on the Mayflower. The thugs involved often use the term 'foreigners' in regard to everyone from legal immigrants to those whose great-grandparents were American citizens. This pattern of threats and intimidation seems to cover an area north from the Civic Center into Greenwich Village. I still have not determined the full extent of this territory. New York's Finest have been muzzled from taking action against these gangsters. Now I am told, with no specifics, to lay off. This leaves three possibilities. One. With much of the world at war, this could be some sort of intelligence related operation where authorities are willing to let a lot of our own citizens suffer to obtain a certain result. Two. Foreign agents, or possibly Bundists, are paying both our street vermin, and some high official, to make divisive trouble. And three. Someone in our own government is assisting some 'pure America' group like the Knights of the Open Palm."

"The Clan," exclaimed Fowler! "Not at all likely, but a speculative case could be built for it."

"Agreed. Now, mostly out of respect for your agency, I will become very quiet on the public side of this. But that does not mean I will stop investigating. Any official who has a real reason for me to stop had better make that reason known very soon. And any government employees who decide to follow me around better identify themselves, as well. I will deal with any stalkers in the most humiliating ways I can think of. Your Director is not the only official who doesn't like being made to look bad.

"Finally," said Jim with a real edge to his voice, "if I continue to get unexplained pressure, or threats, from the government I will go public with that 'not at all likely' theory. My paper is pretty influential. Give me twenty minutes with Frank Heavens and the whole Clarion chain will pick up the story. The Sentinel had a newsboy seriously injured by these vermin. They'll break out headline type of a size they haven't used since the Great War ended if I talk to them at all.

"Have you got all that? Good. I hope your boss doesn't shoot messengers, either!"

That evening Jim's best friend, Tom Gentry, flew Delores, Dawkins the Cockney butler, and even Jim's grandfather Mephito, back to New York from the Catskills.

The night after meeting Dan Fowler Jim donned the heavy greatcoat to go trolling for thugs in the area south of Canal Street. Tom and Mephito waited in a battered wreck of a car in an alley just inside Little Italy. Here they sat until Dawkins' message came over the shortwave receiver bolted behind the back seat.

While Mephito kept watch Jim and Tom bundled the four thugs into the trunk and back seat floorboards. When they looked around the old Indian was nowhere to be seen.

Jim put his hands to his lips. The call of the Peregrine falcon sounded along the street. Tom heard a very faint call in reply. He barely had time to close the back door and grab a spot on the running board before Jim Anthony silently slipped the large sedan into gear. Two blocks north and one east Mephito appeared out of the shadows. He and Jim spoke quickly in Comanche.

As the old man led Jim and Tom to a building around the corner, Jim explained. "He says somebody snuck onto that block. Once he saw me, he hightailed it. He skipped the police call boxes and fire alarms he passed. Went straight to the pay phone in the entry to this food market. My grandfather followed him. As soon as the man asked the operator for a number he cut the line."

They found the watcher peacefully stretched out on the ground with not a mark on him. "How?" began Tom.

Jim shook his head. In a bare whisper he replied, "I never ask. I'm not sure I really want to know how he manages some of the things he does."

Quickly they added the watcher to the pile in the car.

It took two trips to get the five limp bodies up to the penthouse using Jim's private elevator that opened in his closed off garage area. Dawkins pulled tables out of storage to hold them all.

Tom knew what Jim had in mind would probably take all night. He pulled an easy chair into the laboratory so he could both be there to help and doze off.

Jim Anthony monitored all five men as they returned to consciousness. When they woke, or were about to Jim administered an injection based on their body weight. The concoction added an East Indian drug that dulled the senses and boosted subconscious perceptions and reactions to the best known western truth serum. Once the injection took hold Jim fitted the subjects with earphones with receivers that covered the temples. Wires then ran to a table radio like object. When in operation special graph paper marked with a jagged green line exited the side of the machine giving a record of the thought waves of the subject.

With everything ready Jim leaned close to the ear of the subject. He enunciated words key to the case clearly several times while keeping an eye on the laboratory's precision clock. He wrote notes in shorthand. He spoke his own name first. Then he mentioned various street corners. Next came the word "foreigner" which he followed by terms about the origins of the victims of the gang. Jim wasn't quite sure why, but he included the words "Manchuria," "China," and "Chinatown" on his word lists. Lastly came the question "Why?" and "I must report."

Tom woke when the sun came in the laboratory windows, bounced off some test tubes, right into his eyes. He stretched the kinks out of his body as he took stock. All the subjects now wore breathing masks that kept them at the edge of deep sleep. Jim Anthony sat at the map table making very few notes as he studied the green squiggles on the graph paper. Obviously he was not having much success. Nobody outside Jim's in-

"Jim leaned close to the ear of the subject."

ner circle knew of the device. Given Mephito's mysterious abilities, Tom sometimes wondered if the graph paper served a true purpose. Maybe Jim unknowingly really could read minds. He would never suggest that to Jim. He waited until Jim looked up from his task.

"Any luck," he asked?

"Some," said Jim with a weary smile. "As expected, the thugs are just hired muscle. With one exception they don't care about 'foreigners.' In it for the money. On the other hand, it's a darn good thing my grandfather bagged that watcher. I got his reactions to several words about the code sheets. I got a reading that I think comes out as 'map book.' I'll tell Robb at the Star. It may help him.

"I got the only real reactions to the Chinese related words from him. If I'm right, he was thinking 'China Relief, Tomorrow.' I've no idea what that might mean."

"Maybe I can help there," said Tom. "Last night Dawkins was muttering about getting your Tuxedo ready today for a Chinese something Delores mentioned to him."

"That leaves me just a few hours to try and get more out of the watcher."

Jim Anthony tried not to fidget at the table with Delores in the very exclusive restaurant. He wondered again why he was really there. He wished he could be stalking the streets trying to get another code sheet for Robb. Results were still elusive. Yesterday would not be soon enough for the frustrated Jim Anthony.

The Chinese Lantern sat two blocks past the west side of Chinatown. Jim's investigations concerned the area bordering on the east side of the enclave.

A lot of well to do New Yorkers sat around him. All were generous donors to various China Relief appeals. So was Jim Anthony. Tonight's dinner served as a thank you from both the Chinese government and a lot of Chinatown's most influential leaders. All would be briefed on the current China situation and how their donations helped relieve suffering. Jim did not need a briefing. His newspaper had correspondents in Shanghai and several other areas of China. Jim made sure that he saw every "Dateline: China" dispatch that came through the newsroom.

The Chinese Lantern served excellent food. Jim, however, knew a dozen hole-in-the-wall places that served the same dishes as well prepared but without holding back on the spicing of some so as not to incinerate western taste buds. Jim sat at the table chatting with fellow businessmen and their ladies playing a hunch.

With a grandfather who read the future with more than a little accuracy Jim Anthony believed in the value of hunches. He let Delores carry most of the small talk. His eyes swept the tables. Given his near perfect memory and the resources owning a major daily newspaper provided, Jim could identify all but a few of the non-Chinese in the place. He knew the restaurant's owners and managers. He also had a pretty good knowledge of the Chinese New York Consular staff, not to mention the Chinatown big wheels. He even knew a few of the waiters, but strangely none of the busboys.

At a quiet word from Jim Delores let her napkin slip to the floor. Jim unobtrusively waved down a busboy. When the man stopped at the table Jim strained his tiny Cantonese vocabulary pointing to the fallen linen saying, "Another, please."

The man bowed. At the same time his hand swept up the cloth. He returned a few seconds later. With another bow and a flourish he handed Delores a beautifully folded napkin. Jim said, "*Dou Jia,*" meaning thank you in Cantonese. The reply was a very stilted, "Most welcome sir!"

As the busboy departed Jim shifted into the Comanche language. "Those were the hands of a warrior. Stay out of the busboys' way should there be trouble."

Delores took the pronouncement without turning a hair. Instead she taunted Jim a bit, "I'll just bet his English was better than your Chinese."

"You'll get no argument from me. With all the inflections involved Chinese is very hard to get right."

With that Jim returned to studying his fellow diners. A few people puzzled him. Not too far from the raised podium sat six men much younger than most Caucasians in the dinning room. Wearing almost identical suits they seemed to be forcing themselves to relax. Two tables to the right sat a party of four. The older man Jim estimated to be headed for sixty, but hale, hardy, and sharp eyed. Maybe military, maybe not. Ramrod straight with a full head of hair far from fully gray. The two women seemed to be mother and daughter by their looks. Jim would not hazard a guess at the mother's age. She was at least ten years younger than the older man. The daughter's escort seemed a bit ill at ease. His eyes flickered everywhere. There was something familiar about him.

He knew he had seen the fellow in person before. Jim's instincts told his conscious mind that he had seen the other more than once. Neither those instincts, nor Jim's active mental processes gave the slightest reason for alarm. Jim kept half an eye on him while he continued to search the crowd for potential trouble. He left himself a mental note to think about the fellow later.

Four very well dressed couples occupied the next table from the uneasy six men. The money spent coiffing the women's hair would have operated a large Salvation Army soup kitchen for a full day. At least. The table talk seemed animated. The three men whose faces he could see smiled a lot. They kept looking just where the women's fashionable low cut gowns invited them to look. As with the men, Jim could make out only three of the women's faces. Two seemed to have given themselves wholeheartedly to the enjoyment of the moment. The third's laughter seemed forced.

In an undertone heard only by his fiancée Jim asked, "What do you think of the women four tables that way?" He flicked his head in the proper direction.

Delores knew that Jim asked for a reason. She did nothing to make this exchange look more serious than anything else she had said since arriving. "Three of those dresses are not new. Very expensive, but they have been worn before and altered to fit the girls like gloves. Expertly done. The blonde who looks a tiny bit out of sorts bought her dress today. It fits pretty well, but the purveyor would have altered it to perfection for her by noon tomorrow at no charge. Maybe she's worried about paying for the gown without bouncing a check."

A microphone check in Cantonese interrupted their thoughts. They turned their attention to the small raised stage and podium. Chinatown big wheels and representatives of the Chinese government began to gather by the back wall of the room.

The four women in evening gowns at the table next to the six rose together. "Headed for the powder room to avoid some of the speeches," muttered Delores with a low laugh.

The one woman previously only visible to Jim from the back turned to face him. Recognition flashed in Jim's mind. Velma Martin, the professional escort service owner. She seemed to be leading the female exodus. The unaltered blonde hurried at the rear. She almost stepped on the heels of the girls ahead of her.

Jim and Delores watched the four until they almost exited the dinning room. Then a commotion began at the table of the six younger men. One diner apparently spilled something hot on another. Now heated words flew with one side of the table on their feet confronting the other. The volume and vileness of the exchanges continued to grow.

Four busboys, including the napkin barer, converged on the six. Clear, unaccented words came from the formerly broken English speaker, "Sit down!" At the next table nearer to him Jim noticed three right arms vanish under the table at the same instant.

Jim Anthony came out of his chair faster than a human cannonball shot from a circus gun. Like an agile cougar he bounded onto his table. His large crape soled shoe found the only area of tablecloth empty enough not to trip him or smash dishes. With no noticeable pause he leaped to the center of the next table. Then the next and the next. From there he leaped higher, but shorter. Jim tucked his body into a ball. As he turned a complete somersault he thought fleetingly to himself, "If I'm wrong, I'll never live this down."

Jim snapped his body straight as a board. Delores thought sure Jim had miscalculated his final leap. Water glasses, coffee cups and ashtrays flew in all directions when Jim's whole weight impacted the edge of the table just on her side of group making the disturbance. With four people sitting around it, the table's edge stopped far from the floor. Jim twisted to the side in a one hundred eighty degree turn in the tucked position. He landed on cat like feet facing his impact point as the table returned to its normal position. On either side of his landing spot two men tried to shake off the shock of hundreds of pounds of force striking their thighs and right arms. The far side of the table had caught one man in the chin. The other's face showed many scrapes and a bleeding ear.

Instantly a busboy stood on either side of Jim Anthony. Before they could grab for his arms Jim said, "Please wait," in Cantonese. He repeated the phrase in Mandarin. The lead man gave Jim a questioning look. Jim carefully pulled the nearest man's chair away from the table. On the floor in front of him lay a medium sized automatic pistol.

Quickly grim faced "busboys" searched the four. On each of the other three they found the .32 automatic pistols. Too big to be pocket guns. How in the world did they get in undetected, wondered Jim. Then one of the rowdy six tried to slip away from his table. A wisp of an old man in a simple traditional robe appeared out of nowhere. The departing guest ended up twisted like a pretzel with the old man controlling him using only three fingers.

Jim Anthony smiled as he turned and bowed, "SiFu Chan, your students?"

"Yes, Mr. Anthony. They have more to learn."

"As do we all, SiFu Chan."

"Indeed," smiled the old man. "Thank you for your help."

The remainder of the busboy force got the dignitaries, the most likely targets, to cover. Jim himself gave no indication that he had noticed the mother and daughter, plus their companions, make the motions necessary to put away objects that might be weapons. Their faces held relieved looks, but each one still surveyed the room as if looking for other trouble.

A few minutes later New York's Finest arrived in force. Jim tried to get the attention of the Lieutenant in charge to suggest he search for the women of the party. The senior cop recognized him. Before either could speak a loud contralto voice quieted the room. "Get in there you bandy legged witch!"

The unaltered blonde stumbled into the room. One side of her elaborate hairdo was caved in. One glance at her right eye told of a huge shiner in the making. Behind her stalked Velma Martin physically unruffled, but obviously had as Hell. The other two girls followed. One looked very nervous as she held yet another automatic at arm's length. The weapon dangled from a gloved pinkie through the trigger guard. "Hi ya, Fortier," Velma called to the senior cop.

The cop reddened at bit. He drew in a breath, then let it out as he noticed the pistol identical to the others. When he drew breath again he sounded almost normal. "Velma... er... Miss Martin, what's the story here?"

"This is the gun moll, Ronnie. And I mean that literally. The three of us were hired to fill out that table. The men were supposed to corner some prospect with a sales pitch when he wasn't expecting it. Or so we were told. Miss Wilson here is their Gal Friday. Or so we were told. I could tell her legs were real thin. And she walked a bit funny. I thought she might have a leg brace. Anyway we exited to the powder room on cue. We get there she blocks the door. Then she reaches through a slit in her skirt and pulls that popgun out. Linda here squealed a bit. The witch aimed at her, but forgot how close I was."

"Anyway," Velma continued holding up her above the elbow white gloved fist, "I popped her one. She hit the trash can going down. About then it sounded like all Hell broke loose out here. When we were sure there were lots of cops around we came back out. And I don't think we messed up the prints on the popgun much. You know me, Ronnie. I run an above board business. Don't want any trouble."

"Your word is good, Miss Martin. You'll testify if necessary?"

"Just name the time and place. I'll get all three of us there."

"Miss Martin," interjected Jim, "you said that the Wilson woman was literally the gun moll. What did you mean?"

"Why its big Jim Anthony," exclaimed Velma. Her voice changed to a near perfect imitation of Mae West, "Just let me know when you need to be escorted somewhere, handsome."

"I'd be very careful, Miss Martin," said Jim with a wink. "My fiancée is not too far behind me. And she has a right cross Joe Lewis would be proud of."

"Some gals have all the fun," Velma replied as she rolled her eyes.

"Gun moll," repeated Jim?

"Oh that," said Velma with an evil twinkle in her eye. Before anybody could move to stop her she stepped over to "Miss Wilson." She grabbed a generous handful of gown bodice and yanked like a stevedore.

With a loud ripping sound the low cut gown vanished behind Velma. Miss Wilson shrieked as she now stood in only high heels, panties, and brassiere. That is if you didn't count the five small holsters strapped to her legs.

Jim Anthony and Delores entered his penthouse at the Waldorf-Anthony. The police and State Department officials had seemed to want to talk forever. As Jim took Delores' wrap he stopped and sniffed. She noticed the strange fragrance, as well.

"Jim, what is that smell?"

"Sagebrush," said Jim as he quickly worked a combination lock set in the coat closet wall. He whisked Delores into a hidden room. "Mephito only burns sagebrush when something is not normal. Outsiders think it's just another part of his shaman's rituals. Use the exit if I'm not back in ten minutes," he finished as he kissed her firmly on the lips.

Jim closed the door of the secret room. He pulled the closet door shut. This allowed him to open a panel in the door itself. An array of the smallest light bulbs ever made showed any electrical use throughout the penthouse and several other places in the hotel.

Dawkins, the butler would still be at the club he favored on his nights off. Nothing running in his quarters. Nothing in Mephito's area either, but then the old man did not use electrical gadgets much. Lots of juice flowed into the "parlor," however. The room appeared normal to outsiders. It existed to receive "guests" of unknown intent. The ceiling lights and the circuits that normally fed table lights and Stromberg-Carlson console radio were drawing their full load.

A minute and several security checks later Jim Anthony entered the "parlor." If he had not peered into the room from three different angles before entering Jim would have broken out laughing at the scene he found.

The man Jim had noticed so many times in and around Chinatown sat on the couch with his arms spread across the top of the back cushions. In his shirtsleeves, his suit coat hung on the chair of a small writing table. Jim could not say where the contents of his empty shoulder holster might be.

Something pungent still smoldered in a small brazier on the coffee table in front of the couch. In the center of the facing couch sat Mephito in so called "Indian fashion." He recounted an old story of Comanche life that Jim had heard for as long as he could remember. The scene would seem positively folksy except for one thing. The old man's hands, instead of helping to narrate the story, held a Winchester lever action rifle resting at half cock across his folded legs.

Jim ignored the other man for the moment. "Grandfather," he said in formal greeting.

"Grandson," replied Mephito gravely.

"You entertain a guest?"

"I entertain a burglar who spins taller stories than most white men. But he is a polite burglar. He promised to wait peacefully for you if I did not summon the police. As we waited he asked about the Comanche people."

"And you have told him some of my favorite bedtime stories?"

"They are true stories," replied Mephito somewhat indignantly. Then he shifted to the tongue of his people. "You would have me tell him stories with information a burglar might find useful?"

Jim turned to the man on the other couch. "I noticed you at the restaurant. When the action was over I tried to remember where else I'd seen you. I stopped counting at twelve places. All on the fringe of Chinatown since I returned to New York. Now I find you here, apparently handing my grandfather a line of baloney. Please explain."

"Surely. I told him that I am employed by the Federal Government," said the stranger with a rueful smile.

"Given the long and bleak history between federal employees and my mother's people, consider yourself lucky he didn't simply shoot you. Did you break in?"

"No, I just used a rubber covered grapnel to climb on to your balcony. I wanted to talk to you without being seen. I wasn't halfway across the first room when your grandfather seemed to un-blend from the shadows with that cannon of his. Nobody's got the drop on me like that in a long time."

Jim smiled a bit. This fellow seemed naturally likable. He decided he had better be careful. "With no one else in the penthouse to distract him, you didn't have a chance. You could have floated in on a mist like Dracula. He still would have heard you. Now, federal employee, identify yourself."

"Get my wallet from my inside coat pocket. Behind the window covering my driver's license there's a stiff backing card. Take that out."

As he reached for the wallet Jim said, "You do realize that if the wallet so much as hiccups, my grandfather will shoot you?"

"Naturally. Anyway, split the cardboard with your fingernail."

Jim did so, revealing an identification card complete with an embossed photograph. The hair was a different color, but the face was clearly that of the man on the couch. Jim whistled, "Army G-2. Jeff Shannon. Shannon? The Eagle!"

"You are very well informed, Mr. Anthony," said the Eagle. "Through your paper, I assume."

"Partly. The Eagle has been linked to some very unusual situations involving so-called Fifth Columnists, agents of European powers, and the continued enforcement, so to speak, of the Monroe Doctrine. Every news organization keeps its eyes open for the slightest hint of the Eagle. I own part of several ventures down in Venezuela where you encountered intruding aircraft. Several of what G-2 probably calls annalists sifts through any information provided to me by those even indirectly in my employ. That's a whole lot of information first and last. Now, to what do I owe the honor of your keeping my grandfather amused?"

Shannon winched at bit at the mild barb. He smiled ruefully, "Let's hope that part of the story never gets back to G-2. First of all, I wanted to thank you for taking out those four assassins. It saved my party from revealing ourselves. My character is supposed to be a near inflexible isolationist. Even attending that dinner was a risk, but enough intelligence hinted at... Well, that something might happen. I decided I couldn't take a chance not being there. So I concocted a story about how my girl's father would drag me there by the scruff of my isolationist neck to see how evil the dictatorships really are."

"The older gentleman," observed Jim, "looked like he would be capable of doing just that, but where did you find the women that looked so much like mother and daughter?"

"That's because they are mother and daughter. I don't even know their real names, but the daughter, 'Roberta,' is a friendly rival at, shall we say, another agency. I wanted her to be both my escort and backup for the dinner. When we looked at the guest list we seemed far too young to be invited for our own donations and not be well known idle rich. That's how I found out that 'Roberta' had followed in her mother's footsteps. Mother, in turn, suggested we call on a very well to do man with connections all over Asia. Seems twenty-five years ago he did work similar to mine. Seems also that he helped train about half the senior people I report to. There are at least five people at G-2 who may swallow their cigarettes when they see I've been working with Ashton-Kirk."

When the Eagle finished speaking Jim held up his hand. He stepped over to the console radio and changed the radio band. On this particular set the waveband selector switch reached one more position than the stock model. Jim spoke into a hidden microphone, "All clear, darling. I'll be in the lab for a while with a guest. Please make yourself comfortable in the meantime."

As Jim led the way to his lab Shannon smiled and asked, "The Senator's daughter? Sorry to spoil your plans. Does she really have a solid right cross?"

"She did," chuckled Jim as he yanked off the bow-tie Delores spent so much time getting straight, "until I started tutoring her. Now she folds in her first two knuckles in the manner of the Japanese or Korean arts and strikes for the Adam's apple."

"Ouch!" replied Shannon as they entered Jim's fully furnished laboratory. He glanced around at all the apparatus, some very familiar, some totally unknown. "I'll be a monkey's uncle. This looks like something out of Flash Gordon or Brick Bradford."

"A fair percentage of the equipment is my own design," said Jim as he hung up his dinner jacket. "Please grab a chair over at the map table. I'm going to get comfortable."

As he sat down Jeff Shannon watched Jim Anthony's incredible dexterity as his formal shirt studs seemed to almost remove themselves. At the same time Jim kicked off his shoes and guided them under the small coat rack. His highly flexible toes worked off the elastic socks as he hung up the shirt next to the formal jacket. Finally he seemed to leap completely out of his trousers. He caught them before the strange round belt buckle could hit the floor. Deftly he clipped the waistband to a special hanger. Jeff estimated the total elapsed time at under ten seconds.

Now clad only in a gold swimsuit Jim did a couple of quick stretches and began his walk to the map table with two drum major high steps. "I hate those formal monkey suits," he said as he sat down. "Now how can I help you?"

"Actually," replied The Eagle, "I wanted to give you information concerning your current project. I ended up bruising my knuckles on it more than once."

Jim had to consciously intervene to keep his jaw from dropping open. "That's very interesting. I'll be glad of any help you can give. I had expected you were here to explain why I'm getting federal pressure to lay off quote: all actions in and around Chinatown. End quote."

Jeff Shannon sat open mouthed for a brief moment. Then he replied, "I can see you aren't joking. I sure didn't ask for such a thing. I doubt my control did either. Your work actually complimented mine. That street trash was pushing my targets further underground. That made shadowing them harder than usual. Thank heavens my cover character was only an isolationist, not a pacifist. As a "concerned citizen" I rescued two suspect counselor officials from the thugs. Picked their pockets of some very useful items while helping them up. I'm sure they blamed the thugs when the stuff turned up missing.

"My cover had me looking for office and living space for The International Friendship Organization near the Civic Center. That made asking about anti-foreign activities easy. This paper details the locations of incidents I heard about. A couple of days before you hit town, I came across a threesome pushing kids around and threatening their 'foreign' parents. They never saw me coming. I practiced the nastiest Ju Jitsu tricks I know on them. The kids' family, it turned out, traces their family in New England to the 1600's. However, two years ago, a family from the Balkans lived where they do. Does that help?"

Jim nodded, "This helps define the southern end of the area. That last reinforces my theory that the street thugs are just that. Hired muscle following some devious script blindly. But where does the federal leverage come from?"

"I'll inquire about that and let you know. In the meantime, I almost forgot to give you these," with that The Eagle handed over two more of the stationary code sheets.

✳ ✳ ✳

"...Jim did a couple of quick stretches..."

The following morning Jim took a large scale city map to the morgue of the New York Star. All the attacks and threats he uncovered were marked in red and those added by The Eagle appeared in blue.

Robb greeted him, "You were busy last night, Big Jim! The whole place is buzzing. Saved some lives I gather."

"I'm getting more credit than I deserve," replied Jim. "Other measures were in place that prefer to remain out of the spotlight. But the event landed me some new information. First though, here are two new code sheets. See if they support your theory, then come look at this map."

Robb took the sheets to a table with a reading lamp as Jim cleared off space on a newspaper page "make-up" table. As he spread out the map Jim saw Robb flipping the pages of a small folio book with wire binding. In a few seconds his eyes lit up.

"Proved," he said excitedly. "A book code! The gang uses the Manhattan Street Directory as the code base. The first group of characters is the page number. The second group is the page's grid reference. The final number in each group refers to the listing of Counselor offices at the back of the book. A quick reference to the 'foreigner's' origins. A target listing."

"Good information," said Jim, "but no help in finding the leadership. Now look at some new attacks plotted with the others on this map."

Robb came. He looked... and looked... He walked slowly around the table looking. He traced an outline containing all the points with his finger. Suddenly his eyes widened. He let out a wild yell and dashed the depths of the morgue. Jim heard the sound of drawers opening and closing. Finally Robb hurried back carrying a bound volume of the Star.

He opened the book next to the map. Flipping the pages to a business section, with a flourish he pointed to a story with a very similar map. "Behold, New Olympus. Soon to be called Harrison's Folly."

Jim Anthony came over the wall of the remote estate just at dawn with few ideas of what he might find. Woods to begin with. The same woods as outside the wall. Here and there Jim thought he could see little used paths through the large trees. A heavy wooden gate served as the only break in the west wall. The path from it led to the nearby Catholic Monastery. The two properties seemed laid out by the same hand, but Jim knew that the man he sought practiced a Protestant faith.

The woods ended with a short decorative wall. A lush lawn covering many acres began. Here and there beautiful flowerbeds sent new growth to meet the warming spring days. Jim stayed in the wooded area until he reached the closest point to the three story mansion. Soon he peered in the windows of a sitting room by the light of the rising sun. Every piece of furniture was covered in a precisely tailored bright colored fabric slipcover. Every other room he checked was the same, but there was no dust on the floor. Jim scrambled up the ornate wall. The two rooms on the second floor he could see confirmed that the building received regular care, but served as a home to nobody.

Behind the mansion Jim found a garage with six vehicle doors. He detected life in the rooms above. He smelled ham and eggs cooking, heard the heterodyne squeal of a radio trying to lock in to a week signal. Similar sounds and smells came from two nearby cottages of decent size.

Behind the cottages lay a short span of woods. The open space beyond would be invisible in the summer. Jim followed simple flagstone path winding through the wooded segment. He emerged onto another lawn covering about three acres. The path led to a simple but sturdy looking building whose door stood open to the cool morning air.

As he walked to the building Jim noted that the gardens here looked more of Asia, than Europe. Some hardy annuals had been planted. Everything was precise yet peaceful. Something puzzled Jim about the lawn. Finally he realized that grass had been cut by hand with a scythe, giving it a slight undulating appearance.

As Jim raised his hand to knock on the building's front door post a voice from inside called out, "Please remove your shoes before you come in."

Jim glanced around the room as he entered. The word Spartan seemed generous to what he found. To one side sat simple chairs set for conversation. A clothes press and storage chest stood next to a nook filled with a six inch tall stack of Japanese tatami mats. A matching wicker pillow lay atop the precisely folded bed clothes. Before him a thin white haired man knelt at a low table. Two dogs lay beside him, apparently asleep. The German shepherd seemed small compared to the largest Russian wolf hound Jim had ever seen.

"Mr. Harrison," asked Jim?

"I am," replied the older man as he gave Jim a close look. "My heavens, you must be Shean Boru Anthony's son James. News pictures are one thing, but in person I can see both your parents in you."

"You knew my parents?"

"To my long standing regret and shame, not nearly as well as I should have. In those days I was so full of myself that other human beings did not seem important except as they could be useful to me. We did a couple of quick and simple deals together and attended a few of the same business functions the odd times they were in town. I saw you once as an infant. Your grandfather held you looking very proud."

Jim smiled. "You would have trouble getting him to admit that he ever did what he would call 'women's work' in caring for any child. Thank you for sharing that incident. I'm sorry to drop in unannounced, but I didn't want to alert the wrong people to my visit."

"James, I don't normally get up quite this early. However, two of my staff are very distant cousins to you. Iroquois. While adept in the ways of the white man, they take pride in the Woodland culture of their fathers. They are my watchmen. Using telegraph keys hidden all over the property they woke me soon after you came over the wall. If you carried weapons they would have confronted you. I trust their instincts. They did not feel that you were a threat. And even you would have a hard time surviving my canine friends here, if I set them on you. Ulysses, Hercules, kennel!" At Harrison's word the two dogs rose. They stretched briefly and trotted out the door. "Now, how may I help you?"

So much for preconceptions thought Jim as he knelt at the table. "Mr. Harrison, I know this is not a pleasant subject for you, but I need information about New Olympus."

The old man smiled, "Not a single soul has had the nerve to mention Harrison's Folly to my face in over twenty years. It was my fall and resurrection together. I was going to save the world and make a hefty profit at the same time. Rebuild a whole section of the city to house trade officials and central banks' offices from every nation on earth. Prevent war. Keep trade flowing. And collect my high rents."

"I've read the Star's stories about the proposal. The owners then took no position on it."

Harrison smiled grimly, "They must have been the only ones. Just about everybody found reason to oppose it. 'Foreign Entanglements' being the favorite reason. Governments saw it as a threat, too. They pressured the State Department to get New Olympus scuttled.

"I was an arrogant young 'Titan of Industry' back then. I could not be wrong. Could not be stopped. But stopped I was. I had a nervous breakdown. My father kept that covered up. By the time he passed on I could fend for my self again. But why in the name of a Painted Puffin do you need to know about my Folly? And in secret, too?"

When Jim finished relating his experiences of the last three weeks Harrison shook his head. "This makes no sense at all. Sure I railed against foreigners during my breakdown, but I was mad at diplomats and people at my own level of influence, not folks trying to make an honest living. And, James, how can you be sure I'm not behind this whole thing? I told you a used to be a raving mental patient."

"I considered that right after I found out about New Olympus," replied Jim. "Then I put all my resources to work quietly digging for anything about you. Obviously your outlook on life changed radically. Hints popped up of fiercely anonymous good deeds. Then we connected you to Monsignor Kelly. He suggested this visit. So here I am, but nothing gave the slightest hint of this Zen-like life."

"James," said Harrison, with a far away look in his eyes, "two men saved my life and my soul. Archie Kelly, my boyhood friend got me to spend time in the simple lifestyle of Monks in the order next door. They have nothing, and are darn glad of it. And Shiro, my father's old gardener, taught me the benefits of meditation. Rest his soul, he never tried to push his faith on me. Yet he helped me more than any other. And I've tried to pass on what they gave me. Now tell me did you find out who has been bailing out those criminals?"

"The Times Square Law Group, a relatively new law firm with few clients," replied Jim. "We caught one of their law clerks shadowing a team of thugs. The firm's client list does include a couple of suspected Bundist front organizations. Just before I left the Star's legal editor told me that all the partners had previously been with Boyd, Gray, and Studie."

"Bingo! Garvin Studie was my father's personal lawyer. More power hungry than I ever was, if that's possible. Was scared to death of an uncontrolled press. Had lots of Washington connections. The firm probably still does. Garvin would set up practices with him as silent partner to do his dirty work. I let them go after my father died. Glad I did. I hear Garvin's son Harman turned out even worse. If Garvin held a grudge against me, so will the kid."

"Mr. Harrison," began Jim with a wicked smile, "will you help me smoke out this viper's nest?'

"Bank on it, son. Let's put our heads together and see what kind of a bear trap we can come up with."

Soon Jim began to make phone calls. Using a call forwarding service that he owned he spoke with the Sentinel's publisher. A planted speculative story would appear in the next day's edition. More calls followed. Then, very quietly, Jim Anthony and Mr. Harrison headed for the big city.

Above the fold on the front page of the Sentinel's business section the headline read: "New Olympus To Make Comeback?" The story read, in part, "Unconfirmed reports claim that Sherman Harrison will relaunch the long abandoned project later in the week. Sources close to Mr. Harrison say that trade missions from all countries would be welcome to participate in round robin trading to eliminate shortages everywhere."

The next day uniformed messengers delivered embossed invitations, hand signed by Sherman Harrison, to all suspect clients of the Times Square Law Group inviting them to a special meeting about New Olympus. An accompanying letter purporting to be from the law firm encouraged very quiet attendance as their cause would benefit.

At the corner of Hudson and Duane Streets in the city lay a block shaped like a trapezoid. A five story factory filled much of the block, an empty factory. In the middle of the Reade Street side stood an almost empty rooming house that once served the factory's workers. The northwest corner contained a bankrupt five and ten with offices on the second floor and a former Odd Fellows hall on the top floor. On the southwest corner a filling station still operated, but the repair bays above it gathered dust.

All the buildings, at one time, had been served by the steam tunnel system. Within twenty-four hours of arriving in New York Sherman Harrison bought or leased the entire block. Rumors started to sprint around the city. Jim, Tom, a muttering Dawkins, and Sherman Harrison never appeared on the streets as they secretly installed various items in the four buildings.

His grandfather at his side Jim visited a favorite hang out of a certain group of construction workers. Dressed as a Telegraph Delivery Boy, Billy Barton made sure messages got through and numerous questions received answers. The Times Square law clerk now understood that his only hope of long term freedom, or possibly survival, lay in helping Jim Anthony. He quietly took messages to the home of Studie, the younger.

Using information gained from the watcher/law clerk Tom Gentry left new code sheets for all the team leaders at a prearranged drop. The sheets contained additional instructions for the second day following.

Jim Anthony started to feel like a traffic cop or Ziegfeld's choreographer. A lot of events needed to be timed out perfectly. Finally the proper day and time arrived. Things began to happen fast.

※ ※ ※

Around mid-morning groups of two or three men each began to slip into various entrances of the factory. The men who worked behind those doors all wore closed collars and Sam Brown Belts. They gave orders directing the guests to their meetings in various parts of the building. Different work bays of the old factory featured red, white, and black decorations, but no overt political symbols. Art on posters included uniformed men marching and Zeppelins in the sky above them. In each area a forceful man with close shaved hair and Sam Brown belt lectured on unity, purity of thought, and obedience to authority.

In his turn each visitor entered the shift manager's office of that bay to be interviewed. Each man received assurances that amazing things waited for him. He then wrote a brief essay of what he hoped to gain by attending the meeting. Those finished moved on to the top floor of the factory where a man of great importance would address them.

Just before noon the partners of the Times Square Law Office arrived in a panel truck that parked deep in the alley between the five and ten and the rooming house. Soon they entered the apartment of the former rooming house owners. Suddenly the door slammed shut behind them. They heard the lock click. From the bedroom and the kitchen rough looking men with grim faces appeared.

A chauffeured limousine brought key members of the Boyd, Gray, and Studie firm to the stairway leading up to the Odd Fellows hall just after noon. A uniformed doorman received them and directed them to their meeting. As soon as they vanished up the stairs the doorman vanished, too. A few moments later a squad of thugs also ascended the stairs.

Big George, still walking a bit funny, came up the ramp with seven extremely tough thugs to the closed off repair area of the filling station. He found a thick dust curtain hanging where the ramp ended. Listening for a moment, he heard three people speaking in a strange tongue. He peaked through a slit in the curtain. Three men sat around improvised table playing cards by the light of a dangling bulb.

With a smirk, Big George ripped the curtain open. He called out as he led his toughs toward the card table, "Let's get these foreigners started back to the boat, boys!"

Out of the darkness rumbled a fearsome voice, "Who are you calling a foreigner, punk?"

There followed the thumping sound of a big circuit breaker being thrown. Suddenly the upper floor of the garage seemed brighter than day light. Big George found himself encircled by twelve more Mohawk members of the Iron Workers Union.

Finally all visitors to the factory stood in the open area of the top floor. Those who spoke to smaller groups or interviewed the visitors herded them towards a raised platform at the north end. Two uniformed men stood next to a closed door near the platform. When the crowd settled in its proper place one of the men knocked on the door sharply three times. The other waited a count of five and opened the door. Out walked the most perfectly developed individual most of the audience had ever seen. His uniform consisted of a tightly tailored silk shirt, jodhpurs with a wide belt fastened by a strange circular device, and riding boots. Combed straight back, his golden hair contrasted with the dark glasses he wore. His muscles rippled as he walked. Not a single person spoke as the newcomer briskly mounted the platform and strode to the microphone.

"Thank you all for coming," he began. His words echoed back from the other end of the large building. "Today will be an important day for the cause. Today we know true adherent from those who give lip service, or do not care. Are you ready to learn more?"

As one, the audience roared, "Yes!"

"Are you ready to start down the path you have chosen by coming here today?"

"Yes!"

Hands behind the audience gave a prearranged signal.

"Are you certain?"

"Yes!" The walls shook. Dust fell from the roof trusses above.

"Then be ready..." The speaker paused until another signal came. First he removed his dark glasses, then a blonde wig. Whispers began in the crowd. "My name is Jim Anthony. Thank you for giving out your pictures, fingerprints, and handwriting samples. If you have any questions, you may direct them to the members of New York's finest to whom you gave them."

Every uniformed man now wore an NYPD badge on his Sam Brown belt. The crowd bolted for the exits. About half of the audience tripped over a rushing foot or smashed into somebody going a different way.

More cops, in their regular uniforms emerged from the stairwells. Up the main open stairs came twelve men in tight lock step. At their head a grimly smiling Officer Burland.

Jim Anthony's eyes swept the scene. While speaking he had recognized three of the diversion group at the China Relief dinner. Newspaper files allowed him to identify several right wing organizers. Now he looked for weapons. To his left he saw a knot of men pulling out knives.

Jim yanked off his belt. No chance the jodhpurs would fall down. Delores had laughed at him saying that they seemed painted on. Three long steps brought him across the platform as he spun the rope out of the belt so that the circular buckle whirled like one end of a gaucho's bolas.

Jim leaped up from the edge of the platform. He caught the bottom stringer of a roof truss with one hand. Swinging like a monkey he caught the next truss between his feet. Rope in one hand, he swung the round buckle with the other. The knife flew out of the hand of one of the group below him. He guided the back swing to a glancing blow off of another's head. Gathering up the rope as he fell, Jim dropped into the center of the group.

In another thirty seconds the fighting ended.

With the police in full control Jim hurried to the factory basement. Here a dozen court recorders had transcribed every word said in the four buildings.

Done with guard duty Tom gloated as he handed a hand scrawled page to Jim, "Last words from the Studie group. '...but we are the ones that pay you.'"

"Excellent. All that's left now is the cleanup."

Jim Anthony got the red carpet treatment at Children's Hospital. One wing bore his mother's name. Soon he chatted with Tommy Adams, the paperboy hit by the truck.

"Thanks for coming, Mr. Anthony. Your paperboys say you're great to work for."

"You're welcome, Tommy. When I was your age the Sentinel staff taught me a lot about the newspaper business. Good people to work for, too."

"Yer doggon right, young Anthony," came a voice from behind him. Jim turned to find the elderly owner of the Sentinel standing in the doorway.

"This'll save me a trip. I wanted to thank you for cleaning up the scum that hurt Tommy. Be a long time 'fore anybody goes after a paperboy in this town. Put 'er there, my friend."

Jim Anthony took the proffered hand then said, "My pleasure, Dan."

The End

Jim Anthony and the Urban Non-Renewal

I've been to New York City exactly once. For three days in 1964 with the Boy Scouts. Went to the Empire State Building, but it was fogged in above the fifth floor. Took the boat ride around Manhattan. Saw a body floating face down in the river from about three stories up. All this makes me no expert on writing an authentic story set in 1940 NYC. Maybe I should have shipped Big Jim out of town.

Many of the pulp heroes were based in New York City. Too many, actually. It seems like most of them knew THE Police Commissioner of NYC. But all knew different Commissioners. That is except for The Whisperer. He WAS the Police Commissioner. Go figure.

My story takes place in the area now known as Tribeca. Turns out that term originated in the 1960's when some urban renewal person had too much time on their hands. TRIBECA stands for the TRI-angle BE-low CA-nal Street area.

I once had the pleasure of having a story seemingly write itself. This story did its best to avoid having an ending attached.

Warning! Possible SPOILERS if you read past this.

I started with an action intro, followed by a flashback. A whole area that Jim frequents is having problems. Therefore he must have been out of town. Then a separate scene occurs to me. I write it. Then another disconnected scene. I end up writing bridges between them. Problems here. At one point I had Tom and Mephito waiting for Jim's call behind SiFu Chan's apartment. The two older men hit it off. Dawns the light. SiFu Chan has not been introduced yet. The waiting car moves to Little Italy.

I needed a Fed to warn Jim off of his activities in future Tribeca. What better choice than Dan Fowler of the FBI who headlined the G-Men title for a couple of decades. Once Dan showed up, I threw caution to the winds. I added almost every other character I logically throw in.

Officer Burland may, or may not, be the fellow who went on to become The Black Hood of comics, radio, and pulp magazine fame.

Ashton-Kirk, consulting secret agent, appeared in pulp serials. These were collected in four hardbacks beginning in 1910. In 1915 he appeared in three films. The first book, "Ashton-Kirk Investigator" can be downloaded from Project Gutenberg at http://www.gutenberg.org/etext/12314

Jeff Shannon, code name: The Eagle, appeared for about a year in Thrilling Spy Novels. His full speed ahead methods make any version of James Bond seem subtlety personified.

Billy Barton is a hat-tip to multi-talented Billy Barty. In the film "Under The Rainbow" Barty delivered a blow that any pulp hero would have loved a chance at: a sharp jab below Hitler's belt.

Street & Smith editor John L. Nanovic, under the name Henry Lysing, wrote the feature on codes that appeared in most issues of The Shadow magazine. However, credit for introducing me to a "book code" goes to the creators of the Rick Brant Science Adventure books: Hal Goodwin and Peter Harkins. See "The Rocket's Shadow" and Goodwin's later solo title "The Caves of Fear."

"R. Erwin Kennedy" is a by-line I once had to use. Don't ask!

If you need the very last scene explained, please write to me at erwin.k.roberts@gmail.com

ERWIN K ROBERTS was just an empty nester (again!) in Kansas City. That's the *real* Kansas City, not the Kansas wannabe. The city is firmly anchored on the Missouri side of the state line. Now that the kids had left a second time, he lived with just his wife until the last Saturday in 2006. But, you see, there was this Christmas present. A mystery present, from daughter and son-in-law. "But you have to be blindfolded when we take you to get it."

As the wife and I waited for the almost newlyweds to arrive that Saturday, our son mysteriously showed up. Turned out he would be our driver. So away we went, blindfolds and all. Our son pulled into every empty parking lot we passed to drive in circles and figure eights. He kept up a running dialog as we drove through the Kansas City area, "Now on your left is the Statue of Liberty... Wave to the cop, dad!"

Finally we arrived. Still blindfolded, we were led to the entrance of a well known local facility: Wayside Waifs.

Erwin K. Roberts now lives in suburban Kansas City with his wife, and the family supervisor: Xena, Warrior Kitten.

He can be reached at erwin.k.roberts@gmail.com

The Resurrected Killer

by Mark Justice

Five minutes before his death, Alexander Plainview said to his secretary, "Myrtle, my doctor just gave me a clean bill of health. Said my blood pressure was lower than ever and my ulcer has gone away. And you know why?"

Myrtle, a young and attractive woman barely out of school, nodded eagerly. "Is it Mister Flynn?"

The grimace on Plainview's face lasted barely an instant before his smile returned. "Yes, that's right. It's all because of George Flynn."

Flynn had been one of the researchers at Eagle Chemical, the company that Plainview and three other board members managed. Some months ago a state-run European company began manufacturing the same products as Eagle Chemical, so close as to be identical. These new items were being sold at a much lower price, threatening to drive Eagle out of business. After many sleepless nights, Plainview and his fellow board members hired a detective to discover who was leaking Eagle's proprietary information.

The culprit turned out to be George Flynn. He had sold company secrets to a foreign power. Plainview fired Flynn with police present, just before the traitorous researcher was hauled off to jail.

But before he could face the law for his crime, Flynn hanged himself in his jail cell.

Plainview had slept wonderfully ever since.

Of course, the revelations about Flynn had not stopped the European company from selling the product, but an investigation was underway, and the sales pendulum was swinging back to Eagle Chemical.

"You're witnessing a new era, Myrtle," Plainview said, "one rife with opportunity for all of us." He allowed his gaze to linger on the secretary's nylon-clad legs.

"That's swell, Mr. Plainview," Myrtle said, oblivious to the attention of her boss. "Now about that correspondence…"

"Yes, of course," Plainview said. He wanted to dictate the letter to his secretary. He really did. Yet he was far more interested in examining the curve of her ample bosom against her tight sweater and the way one shapely thigh had been revealed when she crossed her legs.

I have become a randy old goat, he thought. Not that his wife would notice. She was too busy with her bridge club and babysitting their young grandchildren. For months he had existed as a condemned man, waiting for the hangman's arrival. Since the Flynn matter had…been resolved,

Plainview felt strong again, felt young, and he certainly wanted to enjoy all the pleasures that life offered.

"Myrtle," he said, emotion thickening his voice, "in the short time you've been here, you have demonstrated and enthusiasm for the job that is rare among today's young people. Eagle Chemicals needs good and faithful employees to lead us into our bright future. I would like to speak with you soon about your opportunities for advancement."

Myrtle was stunned. Her mouth – framed by those thick, luscious lips – hung open. Her cheeks flushed with color.

"Really, Mister Plainview?"

"Really."

"Anytime, sir," Myrtle said, flashing a large and genuine smile.

"Hmmm," Plainview said, making a show of careful consideration. "I suppose it would be wise to hold our meeting away from the office."

"Why?"

"Because, my dear, not every girl at Eagle chemical is worthy of the same consideration for promotion. We don't want to stir up jealousy. That would lead to a slow down in productivity. Do you understand?"

"Of course, Mr. Plainview."

"Fine. Why don't we discuss the matter over dinner? Let's say 8 o'clock at my club?" This would be perfect. Jenkins would certainly be there. The president of Northeast Chemical was always parading his latest tomato at the Seacoast Country Club. Wait until he got a load of Myrtle. Plainview smiled with delight.

"I—I was supposed to dine with my mother tonight," Myrtle shyly offered.

"Call her," Plainview said. "I'm sure she would understand. After all, she must be very proud of her daughter, and I know she wouldn't want you to miss out on this amazing prospect for advancement."

Myrtle's lovely smile returned. "Of course. May I call her now?"

"Certainly."

Myrtle stood. As she walked to the door, Plainview took careful note of the way her backside swayed against the taut material of her skirt. He must call ahead to the club and have a good bottle of wine chilled. Perhaps two bottles.

Plainview allowed his imagination to wander to the end of what he was certain would be a magnificent evening. Myrtle would be overwhelmed by the grandeur of the dining run at the Club. The prime rib and shrimp would be grilled to perfection, and her head would swim from the expensive wine. She would be so grateful she would—

She screamed.

From the outer office, her shriek was piercing. Plainview took a step toward the door. But he stooped when he heard the sound. It was a sizzling, like bacon frying in a pan. The smell was all wrong, though. It was electrical, and the noise was accompanied by a series of flashing lights. The light threw freakishly distorted shadows across his open doorway.

Myrtle's scream was suddenly cut off, as though a switch had been thrown. Or someone had silenced her.

"Who—who's out there?" Plainview tried to sound confident and brave. He failed. "Myrtle? Are you hurt?"

The sizzling noise grew louder and the flashes of light came closer to his door.

Plainview stepped behind his desk, and then decided to back up. He continued until his buttocks touched the rear wall of his office. At virtually the same instant, something stepped through the doorway.

It had the shape of a man. Plainview couldn't make out any of its features, for this thing was the source of the noise and the light. If it was a man, he was surrounded by some sort of contraption, a metal framework that encased his upper body. The frame must have been made of metal, since sparks flew from various points along its surface, thus providing the oddly flashing lights.

The electrical smell grew stronger. To Plainview, it was the unmistakable odor of overheating wires, ready to catch fire. His thoughts immediately went to the storage facility in the back of this very building, to the combustible chemicals stored there and the result if a fire reached those stores.

But the man who approached him seemed unaware of the danger he posed. At least, the danger to the building. He appeared to be quite cognizant of the threat he presented to Plainview. Those arcing flashes of electricity might be enough to kill a man, even without knowing what other nefarious purpose that contraption served.

Plainview trembled as the strange man approached. Though he was frightened, part of him was fascinated by the metal framework that circled the head and chest and arms of the man. It appeared to be connected to a box-like contraption on the man's back.

The man stood so close that Plainview could feel the heat emitted by the metal suit. The crackling bolts of electricity sent a tingle over Plainview's face and hands.

"Who-who are you?" Plainview said.

"You know me, Alexander." The voice was oddly distorted, as if it were traveling over a long-distance telephone wire.

Plainview raised a hand to shield his eyes from that awful glare. At the same instant, the strange man leaned forward. A spark from his metal gizmo touched the tip of Plainview's nose. Plainview threw his head back and it thudded into the wall. A cascade of colors exploded before his eyes. When they faded away, he realized he could see the strange man's face.

And it was the one man it couldn't be.

"You!"

"Time to pay for your sins, Alexander," the weird, distant voice said. "Do you know how long I've waited for this?"

"It can't—you can't be here!" Plainview voice was pitched as high as a girl's. He couldn't help it.

"It wasn't easy, Alexander. In fact, getting here was the most difficult thing I have ever done. You might say it's been my life's work."

"'Life's work'? I don't understand."

"I know," the stranger said. "And that makes this all the more delicious."

He reached for Plainview with his sparking, metal encased hands.

Plainview felt a second of searing heat, followed by an eternity of white-hot agony.

The big man strode up the front walk with an easy confidence.

He was dressed in a superbly-tailored, expensive business suit, though he far preferred must less formal attire. But Jim Anthony was in Maine on family business, so in a sense he was representing his late father, and, in this case, that required a nod toward conventional business tradition.

Jim's late father, Shean Boru Anthony, the Irish adventurer and mul-timillionaire, had left his fortune to his only son. The wealth consisted of a lot of cash and several enterprises, primarily a chain of newspapers. While the money allowed Jim to pursue an education in several disciplines, it mostly allowed him to vigorously follow his love of adventure. Occasionally, however, he had to attend to business. Jim made it a point to personally visit each newspaper at least twice a year. This morning had been spent with the editorial staff of the Bangor Morning Bulletin.

Urgent business required him to leave the country as soon as possible, preferably that very day. In fact, his lifelong friend and pilot Tom Gentry was waiting for him at the airport, the plane fueled and ready to depart for

France, where the authorities had requested Jim Anthony's help in tracking down a macabre killer.

Jim's reputation as a hunter of murderers had grown to the point that he was forced to turn down many petitions of aid. The Paris case had been far too enticing to pass up. He was anxious to get in the air.

First, though, he had to visit an old friend of his father's. Alexander Plainview was a chemical engineer who now ran his own company. Shean Boru Anthony had been an early investor in Eagle Chemical and believed Plainview and his company were important to the defense of the nation. Jim had kept in touch with Plainview since his father's death.

Jim asked the cabbie driver to wait in the parking lot of Eagle Chemical while he popped inside to say hello. Frankly, his thoughts kept returning to the crazed killer in France. It was just the sort of exciting case he lived for.

All thoughts of international murderers were driven from his mind by a woman's scream from inside the office. Jim Anthony jumped forward as if he'd been launched from a cannon. He threw open the doors and hurtled into the lobby of Eagle Chemical.

The first thing that registered on his senses was a sharp electrical odor, one that was quite familiar from the many hours he spent in the lab working on new inventions that he hoped would someday serve mankind.

The office held several nice leather chairs and two desks. The walls were hung with prints of well-known paintings, giving the lobby a professional yet serene atmosphere. Or, it would have been serene were it not for the screaming woman. There were actually two women in the lobby. The first, an older specimen, stood behind one of the desks, a look of shock upon her soft features. The second girl was the screamer.

She was young and, he couldn't help noticing, quite attractive, despite her hysterical demeanor. Jim took her by the shoulders and shook her roughly.

"Here," he said, "get hold of yourself. What's happened?"

The girl screamed once more, to which Jim responded by another firm shake. Then, looking like a sleeper waking from a particularly horrid nightmare, the girl became aware of Jim Anthony.

"Oh. It's—oh, I'm sorry. But he's in there with Mr. Plainview. Only it can't be him. Don't you understand?"

Jim released the girl and started toward Plainview's office. He'd been here before, so he knew which door to open. Before he could touch the knob, the door flew open and a most unusual man ran out.

The man was old, but not elderly. His head, upper body and arms were encased in a framework of metal tubing. That was the source of the hot electrical smell. Sparks flew from the apparatus. The gadget appeared to be powered by a case strapped to the man's back. The man extended a hand toward Jim Anthony. The fingertips danced with blue flares.

Jim sidestepped the man's touch. In one smooth movement, he picked up one of the leather chairs and hurled it at the man. There was a crackling flash of light and the man was knocked to the floor. At least Jim thought he was. For a second his vision was blotted out by a white blob of an afterimage, as from the flash of a photographer's camera. When he blinked the image away, the man with the weird contraption was gone. He had vanished.

"What happened to him?" he snapped to the women. Both of them looked as surprised as Jim.

"Where's Mr. Plainview?" the older woman asked. If Jim remembered correctly, her name was Vera.

Jim didn't take the time to answer. He rushed to the open door of Plainview's office.

The man who been a friend to Shean Boru Anthony was dead. It was a death that had been horrific, and a death that was completely alien to Jim Anthony.

Alexander Plainview's head was stretched out of shape. The skull had been compressed and lengthened through some means that Jim did not understand. The head had also been twisted, with Plainview's forehead and chin facing in opposite directions. The man's mouth was open in what must have been a primal scream of agony. Even Plainview's eye sockets were elongated into a configuration that was so unnatural, even Jim Anthony's blood ran cold.

He took a step back and forced his eyes away from the corpse. He quickly examined the room. Nothing seemed out of place. There was no weapon left behind, no arcane instrument of sadistic torture.

Of course not, Jim realized. The instrument of torture was worn by the strange man. Plainview's killer had vanished in a flash of light.

Jim heard a gasp from the doorway. He spun to find the young woman standing there, one hand over her mouth, her eyes wide with fear. Jim moved to block her sight of the corpse. He led her back to the lobby.

The woman began to tremble, her knees buckled. Jim deftly caught her. He carried her warm, soft form to one of the comfortable leather chairs. He sat her in it, and guided to her to her knees.

"Sit like that for a minute until the dizziness passes," he said.

Jim faced the older woman. She was afraid, yet she was also capable of taking orders. The woman came from hearty Yankee stock.

"Vera, please call the police."

"Yes, Mr. Anthony," she said. She lifted the telephone receiver, then asked, "Is Mr. Plainview dead?"

"Yes," Jim said. "I'm very sorry. The scene in there is among the most gruesome I've ever witnessed, You'll sleep better if you don't see it."

Vera muttered something under her breath. She dialed for the police. He had the feeling that Vera would sneak a look in the office at her first opportunity.

Jim intended to check on the younger woman, but as he took a step toward her, something else caught his eye.

The chair he had thrown at the killer was on its side against one wall. He walked over to examine it. He took hold of the exposed arm and turned the chair over.

The other arm was warped and twisted, like a wax candle held too close to an oven.

He sat the chair down.

Who was that strange man? And what power did he possess?

※ ※ ※

The older woman had finished her report to the police. She stood watching Jim Anthony.

"Vera, did you recognize the man who went in Mr. Plainview's office?"

"No, sir. I was typing a letter when he came in. I only caught of glimpse of him as he ran by poor Myrtle. Then, when he came out, you immediately threw the chair at him and then there was that flash, and he was gone." Vera's tone held a note of disapproval, as if Jim had caused this disruption to Vera's office routine.

Jim stepped outside. He knew the man with the odd contraption didn't get past him, but he had to check. As he expected there was no sign of the man or his unusual machine.

He retuned to the office. The young woman—Myrtle—still sat with her head on her knees. Vera stared at him.

"Are you going to find him, the man who murdered Mr. Plainview?" Her arms were crossed over her chest. Jim could hear her foot tapping on the floor tile. "You're Jim Anthony. Finding killers is what you do."

It was. The moment the strange man had emerged from Alexander Plainview's office, Jim knew he had to postpone his trip to Paris.

"I need use your telephone," he said.

Vera moved aside as Jim placed a call to Bangor's airport. He asked for Tom Gentry. In a moment, Jim's friend came on the wire.

"Tom? Shut her down. We can't leave yet. Something has happened. Yeah, our kind of trouble. We'll need the standard equipment. Get the car and meet me here." He recited the address of Eagle Chemical before breaking the connection.

Vera had listened attentively. She gave Jim a small nod of approval.

"Vera, do you know anyone who would want to hurt Plainview?"

"No," the woman replied. "At least not anymore."

"What does that mean?"

"It means you're wasting time giving me the third degree while a murderer is on the loose."

Despite the gravity of the situation, Jim smiled. This tough-as-nails northerner would be a good woman to have on his side.

"Yes, ma'am," he told her. "You're right."

He returned to the spot where the chair had lain. Jim had been certain that the man had been knocked off his feet by the chair, yet that flash of light had obscured his vision at the point of impact. He knelt on the floor and carefully examined the linoleum. The surface of the material was immaculate, appearing as if it had been installed that very day. Eagle Chemical certainly spent good money on a cleaning service. Jim had no doubt that Vera was ultimately responsible for the tidiness of the office.

He was about to give up when he noticed an anomaly. There was a deformity of the floor four feet away from where the chair had landed. Jim smiled. He must have struck the murderer harder than he had known. He definitely had landed on the linoleum. The surface of the material was indented and uneven. It had been reshaped, perhaps through great heat or tremendous pressure. Jim would have given a sizable chunk of his fortune for a chance to examine the mechanism that the killer had worn.

He stood up just has the first police officer entered the building. For the next several minutes, Jim related what had happened. In the middle of his recitation, a young cop went into Plainview's office. He exited hastily, holding his hand over his mouth until he could get outside. Jim heard the retching sounds he made.

When the first police officer finished with Jim, he turned his attention to Vera. The older woman told her version of the event in clipped, even tones. Jim strolled over to Myrtle. The young woman sat up, looking back at him with bleary, reddened eyes.

"I can't believe this happened. It's impossible," she said.

"I know. Something like this is always hard."

"That's not what I mean," Myrtle said, her voice barely above a whisper. "I mean it was impossible. The man who killed Mr. Plainview couldn't have been here."

"Why not?"

"Because he's dead. George Flynn killed himself weeks ago."

Jim took Myrtle by the arm. He led her to the door. The cop who was question Vera looked at him.

"Just getting her some fresh air," Jim said. "She was feeling faint."

The cop nodded his permission. Jim and Myrtle stepped outside.

Two patrol cars were parked near the sidewalk. Another young policeman smoked a cigarette while leaning against one of the cars. The cop who had gotten sick was trying to light his own tobacco but his hands were shaking. An ambulance turned into the drive, and Jim realized that his cab was still waiting.

"Come with me," he said. He put Myrtle in the backseat of the cab and climbed in next to her. "Is there someplace we can talk?"

"The Marquis Room, downtown," she said.

"You know where that is?" Jim said to the cabbie.

The man said he did. With a grinding of gears, the cab streaked out onto the street. The driver seemed pleased to leave the phalanx of law enforcement behind.

The Marquis Room proved to be a restaurant and bar near the center of Bangor. It was old. Very old. But it was clean and quiet, and they got a booth in the back where it was even quieter. Jim had a cup of coffee. Myrtle ordered a martini.

"I never do this," she explained. "But I really, really need it. And I'm pretty certain work has been canceled for the rest of the day."

When her drink arrived she took a long, slow sip and made a small satisfied sound.

"Okay," Jim said. "Give."

Myrtle took another sip of the martini.

"You're Jim Anthony, right?"

"Right."

"The millionaire. The guy who tracks down murders."

"Sometimes."

"Are you married?"

"No."

Her face brightened.

"But I'm engaged," he said.

"Oh." Myrtle lifted her glass and drank until it was empty. She signaled the waiter for a refill. "Sorry. I'm a little upset. See, Mr. Plainview told me I was going to get a promotion. He was taking me to dinner tonight to talk about it."

"That's nice," Jim said. "Now let's talk about what happened at your office."

Myrtle slumped back in her chair. She looked down at the table.

"Who is George Flynn?"

She sighed before she answered.

"He worked for Eagle Chemical. When I started there, everyone was upset because some company in Germany was selling something called, uh, rocket propellant, I think. Do you know what that is?"

"I do."

Myrtle nodded.

"Good. Maybe you can explain it to me sometime. Anyway, this rocket stuff was the same kind of rocket stuff Eagle made. It had a secret formula or something, so they knew somebody here had told the company in Germany what was in it. It turned out to be George Flynn."

"They were sure?"

She nodded again. She smiled when the waiter brought her second martini.

"Mr. Plainview and the other directors hired some detective. He took pictures of George meeting with the Germans. Then Mr. Plainview turned the pictures over to the army, because that's who we—I mean Eagle Chemical—sell the rocket stuff to. They arrested George."

"Did it go to trial?"

She took a slow drink. She closed her eyes as she swallowed.

"Nope. See, he hanged himself in jail. It never went to trial. George was dead."

Jim was confused. He tried to read one edition of each of his newspapers each day, and he had heard nothing of this. Myrtle must have noticed his puzzled expression.

"Myrtle slumped back in her chair."

"Mr. Plainview and the others talked the newspaper into not running the story. Eagle Chemical employs a lot of people around here, you know."

Jim nodded grimly. It seemed he would have to visit the offices of the Bangor Morning Beacon again before he left town.

"And," he said, "you believe Plainview's killer was the deceased George Flynn?"

Myrtle nodded vigorously.

"Yea. He looked a little older, but that's makes sense. Hanging yourself would really age you, wouldn't it?"

"Did Flynn have any family?"

"Oh sure. A wife and little boy. Tim. He's a cute kid. He still comes by the plant just to hang out. Poor little guy."

Myrtle looked as if she might cry. The alcohol was obviously taking effect. Jim needed to keep her talking.

"What about other family? Brothers? A dad?"

Myrtle wiped one hand across her eyes.

"Nobody. He was an only child and his parents were dead. He told me his life story one day in the break room. I have that kind of face, you know? People want to tell me things. Like Mr. Plainview telling me I was going to get a promotion."

She sobbed very softly.

Deciding he had extracted all the information he could from Myrtle, Jim paid the check and escorted her back to the cab. Within ten minutes, they were back at Eagle Chemical. There were more police cars in the lot. And Tom's big sedan was parked there, as well. Jim paid the cabbie and entered the office.

Fresh-faced and freckled Tom Gentry was perched on the edge of a desk, his long legs swinging like a kid's. He smiled when he saw Jim.

"There he is. Did you slip off for a spot of lunch time romance, old boy?"

Myrtle blushed. She pushed past the policemen in the direction of the washroom.

A man in a cheap suit and a bowler scowled at Jim.

"Anthony? I'm Inspector O'Donnell. I know you're a big shot an' all, but you're nuts if you think you can skip out with a witness in my town."

Jim stepped forward until he was toe to toe with the smaller police inspector.

"Yeah? Well, I'm back. And I'm conducting my own investigation."

"No, you're not."

Jim simply stared at O'Donnell. The cop had a face like a bulldog and he never broke his steady gaze.

"Alexander Plainview was a family friend and I'm going to find his killer."

"What makes you think I'm going to let that happen?"

"Did you see the body?"

O'Donnell swallowed hard. This time he did look away.

"Check my references, Inspector. You'll find I'm qualified to look into… unusual crimes."

A flush spread from O'Donnell's neck to his cheeks. He looked up at Jim Anthony with fire in his eyes.

"I don't know what you have on the New York Police, but we're pretty tough here in Maine. Maybe we don't need your fancy help."

Jim smiled.

"Then why don't we try working together? Cooperation might get us farther than butting heads. I'll start."

Jim told O'Donnell everything Myrtle had revealed to him in the bar.

The inspector squinted one eye and stared at Jim with his mouth open, which resulted in an even stronger resemblance to his canine counterpart.

"You're on the level with that story, Anthony?"

"That's what she told me."

"That's impossible."

"What happened to Plainview doesn't make any sense either. Or do you need to check the body again?"

O'Donnell's face lost a bit of its color.

"It's been, ah, taken to the morgue," he said.

"Listen, was Myrtle right about Flynn's family?"

"I'll have to double check, but that sounds right."

Myrtle emerged from a hallway in the back of the lobby, accompanied by a boy.

"Look who I found," she said.

They all turned to see the new arrival. The child was perhaps ten years old. He had a friendly open face, though it was somewhat guarded, thanks to the presence of so many police officers. Still, Jim thought he could detect a resemblance between the child and the killer.

"You must be Tim Flynn," Jim said. He stuck out his hand.

The boy did not hesitate he stepped over to Jim and shook.

"Nice to meet you, sir," the boy said. He smiled at Jim, but there was a deep sadness in his features, though he tried hard to hide it.

"Tim here is our official mascot," Myrtle said. She slightly slurred the S in "mascot." The boy seemed embarrassed by the attention.

O'Donnell spoke up, much to the relief of Tim Flynn.

"I'm going to get back and check on, ah, that question you had," he said. "Stay in touch, you hear?"

"You got it, Inspector," Jim said.

O'Donnell stared at Jim while he got a cigarette between his lips and lit it. Then the cop turned to Vera.

"Nobody goes into that office until I say so."

"Of course, Inspector," Vera said.

O'Donnell walked to the door. He was halfway outside when he turned around and said, "Dinner on Sunday?"

"Of course," Vera replied.

"Meat loaf."

"If I must."

O'Donnell smiled for the first time. He whistled as he left the building. The other cops followed him.

Jim and Tom Gentry looked at the older woman.

She shrugged.

"He's my son-in-law," she said.

The door opened again. The new arrival was a tall, distinguished man in a tweed overcoat and an old Homburg hat.

"Vera, I got here as soon as I could."

The older woman crossed the room in a hurry to hug the man.

With her face pressed against his chest, he said, "I can't believe he's gone."

After a few seconds, Vera pulled away, straightened up and smoothed out her blouse and skirt. The man looked at Jim for the first time, extending a hand.

"I am Claude Martin, one of the directors of the company."

"I'm Jim Anthony."

"I know who you are."

"And this is my colleague Tom Gentry."

"The pilot? It's a pleasure. A real pleasure." He shook with both of them. Tom seemed genuinely pleased to be recognized on his own merit.

"A terrible thing. Terrible," Martin said. "The police told me what happened. Or as much as they knew. I'm afraid it didn't make a great deal of sense."

"I hope to change that," Jim said.

"Yes!" Martin cried. "By God, I'm going to hire you."

"You can't," Tom said.

"Excuse me?"

"Jim Anthony can't be hired, and, if he could, you couldn't afford him."

"Now see here," Martin declared, "I'll have you know—"

"Easy," Jim said. "All Tom means is that my...financial circumstances allow me to pick and choose the cases I want to follow."

"And this one?" Martin said, one eyebrow arched.

"This one is personal," Jim told him.

"Excellent!" Martin clasped Jim's hand again. "So do you really think this has anything to do with that thief, George Flynn?"

Jim glanced at Tim. The boy stared at the floor. There was a lot of color in his cheeks.

"Myrtle," Jim said, "do you think you could take Tim to find a snack?"

"Huh? I mean, sure." She took the boy by the hand and guided him back to the hallway, which presumably led to a cafeteria or break room.

For his part, Martin seemed taken aback by his own insensitivity.

"I was a thoughtless fool. I apologize."

"We're not the ones who need the apology," Tom said.

"Of course, of course." Martin removed the Homburg. "Will you gentlemen join me in my office? I have a few questions, and I thought you might have a few, as well."

Martin crossed the lobby to a door on the other side of the room from Plainview's office. He produced a ring of keys from his coat pocket and unlocked the door. He walked inside.

"Come on in and make yourselves at home."

Before Jim could cross the threshold, he smelled it.

A hot, electrical odor, like melting wires.

"Martin, wait!" he called out. But it was too late.

"What the deuce? Flynn? It can't be you!"

Jim stepped into the office. The killer stood in front of Martin's desk. Claude Martin was between Jim and the man with the strange machine. Jim planned to lunge forward, shove Martin to safety and face down this man, whether he was George Flynn or someone else.

Too late.

The killer reached out and touched Martin with both hands. The sparks around the man's metal framework hissed and popped. And Martin... changed.

From Jim's perspective, it was like watching a frame of a motion picture as it was trapped in the projector. Martin's body stretched until he was taller and warped, a fun house mirror distortion of his former self. The burning smell grew worse, too, though nothing was as terrible as the scream that came from Claude Martin. It was an incoherent cry of torment, a keening wail that reached a crescendo before ending abruptly.

Martin was dead.

The misshapen corpse of the chemical executive fell to the floor. Jim couldn't spare even a second to look at the dead man. The killer stepped over Martin's body and advanced on Jim.

Without turning around, Jim said, "Tom, get out of the room."

He heard Tom's footsteps retreat. His friend was a good man to have in a tight spot. No argument. No questions. The two of them worked together like a precision machine.

Jim backed through the doorway into the lobby. The killer continued to come after him with a slow, steady stride. Jim studied the man's face. The killer was older, certainly, but there was a fire in his eyes that was born of anger. Or madness.

"Jim Anthony, it's been a long time," the man said. His voice was strangely distorted. It seemed to originate from very far away.

"I don't know you," Jim said, still walking backward.

"You can't hope to stop me, you know. From my perspective, you are little more than a child, playing at a game you can't possibly understand."

The killer stepped over the threshold and entered the lobby. He extended his hands toward Jim.

Tom Gentry stepped behind the man, and smashed the red metal fire extinguisher into the man's head. Or more accurately, he tried to strike the killer. The cylinder stopped an inch or so from the metal tubing that surrounded the back of the man's skull, amid a shower of sparks and a high-pitched whine.

"Tom, get down!" Jim shouted. Tom instantly flung his body away from the killer, just before the fire extinguisher exploded.

Tom raised an arm to shield his face from debris. He felt the bite of hot metal on his hand. The blast threw the killer to the floor, and this time he did not vanish. In fact, the man quickly stood. His face was contorted with rage. He stalked toward Jim once again. Now, his metal armor sparked more fiercely. Jim wondered if the explosion managed to damage the mechanism.

Hopefully, there would be time for musing later. Jim vaulted over Vera's desk. The older woman was standing halfway out the front door. The killer reached the desk and reached across it toward Jim. Remembering the hellish scream that had come during Claude Martin's death throes, Jim took hold of the edge of Vera's large desk and flipped it onto the killer.

Another blinding flash of light strobed through the office.

When his vision cleared, Jim saw the killer had disappeared again.

Tom was on his hands and knees, trying to stand. The back of his leather jacket was smoking in several places. Tom gently forced him to the floor and rolled him over to extinguish the small flames. He took Tom's hand and helped his friend to his feet.

"Wow," Tom said. "Is the phone ringing or is that inside my head."

Jim took the freckled aviator's head in his hands and carefully examined him.

"Is your vision blurred? Any dizziness?"

"No and no. Please tell me I look better than you, pal."

Jim touched his own face. His fingertips were smeared with blood. Apparently, some of the debris made it to his face. He was lucky none of it landed in his eyes. He also noticed several burn marks on the sleeve of his coat. He jerked the garment from his body and tossed it over a chair. While he was at it, Jim removed his tie and unbuttoned his collar. God, he hated suits.

When he had rolled up his shirt sleeves, he found Vera standing next to her overturned desk.

"I think you can take the rest of the day off," Jim said.

"Like hell," she said. "Someone has to telephone the police and tell them there's been another murder."

"Fine. While you're at it, I need to speak to your son-in-law."

Vera knelt to grab a corner of her desk. She tugged on it for a few seconds.

"Give a lady a hand?"

Jim took hold of the edge of the wooden structure and set it upright. Then he scooted it back where it had been. Vera placed the phone in the exact spot where it had previously rested. The floor was littered paper and framed photographs.

"I suppose I'll have to do something about that," she said.

Jim looked where she pointed, a spot in the center of the desk. A section of the wooden surface was warped and blackened. In the center of the damaged area were two handprints.

"This must have been where he tried to stop the desk," he said.

He leaned in closer to examine the handprints. He wasn't certain at first, but he got as close as he could and there they were: whorls and ridges.

"Tom, did you unload the equipment cases from the plane?"

"Sure thing," Tom said. "They're in the car."

"I need number two."

"What's going on?"

"The killer left behind his fingerprints."

While Tom began to collect the fingerprint information, Vera waved Jim Anthony to the phone on Myrtle's desk.

"Ronnie's on the line."

"Ronnie?" Jim said.

"The, ah, inspector."

Jim lifted the receiver and heard O'Donnell's thick voice.

"Anthony? I've got cops headed over there. Vera said it was the same man."

"It was. He vanished just as mysteriously as the first time."

"Geez Louise. I've never seen anything like this mess. What's behind it?"

"I don't know yet," Jim said. "But I think it's safe to assume it has something to do with the men who run Eagle Chemical. If we can locate the other two directors, can you gather enough men to keep an eye on them?"

"Yeah, sure. But what can my boys do against that machine he's wearing?"

"They can shoot him. Tell them not to hesitate to fire."

"Okay," the stocky cop said. "Now I have something for you. The girl was right. Flynn was survived by his wife and kid. He had no other living relatives."

Jim was silent.

"What? You don't really think he returned from the dead?" O'Donnell laughed, but the sound came off as forced.

"Are you sure he is dead?"

"Oh, yeah. Saw him swinging from the end of that sheet myself."

"Was he cremated?"

"No. They planted him in one of the cemeteries in town."

"Good," Jim said. "Then dig him up."

"Huh?"

"We have to be sure."

"The judge will think I'm nuts."

"Then tell him it was my idea," Jim said. "One more thing."

"Yeah?"

"When Flynn was arrested, was he fingerprinted?"

"No. Why would we? He confessed."

Jim sighed.

"Anything else, m'lord?" O'Donnell asked

"That'll do," Jim said, "For now"

He hung up, and addressed Vera.

"The other two directors, are they here in town?"

"I believe so," she said. "They don't come in every day but they would have informed me if they were going to be gone."

"Call them. Tell them to stay home. The police are on their way."

"Very well," she said. "Do you think the police can protect them?"

Once more, Jim Anthony was silent.

The flash of a camera bulb drew his attention. Tom photographed the killer's fingerprints. The boy, Tim Flynn, had returned from the bowls of the building and stood watching.

"What are you doing, mister?" he asked.

"Getting the bad man's fingerprints," Tim said.

"Neat! Will you get mine, too?"

"Sure." Tom removed a piece of thick white paper and a fingerprint ink pad from the equipment case. "Ready to get your fingers dirty, kid?"

"You bet," the boy said.

Jim saw Myrtle leaning against the wall, near the entrance to the hallway. He joined her. She studied him through half-lidded eyes. She smelled strongly of booze. Jim imagined she had a bottle hidden away somewhere in the building.

"Great day, huh? Took away my promotion, now he's killing all the bosses."

"Bosses" came out as "bosh-ez".

"I think it's time to call it a day, Myrtle."

"Sure, sure. So I can go home and listen to my mother tell me how I'm wasting my life. She thinks I should marry a rich man." She leaned against Jim's arm. "You want to marry me, rich man?"

He took her by the shoulders and guided her to a chair, just as he had earlier in the day.

"Excuse me a minute," he said.

Vera had her coat on.

"Mr. Anthony, should I wait on the police?"

"I'll be here," Jim said. "Did you reach the other directors?"

"Mr. Bane and Mr. Wells are both at home. I gave them your instructions, then relayed that information to Ron—the inspector."

"Vera, you're a hell of a woman."

The tough old Yankee blushed and looked away.

"I need one more thing, if you don't mind," he said.

"Do you need me to build a Buck Rogers ray gun to use on that character?"

"Not a bad idea," Jim said. "Actually, I was hoping you could call a cab for Myrtle. She appears to be…done in by today's events."

Vera shook her head. "You mean she's drunk as a skunk."

Jim shrugged. "It may be my fault."

"You didn't hide that flask in the ladies room, did you, sir? No, I won't call her a cab. But I will take her home. Young Tim, too."

"Thank you," Jim said.

"I take it you're staying in town tonight, sir."

"Looks like it."

"Then you'll need a room. The company keeps a suite at the Windsor Arms downtown. I told them to get it ready."

"Vera," Jim said with affection, "will you come to New York and organize my life?"

She snorted. "Shall we wait and see if I still have a job here?"

"Of course," Jim said.

Tim ran over to show off his black fingertips.

"Vera, look!"

"Oh no, you don't, young mister. We'll be scrubbing those paws before you get into my car."

She took him back to the washroom.

Tom had packed the fingerprint equipment in the case and was carrying it to the door.

"I saw a photography studio on my way over here. I'm going to borrow their darkroom," he said. "These fingerprints may turn out to be a dead end, but it beats cooling my heels."

"Fine," Jim said. "Just hurry back. I'm sure O'Donnell will need a statement from you."

"That shouldn't take long. 'Swung a fire extinguisher. Couldn't connect. Got knocked into next Tuesday.' What are you going to do?"

"Besides waiting on the cops? I'm going to think."

"Now we're in trouble," Tom said with a smile.

"Get out of here," Jim said.

Tom left, trailing laughter as he went.

In a moment Vera, Tim and an unsteady Myrtle also departed, leaving Jim Anthony alone with Claude Martin's corpse.

He stood in the dead man's office and studied the grotesque, elongated body. Whatever had done this was far beyond anything in Jim's experience. He didn't believe in ghosts, so this had to be a super-science both futuristic and macabre.

An idea was tickling the base of his mind, a fleeting notion, really. Jim preferred not to hypothesize until he had evidence. However, evidence was proving difficult to obtain in this case.

This tiny thought was strange. No, even worse, it was impossible as he understood the laws of the universe. Yet it tugged at his mind, demanding room for consideration.

Ridiculous, Jim decided. He had no way to prove it. Even if this fantastic concept amazingly turned out to be true, how could he do anything about it?

He shoved it out of his head. He needed to concentrate on practical matters.

The sound of sirens alerted him to the arrival of the police, returning to Eagle Chemical for the second murder of the day.

Jim feared it wasn't to be the last.

✳ ✳ ✳

Jim was leaning against Vera's desk, his arms crossed over his chest, when Inspector O'Donnell strode into the office, followed by five more uniformed officers.

"You look like hell," the pugnacious cop said.

"I'll heal," Jim said, "but you'll still look like a mad bulldog."

O'Donnell smiled. "Mad bulldog. I like it."

"You took your time."

"Yeah. I had some work to do. When I get a minute, I'll explain what that is. Where's the body?"

Jim pointed to Martin's office. He stayed where he was and allowed the inspector to view the corpse. Judging by the oaths muttered by O'Donnell, the cop managed to locate Martin's body without difficulty.

Two of the younger cops hurried from the office and went outside. Jim heard one cough and the other suck in deep gulps of fresh air. O'Donnell stayed for a while, and when he finally returned, he looked shaken. He didn't try to hide his unease. Jim could respect that.

"Never in my life have I felt so unqualified to do my job," the inspector said. He pulled a red and white checked handkerchief from a rear pocket, and wiped it across his brow.

"Nobody's qualified for something like this."

"Except you," O'Donnell said. "This must be just another day at the office for the great Jim Anthony."

Jim shook his head and resisted the urge to smack the cop on the side of his head.

"Actually, it's the strangest thing I've ever encountered."

"No kidding?" O'Donnell looked impressed. "So you're just as lost as us?"

"I didn't say that."

"Nice," O'Donnell said. He pulled a cigar from his coat pocket and struck a match on the edge of Vera's desk.

"Did you make any progress on getting Flynn exhumed?"

"You might say that." O'Donnell puffed deeply on his cigar, making Jim wait for the answer. He exhaled a cloud of blue smoke. "Eagle Chemical is a big employer. The first judge I called signed the papers. They're digging him up right now."

"Then I need directions to the cemetery," Jim said.

"Naw, you don't. I'm on my way over there now. My boys can wait for the meat wagon. You can ride with me."

"Do you know a photography studio near here?"

"Yeah. Why?"

"We have to pick someone up."

After a fast ride in O'Donnell's surprisingly spotless coupe, Jim decided to join Tom in his sedan, and follow the inspector to the cemetery. It gave him a chance to explain to Tom what he wanted, and give Tom a chance to prepare himself.

"It's not the first dead guy I've seen," Tim said. "Not by a long shot."

"I know."

"It'll be the first one I've fingerprinted, though. If he's there."

"Do you think he came back from the dead?" Jim said with a smile.

"Jim pointed to Martin's office."

"More like he was never dead to begin with. He faked it somehow. Maybe the coroner was in on it. Then he hides out while he builds that sparking gizmo."

"And if Flynn is in that grave?"

Tom waved a hand.

"Forget it, pal. He can't be, not if he's the guy everybody has identified. We know he's not a ghost, so what else could it be?"

Jim didn't answer.

They followed O'Donnell through the center of town and past the bar where Jim had gone with Myrtle. That seemed like it had been days ago. The cop led them through a part of Bangor Jim had never visited, finally turning through the open gates of a cemetery that looked as if it had been founded before Maine became a state. They drove slowly past the plumb real estate – the fancy mausoleums and large statuary – until O'Donnell stopped at the bottom of a hill that seemed to be covered in perpetual shadow. The grass grew sparsely here, and there had been few attempts at landscaping. Two young men leaned on shovels next to a pile of dirt. An old tractor outfitted with a big blade on the front sat behind the dirt. A man in a rumpled suit stood next to a mud-stained coffin.

Jim and Tom parked a few yards away from the open grave. Tom retrieved an equipment case from the back seat.

"Did I ever mention that I hate graveyards?" he said.

"Not that I recall."

They caught up with O'Donnell, who introduced them to the man in the suit. His name was Clemmons and he was the coroner.

Once they were all assembled, Clemmons nodded to one of the young men, who replaced his shovel with a crowbar. He slipped one end in the crack between the casket lid and the casket, and pried. The lid opened with a snap, and the sickening sweet odor of corruption rose from the interior of the box.

O'Donnell had his handkerchief over his mouth. The coroner behaved as though he couldn't smell it. The man who had opened the casket walked away to stand with his co-worker. Tom coughed once.

"Okay," he whispered to Jim, "the other dead guys didn't smell this bad."

"They were fresher," Jim said. "Come on".

O'Donnell used his free hand to raise the coffin's lid.

The body in the box was emaciated, the skin turning the color of an old piece of fruit. The skin had drawn tight, bringing the bones of the face and hands into stark relief. The corpse's yellowed teeth were set in a grimace.

The dead man was dressed in a blue suit that was stained with the fluids of decomposition.

"For the record," O'Donnell said, "That's George Flynn."

"Why wasn't he embalmed?" Jim said.

O'Donnell shrugged. "It costs a little more. The family decided to skip it."

Jim leaned over the casket and tugged at the dead man's collar. The exposed skin was deeply grooved by an indentation that was a shade darker than the rest of the skin.

"He hanged himself with a sheet?" Jim said.

"Yeah," O'Donnell said. "He tied it high on the bars of the cell door so he would dangle."

"How long ago?"

"It'll be four weeks this coming Saturday."

Jim stood and faced his friend.

"Okay, Tom. Your turn."

While Jim examined the corpse, the freckled aviator had donned leather driving gloves. He opened the equipment case and removed his ink pad, paper and other supplies. He lifted one of the corpse's bony hands and applied ink to each finger tip. Then he carefully pressed each fingertip against the paper. He repeated the process with the other hand. When he finished, he sat the ink pad and papers atop the equipment case before walking for several yards. Jim noted that Tom was pale, but he had carried out the task without complaint.

"You need anything else?" O'Donnell asked.

Jim shook his head. "I doubt it. But if we do we know where he is."

Clemmons, the coroner, gestured to the two young men, who were sharing a smoke and laughing about something. They came over and closed the casket lid in preparation for reburial.

Jim met Tom at the car. Tom's leather gloves were gone, probably tossed away nearby.

"You okay?" Jim said.

"Sure. As soon as I get to that fancy hotel and have a couple of drinks."

The Windsor Arms turned out to be a fine hotel. Their suite was spacious, with two large bedrooms and a large sitting room. Jim ordered food for them both and whiskey for Tom. It turned out the aviator didn't have much of an appetite. While he had a drink, Jim had dinner and listened to the news on the radio. The killings at Eagle Chemical were the top story. There were no new details. Thankfully, the other two directors were still alive. Jim pondered that. Why hadn't the killer tried again? It had been several hours since the death of Claude Martin.

Perhaps the mechanical contraption had been damaged by the desk Jim had tossed on him.

Or maybe he only wanted to kill Martin and Plainview. He could have no interest in the other two, Bane and Wells.

Tom finished his drink and cleared off the desk in the corner of the sitting room. He turned on a lamp and retrieved the photographs of the killer's fingerprints, along with the samples from the dead man. He used a magnifying glass to examine the material. Tom muttered to himself, as he was wont to do when he was deep in thought.

Jim stood at the suite's window and studied the lights of downtown Bangor. He needed to send a wire to the authorities in Paris, explaining his delay. Unfortunately, he wouldn't be able to tell them how long he would be in Maine. He didn't know. Jim had been honest with O'Donnell. This was the most confounding matter he had ever investigated it. It appeared the killer was using some sort of supernatural abilities to appear and disappear as he had. Of course, Jim knew that was hogwash. There was no supernatural. Super-science, perhaps. Even though Jim Anthony was on the cutting edge of many of the world's scientific disciplines, there were still some matters of which he remained unaware, including the science used by the Eagle Chemical killer.

However, Jim did not intend to remain uninformed about the killer's methods. Not for much longer.

"Son of a gun!" Tom stood up from the desk and waved his arms in the air.

"What is it?"

"I'm not sure if I'm happy or sad."

"What did you find?"

"The fingerprints," Tom said, "do not belong to George Flynn."

A small flicker of disappointment passed through Jim's thoughts. After seeing the body, he was fairly certain of the results of the fingerprint comparison. Still, one dead body could be substituted for another. That would have made George Flynn a criminal genius. In this case, the real genius must be the person who invented that machine the killer wore.

"How certain are you?" Jim said.

Tom shrugged. "Ninety percent. Let me fix another drink and I'll double check it."

While Tom worked, Jim went down to the lobby of the Windsor Arms, where he filled out a telegram and gave it to the concierge, along with a generous tip. At least the Paris authorities would know he hadn't forgotten them. He stepped outside for the latest edition of the evening papers. The murders were front pages stories. One of the papers—Jim's own, it turned out—ran a sidebar on Jim and his career as a crimefighter. Jim didn't like it. He had never sought publicity, and the last place he expected to find it was within his own business. He added another item to the mental list that he intended to share with the editor of the Bangor Morning Bulletin.

When he returned to the lobby, he was greeted by the sight of Tom, sprinting across the expensive carpeting. His face was as pale as when he'd been working with the corpse earlier in the day.

"What is it?"

Tom moved his lips silently for a moment. For the garrulous aviator to become speechless, the event must be spectacular.

Finally, Tom managed to say, "Something. I've found something."

"What?"

He shook his head. "Telling you is no good. You'll want to see for yourself. So just come along."

With that, Tom turned and retraced his steps across the lobby. Jim followed, barely able to restrain his curiosity.

When they entered the suite, he said, "So what has you so excited?"

Tom went to the desk, handed the magnifying glass to Jim, and briefly explained.

Jim looked at him in disbelief.

Then Jim checked for himself. And checked again, followed by a third examination.

When he had finished, no one spoke for a long time.

Tom slumped in a chair and sighed.

"I feel like I'm stuck in a dream."

"More like a nightmare," Jim added.

"How can this be?"

"There can only be one explanation. But it's the craziest thing I've ever considered."

Tom slapped his own leg.

"Give, brother. This I have to hear."

Jim told him.

Jim and Tom talked for over an hour, examining the problem, and Jim's conclusions, from many different angles. Tom hated the idea, but he couldn't come up with another scenario that conformed to the facts.

"Damn," he finally said, slumping against the cushioned couch.

"I know how you feel," Jim said. He stood gazing out at the city lights.

"This makes my head hurt."

"Take an aspirin. I'm going to need you later."

"Yeah, yeah." Tom stood up and stretched. "I'm going to find a drugstore."

"Did you pack the guns?"

"Sure. Do you think I'm nuts?"

"Sometimes," Jim said. "But I'm sure I often make you feel the same. Grab the weapons on your way back."

"Okay." Tom shrugged. "I'm not sure how much good a bullet will do. I couldn't touch him with the fire extinguisher."

"I hope the guns will work a little better. Now get going."

"Aye aye, skipper." Tom threw his friend a mock salute. When the door closed, Jim Anthony sat his empty glass down next to the ice bucket. He thought about fixing another drink, then decided against it. He needed his head clear for what was to come. Besides, most of the ice had melted. Jim decided to wait for Tom to get back for calling for more.

Jim stripped away the rest of his business suit. He dressed again his familiar yellow swimming trunks and leather moccasins, the clothing in which he felt most comfortable.

He rubbed his temples and tried to force his body to relax. This was easily the most spectacular and unbelievable case he had ever investigated. Over the course of his career, Jim had witnessed incredible events that, if revealed, would shock the world. But these murders were like nothing he had even imagined. If it were true…

Jim shook his head. Of course it was true. Facts didn't lie. His conclusions, improbable as they were, fit the facts. Now Tom had only one question. How was this far-fetched feat accomplished?

He hoped there would be an opportunity to question the killer, as unlikely as that sounded. Later, Jim would muse that the universe loved to pull the rug out from under you. At that instant, however, he was only thinking of the smell.

The hotel room was filled with the distinctive odor of an electrical fire.

For an instant, Jim thought of trying to escape the room, to find a battlefield that offered more space to maneuver, but he couldn't bring himself to put others in unnecessary danger.

There was a ripple in the air, directly in the center of the room. A tear appeared, as though the very fabric of reality was being ripped open. A light shone through the opening, growing brighter as the size of the tear increased. With a rush of air and a sizzling noise, the killer appeared.

He looked just as he had when Jim last faced him. The weird apparatus was unchanged. If anything was different, it was the killer's face. It was without expression, quite a contrast to the mask of anger he had earlier worn.

"There you are," he said, his voice again pitched as though it was being delivered over a transatlantic cable.

"I know who you are," Jim said.

"You can't."

Jim spoke his name. Surprise briefly flashed across the killer's features.

Jim smiled. "Thank you for the confirmation. Now tell me how you did this. Did you invent this apparatus?"

The killer snarled as he lunged for Jim, one hand outstretched to touch the crimefighter. Jim nimbly avoided the hand, even as he noticed that the killer's entire body was sheathed in a faint glow, nearly invisible.

The killer's lunge caused him to lose his balance. As he fell forward, Jim got a good look at the back of the unusual contraption the man wore and the many wires and hoses that radiated from it. Jim was careful not to let any part of the machine touch him.

The killer spun, the now-familiar rage contorting his features again.

"You're ruining everything," he snarled. "It's time for you to go."

Jim backed up until he was against the table. The killer leaped at him again. Jim's fingers found the ice bucket. Jim dropped to the floor, allowing the killer to sail over him. Jim sprang instantly to his feet and he poured the water from the ice bucket over the killer's back.

The result was immediate and impressive. The strange contraption on the man began to spark and smoke. The killer made a sound of inarticulate raged mingled with confusion.

Jim stood back, watching carefully as the sparks traveled the length of the apparatus. Finally, he saw what he'd been waiting for.

The almost-undetectable glow that surrounded the killer flashed once, twice, and disappeared.

Where other men would have hesitated, riddled with doubt, Jim Anthony acted. He reached out for one of the many wires that dangled beneath the main body of the unit. He chose one that was thick and snaked around to the front handles of the gizmo. Jim yanked hard, and the cable came loose. He pulled the end of it from beneath the killer's body.

The electrical smell grew faint, as did the sizzling sound that always accompanied the killer.

"Shoddy workmanship," Jim said.

The killer rolled over and got to his feet.

"Damn you," he said.

"It's over. You have to give up."

"If you know who I am," the killer said, "you know I can't do that."

Jim shifted his weight to the balls of his feet. He was perfectly balanced and ready to take down the killer. Without the science-fiction machine, the murderer was just another man, one that Jim could easily dispatch. He relaxed into is fighting stance. This was familiar ground. Jim even felt the hint of a smile spread across is face.

The door to the hallway opened.

Tom stood, with a small case in one hand, the room key in the other. "Hey, I thought I should get the guns first—"

The killer took advantage of the split-second of confusion to shove Jim toward the door.

"Shoot him," Jim said. "Now!"

Tom fumbled with the latch on the case. Jim twisted around. There was still time to stop the murderer.

The killer plugged the loose cord back in the socket on the front of his machine, the part Jim thought of as the controls. The glow appeared again and disappeared just as quickly.

Perhaps the machine had been too severely damaged by the water. This could work out, after all. It could end tonight, in this room.

Jim launched a blow at the killer's face. At the last second the glow again shimmered into existence around the man. Any man with slower reflexes would not have been able to stop his momentum. Jim saw the glow and forced his entire body to turn to the left. The punch missed the killer, but the motion carried Jim past his target and off his feet. Jim rolled with the fall, turned it into a somersault and came up on his feet.

Jim spun to face the murderer again, and saw that Tom had found one of the guns. He pointed the flat automatic at the killer.

"No!" Jim's cry was too late. Tom fired the gun. The shot struck the glowing field near the middle of the murderer's chest. The bullet ricocheted against thick frame around the mirror on the wall, then changed direction again. It plowed into the wood of the door frame two inches from Tom's head.

"Geez!" Tom said.

Jim searched for the ice bucket. It was six or seven feet away, resting on its side, and he could clearly see that only a few beaded drops of moisture remained. There was no other source of water in the room. He snatched up a chair from the desk. It wouldn't keep the killer at bay for long, but it would hold off the lethal touch for a couple of seconds.

To Jim's surprise, the killer did not attack.

"It's been fun, Anthony." The man's voice once more sounded like it originated from a great distance.

The murdered winked out of existence.

And suddenly reappeared. He looked as shocked as Jim felt.

He disappeared again. This time he did not return.

Tom stood in the doorway, his gun hand extended toward the spot the killer had occupied.

"Holy smokes," he said.

"I couldn't have put it better myself," Jim said.

✳ ✳ ✳

"Shouldn't we get out of here or call the cops?" Tom asked.

Jim shook his head. "The police can't do anything. And I don't think he'll rush right back."

"Why not?"

"He has to repair the damage from my dowsing. But that gives me an idea. We need to reach O'Donnell. The police detail protecting the other two men should keep buckets of water standing by. Better yet, see if they can get a pumper truck from the fire department at each location."

"Think that will stop him?"

Jim shrugged. "Hard to say. I suppose it depends upon his ingenuity. If can make all the connections on that gizmo watertight, then it won't work. But I bet he won't. He doesn't strike me as the patient type."

Tom went to the phone and placed the call to Inspector O'Donnell. Jim could hear the cop's bark from across the room. Tom hung up.

"Gee, is he always that friendly?"

"Always," Jim said.

Tom paced the hotel room, unable to settle down. "So what do we do now?"

Jim considered the question. "Frankly, I'm at a loss. The only thing we know for sure is that the killer has it in for the Eagle Chemical board of directors. We don't know which one he'll strike next, but he'll make it to both houses eventually."

"Unless we stop him," Tom said.

"Sure, sure," Jim said. "I admire your optimism. All our scientific knowledge, and the best idea I have is to douse him with water."

"It could've worked, if only I had been quicker with the damn gun."

"Don't be so hard on yourself, pal. We're exploring unknown territory. We need to learn from our mistakes and move forward."

Tom sat down on the edge of the couch. "Yeah, you're right. I just hate feeling like we're in over our heads. It's driving me nuts!"

"I would think you'd be used to it by now."

"Very funny," Tom said. "So which guy do we cover – Wells or Bane?"

"Both of them," Jim said. "We're going to split up."

Tom sprung from the couch as if he'd been launched by a catapult.

"A fine idea. This sitting around is making me antsy. So where do you want me?"

"Take your pick."

"Banes it is. Tell Wells I said howdy."

After dressing again in slacks and shirt, Jim dropped Tom off in front of Banes's impressive home on the outskirts of town. The house was illuminated by spotlights on the lawn. Two police officers were stationed in front. From an earlier conversation with Inspector O'Donnell, Jim knew there would be at least two officers in back of the house and several inside. He watched Tom wave to the cops and enter the structure. When the front door closed, Jim turned around and drove back to the town. On the way, he passed a fire truck with its siren wailing, heading to the Banes house, as Jim had requested.

"What's the hurry?" Jim muttered.

Surprisingly, Taylor Wells lived on a middle-class street on the east side of Bangor. It was what Jim's father would have called a "working man's neighborhood". There were no flashy homes in this part of town. By comparison to the Banes residence, Wells lived in humble surroundings. The house was indeed larger than most of the neighboring abodes, thanks to an addition that appeared to have been built in the past couple of years. The houses were much closer together in this part of town, which made the police presence all the more obvious. The officers and emergency vehicles – including, Jim was pleased to note, a pumper truck from the fire department – certainly drew the curious. Neighbors lined the sidewalks and the porches, smoking cigarettes and drinking beer from dark brown bottles, sharing gossip in murmured voices, punctuated by the occasional bray of laughter.

Murder as entertainment, Jim thought.

He had to park the car up on the sidewalk in front of the Wells house. A cop hurried over to shoo him away, only to recognize Jim and toss him a salute. Jim had to weave his way through a throng of onlookers. As he shouldered past, a man said, "Watch it, bub." Another cautioned his companion, "Don't you know who that is? It's John Anthony, the super-detective."

An older cop was stationed by the front door. He waved Jim through the entrance.

Once inside, Jim realized he had stumbled into chaos.

Three young boys ran through the living room carrying toys guns and making the sounds of gunshots with their mouths. Two women sat on a big couch, speaking furiously in whispered voices. They looked so alike they had to be related, probably sisters.

Jim continued into the dining room, where it looked like a portion of the police station had been transferred to the Wells house. Inspector O'Donnell sat at a big oak table, which was covered with newspapers and two telephones. The cop was talking loudly into one of the phones. Jim noticed that the telephone wires ran out the kitchen window. The police command center had been set up in haste.

In the adjoining kitchen, two men in fire department uniforms were eating sandwiches by the icebox. A tall man in a rumpled suit stood gazing out the window. His tied was undone and he held an empty wine glass in his hand.

"And I want an update every ten minutes. No, don't make me call you!" O'Donnell slammed the telephone receiver into its cradle. Jim was surprised it didn't shatter.

"Anthony," he said around an unlit cigar. "We got your message." He

"An older cop...waved Jim through..."

pointed to the bucket of water in the corner of the dining room. "Got one in every room." O'Donnell nodded toward the two feasting firemen, before adding in a louder tone, "And if you-know-who does show up here, maybe they can subdue him with pastrami on rye."

Both firemen meekly shuffled out the back door, sandwiches in hand.

"Let me introduce you to our gracious host." The inspector led Jim into the kitchen and the man with the wine glass. "Mr. Wells, this is Jim Anthony. He's giving us a helping hand on this."

"Oh, yes," Wells said. He shook hands with Jim. "I've heard of you, of course. I appreciate your assistance." Taylor Wells had the look of a man who had been hit with the news of a serious medical diagnosis, and hovered between disbelief and acceptance. His eyes had a faraway cast and his voice was so soft, Jim had to strain to pick up the words.

"Mr. Wells, are those your kids out there?"

"What? Oh, two of the boys are. The other is my nephew. That's his mother, my wife's sister, sitting on the couch."

"I know it's been a tough day," Jim said. "And I have no desire to upset you further, but what the hell are you thinking?"

"Excuse me?" Wells wrinkled his brow, trying to make sense of Jim's comment.

"Just a minute – " O'Donnell began.

Jim held up a hand to silence the cop.

"Mr. Wells, I've seen two of your partners murdered in the most horrible manner I have ever experienced. This same man is coming here. He doesn't care who he hurts. Do you want your family to die today?"

"Of—of course not. But Grace refuses to leave."

"Fine. She's an adult. Not a bright one, apparently, but an adult. Get those children out of here now, sir."

Wells started to say something, possibly a defense of his wife's mental acuity. Instead he shook his head and went to the living room. He bent over and spoke close to the ear of one of the women.

"Did you have to be so rough with him? He's friends with the mayor," O'Donnell said.

"It was necessary. Didn't you notice he's in shock? I had to get through the fog in his head."

"Still…"

"If he's still alive tomorrow to complain to the mayor, I'll be happy to buy you a steak dinner."

"You're on." O'Donnell scratched a match on the sole of his shoe and lit the cigar. When he had it going, he jabbed it toward Wells. "Guy considers himself one of the boys. He's stinking rich, but he lives right here in the neighborhood where he grew up. He donates a ton of money for civic projects. Did you notice that park about four blocks from here? He paid for that last year. He sponsors the kids baseball league for the whole damn town."

"Okay, he's a good guy," Jim said. "What's your point?"

O'Donnell lowered his voice. "My point is he's a real asset to this city and I don't think we can keep him alive."

Jim said nothing.

One of the telephones on the dining room table rang. O'Donnell practically dove over the table to answer it.

"Yeah? Huh? Hold on." He held the handset out to Jim. "For you. It's Gentry."

As Jim took the phone, the other line rang. O'Donnell scooped it up.

"Tom," Jim said.

"Bane's dead," Tom said.

"When?"

"Two minutes, maybe. He stepped into the bedroom, probably to visit the facilities. We heard a scream and saw a flash of light, and by the time we got into the room, we found…well, you know what we found."

Jim considered Tom's words. There wasn't anyway to predict when the killer would arrive. It could happen in the next second or not for hours. He hoped they had a little time. He had an idea, if Inspector O'Donnell would help.

"See if one of the cops can give you a ride over here. I might need you."

"I don't know why," Tom said. "I've been completely useless in this whole mess."

"Stow that. If it weren't for you, we would have never figured out who the killer is. Now I hope that information will help us save a life. See you when you get here."

Jim handed the phone back to Inspector O'Donnell.

"You know, huh?" O'Donnell said.

"He could be here at any time," Jim said.

O'Donnell swallowed hard. "I'm good at my job, you know? I always knew I might catch a slug. It's part of the risk, and I've always accepted that. But this…"

"It's not over yet."

Jim walked back to the living room. Taylor Wells was still conferring with is wife and her sister.

"Rudy Bane is dead," Jim said.

Grace Wells gasped and cover her mouth with a hand. Taylor Wells paled, but otherwise remained silent.

"The women and children must leave now."

"No!" Mrs. Wells took her husbands arm. "I won't leave Taylor."

"It's not safe here," Jim said.

"If we leave," she said, "then he's coming with us."

"That's no good," Jim said. "The killer wants your husband. Wherever you go, he'll find you. If your husband goes with you, then it's quite likely that you all will die."

One of the boys started crying. Both women sobbed. Jim looked at Wells.

"He's right," Wells said, patting his wife's hand. "Nothing is more important than the safety of you and the boys. You have to go."

"I'll have an officer take you someplace safe," O'Donnell said.

Taylor hugged his family. Jim turned to the beefy police inspector.

"Now I need something from you."

"This I've got to hear," O'Donnell said.

"The boy, Tim Flynn. I need you to have him brought here now."

"Flynn's kid? Are you nuts?"

"Send your best driver. The boy needs to be here as soon as possible. Wells's life – hell, all of our lives depend on it."

O'Donnell shook his head. "I can't believe you, Anthony. You want to bring a child into this death trap?'

"Believe me, O'Donnell, that boy will be safer than anyone in this house."

O'Donnell stared at Jim for a long moment. Jim pitied the criminal that was interrogated by this bulldog.

"Okay. I'll do it," the police inspector finally said. "If it goes wrong, I swear I'll find a way to live just long enough to shoot you."

"You're on," Jim said.

For all of them, time slowed to a painful crawl.

With each second bringing the possibility of instant death, everyone was on edge. While Inspector O'Donnell paced the dining room, Jim tried to keep busy. He sat a sullen Taylor Wells at the dining room table and stationed police officers on each side of him. He then had all of the water buckets brought into the dining room and divided up between corners, so one would always be handy. He also made certain the two firemen were prepared outside. They uncoiled the big hose from the truck and held it at the ready.

When he had done everything he possibly could, Jim looked at his watch. Barely ten minutes had passed.

He removed the automatic from the waistband at his back and checked the ammo. It was fully loaded, for all the good it would do. He returned it to his belt. Another 30 seconds passed.

O'Donnell passed him, puffing heavily on his cigar.

"How much does the boy know?" Jim said.

"About what his old man did?" The inspector pondered the question. "I really don't know. They kept it out of the papers. I suppose it depends on how much the kid's mother shared with him."

Jim nodded.

"Hey, Anthony, do you still think there a change this killer is really George Flynn come back to life?"

Jim shook his head. "It's not George Flynn."

A clamoring came from out front and everyone tensed. Jim had a hand on the gun at his back. The front door was thrown open and one of the police officers entered, accompanied by Tim Flynn. Through the door, Jim saw the front of a police car. The cop had driven the vehicle over the sidewalk and right to the front door of Well's house. Two other people climbed out of the back of the patrol car and entered the house. It was Vera and Myrtle from Eagle Chemicals.

"When I took Tim home, his mother asked if I could watch him," Vera said. She had to go out of town. Her sister down in Augusta is having a baby and there were some…complications. She'd already cooked a big meal, so we just stayed there. Besides this one didn't wish to go home to face her own mother."

Myrtle, red-eyed and disheveled, said nothing.

"Hi ya, Mr. Anthony," Tim said. He was friendly, if slightly apprehensive.

"Hello, Tim. Will you come over to the table and sit for a bit?"

"Sure."

Jim pulled out a chair for Tim. The boy sat, and Jim settled in to the chair next to him.

"Tim, do you know Mr. Wells?"

"Sort of. He was one of my dad's bosses."

Wells gave the boy a wan smile. It was apparently the best he could muster under the circumstances.

"Do you know what's been going on?"

Tim swallowed. When he spoke, he chose his words carefully. "Some people got…killed."

"Yes, unfortunately."

"Does it…does it have anything to do with my dad?"

Jim nodded. "I'm afraid it does."

The boy looked down at the table.

"Tim, do you know what your dad did."

With his eyes still downcast, Tim nodded. "I know what they say he did."

"And what's that?"

Tim drew in a big breath. He let it out and lifted his head to meet Jim's eyes.

"They say he stole something from where he worked, and they put him in jail, and he committed…he hung himself." As he said the last words, Tim shifted his gaze to Taylor Wells. Wells looked away.

"You don't think he did it?"

Tim shook his head. "My dad is…was a good guy. Somebody made a mistake."

"How does that make you feel?"

Tim looked at the top of the table again. "Sad, I reckon. And mad. My mom cries all the time. I miss him a lot."

Jim patted the boy's shoulder. "You seem like a good kid, Tim. I guess your parents taught you about right and wrong."

Tim nodded. "Mom says I have to always do the right thing even when I don't want to."

"Sounds like you have a great mom."

Tim nodded again. His lower lip trembled slightly. He wiped his hand across his eyes.

"Tim, there's a man who is trying to kill Mr. Wells. Now this is going to be hard to hear, but – "

The front door flew open again. Jim jumped to his feet. Vera gasped. Myrtle let out a squeak.

It was Tom Gentry.

"What did I miss?"

"Vera, why don't you take Myrtle and go to one of the bedrooms?" Jim said.

"No, sir," Vera said. "That boy's mother entrusted me with his well being and I will not let him out of my sight."

Jim sighed. "Very well. Could you at least stand away from the door?"

As soon as the words were spoken, a scream came from outside, followed by a load roar. Two more screams followed.

One of the firemen. The hose. The other fireman and at least one of the cops.

"Get away from the door!" Jim shouted. He crossed the room in two great strides and yanked the arms of Vera and Myrtle, tossing them toward the couch as though they weighed nothing. Tom was on the move to the dining room.

The doorknob on the front door turned. It went to the left, then to the right.

He's teasing us, Jim thought. He wondered if the firemen missed the killer with their hose.

The door slowly swung open. Halfway through its arc, the hinges squealed softly.

The killer stood in the doorway. In addition to the glow that surrounded his body, Jim saw droplets of water form a nimbus around the man.

The fire departments hose had been useless. The water did not penetrate the killer's machine.

The murderer raised a hand to wipe away the moisture that appeared to hover in front of his face. When he spoke, it was in that tinny, faraway voice.

"I suppose this was your idea, Anthony."

"For all the good that it did," Jim muttered.

From behind Jim, one of the police officers yelled, and rushed the killer. The cop carried a bucket of water. He had missed the point of what just happened, or he was simply desperate. He emptied the contents over the killer, who shook his head and made a tsk sound. The murderer reached out a hand and touched the bucket bucket-toting copper. The officer screamed as his body began to melt and elongate. He fell to the carpet, dead before he touched the floor.

The killer stepped over the body and walked to the dining room. Jim backed up, making certain he remained in the man's line of sight. From the corner of his eye, Jim saw the Flynn boy standing next to the couch. Vera's arm was around him. Tim pulled away from the older woman and made his way toward the front door.

"I've made some improvements," the killer said. He gestured to the gizmo he wore. At every junction where a wire or hose went into the machine, a silver substance wrapped around the connection. "It's called duct tape.

It's the greatest invention of the 20th Century. Other than this machine, of course."

"What's he talking about?" Wells said. "What do ducks have to do with this? Why are you trying to kill me?"

The killer pointed a shimmering, deadly hand at Wells.

"Because you killed my father."

"Wells," Jim Anthony said, "meet Tim Flynn."

The room erupted in noise, from Tom, Inspector O'Donnell and at least one of the women.

"It's true," Jim said. "As incredible as it sounds, you're looking at Tim Flynn, from some distant point in the future."

Jim tried to locate the boy, but his line of sight was blocked by the killer.

"It's true," the older Flynn said. "I'm from about fifty years in what would be your future. To me, of course, it's the present."

"For time travel to be possible, incredible scientific advances would have to be made over the next half century."

"Or," the killer said, "you could raid the technology found in a crashed UFO."

"A what?"

"A flying saucer. Oh, wait. You won't hear of those until after the war."

"War?" Tom said.

"Never mind that," Jim said. "You have the time travel machine but it's not perfected, is it?"

"No. It draws a tremendous amount of power, and requires frequent re-charging. And it's not completely accurate. It won't allow me to make too many visits too closely together."

Jim nodded. "So that's why you didn't simply appear in a new location one second after each killing."

"That's right," the older Flynn said. "Oh, and it had a vulnerability to moisture. But you already know that."

"It seems like a lot of trouble to avenge your father's suicide. After all, he did commit the theft. And he was conspiring with enemies of America."

"Don't say that!" The killer stepped closer to Jim. "You don't know any-thing. Those men, the rich bastards took away my father. Do you know what that's like? It ruined my life. I was going to be an engineer, but I started drinking. I barely graduated college, then I lost every job I had. And a couple of wives along the way. Finally, the only job I could get was an assistant in a lab that did contract work for the government. When I saw what was being done with this retrieved technology, I started to realize I could change everything."

"But what did you change?"

The killer glared at Jim. "I went back as far as I could. That was the day of my father's funeral. The time machine has a limited range, you see. So I was left with only revenge. The directors of Eagle Chemical had to pay for what they did to me."

"Is it true?"

The killer turned to see who had spoken to him.

Young Tim Flynn stood behind the man.

"Is it true? Are you really me?"

"Yes," the older version of Tim said.

"I will really have that terrible life?"

"I'm sorry, but yes. You will."

Jim watched the eerie exchange. He wanted to take action, to protect the boy, yet he knew of nothing he could do.

"And this bad life and all that drinking and stuff, that will make me kill a bunch a people, like you just killed that policeman?"

"You don't understand." The killer said. "They destroyed my life. Our life."

"Mr. Anthony?"

"Yes, Tim?"

"Can I ask you a question?"

"Of course," Jim said.

"You have to be honest with me."

"Of course."

Young Tim closed his eyes. "If I die before I grow up, would that stop this from happening?"

"Tim, don't do anything foolish."

"You said you'd be honest with me."

Jim sighed. "Okay. I don't know, Tim. I just don't know enough about time travel to be able to form an opinion. On one hand, the fact that's this has already happened could mean events cannot be changed."

The older Flynn looked back and forth between the boy and Jim.

"Of course, it is also possible that your death would erase everything that's happen since he killed Mr. Plainview. I'm sorry, but that's the best I can do."

The boy nodded. "I appreciate it."

He reached under his shirt and removed a gun. Jim was almost certain it was the dead policeman's service revolver. Tim must have taken it when the killer was focused on Jim.

"What are you doing?" the killer demanded. "You can't hurt me with that. The machine generates a distortion field that bends time and space."

"Who said I was going to use it on you?" Tim lifted the barrel to his own temple.

"Didn't you hear what Anthony said? Your death might not change anything."

"Let's find out," the boy said.

Jim stepped around the older Flynn to kneel by the boy.

"Tim, don't do this," Jim said.

"I have to," Tim said. Tears ran down his face. "Even if it doesn't change anything, being dead is better than ending up like him. I won't be a killer, even if my dad really did what they say."

Tim used his thumb to pull back the revolver's hammer.

"No!" There was a loud click, and the shimmering light around the killer faded away, along wit the sizzling sound. He shoved Jim out of the way and squatted next to the boy. Tim took a step back so the older man couldn't grab the gun. Instead, the older version of Flynn touched the shoulder of his younger self.

"Tim, I did this for us. Maybe you can have a different life if you know Wells and the rest are dead. They are responsible for what happened to Dad. You'll grow up knowing there was justice for our father."

"I know I'll never be you," Tim said. "Because I'm never going to be that stupid."

The boy pulled the gun away from his head, pointed it at the killer and fired.

The bullet struck the older Flynn in the center of his chest, knocking him to the floor.

He looked up at Tim. Blood ran from the corner of his mouth, and Jim knew the bullet had struck a lung.

"Wh—why?"

Instead of answering, Tim took a step over to his older self and thumbed back the hammer of the gun again.

The killer reacted immediately. He touched a spot on the mechanism around his shoulder. The shimmering aura appeared again. There was a flash of light and the killer was gone.

Tim dropped the revolver of the floor. He turned to Jim.

"Did I do okay, Mr. Anthony?"

Jim stood up. He tousled the boy's hair.

"You were perfect, son."

Vera appeared next to the boy. She gently pulled him to her.

Tim hugged her waist and sobbed.

Jim returned to the dining room table. Wells stared at the spot where the killer fell. His mouth hung open.

"It's over," Jim told him. "I've seen that wound before. He's through."

Wells stood up and went to a small table next to the wall. He poured a staggering quantity of whiskey into a thick glass and drank it down in one gulp.

"Did that really just happen?" Tom said.

"Unfortunately," Jim said.

"Okay, now you can answer my question. In 50 years, I'll be a spry seventy-nine-year-old handsome man. If I look up that Flynn character and shoot him before he comes back here, will that wipe away everything that happened?"

"I'm not sure."

"A lot of help you are."

"Here's something I do know," Jim said.

"What?"

Jim pointed to Tim. The boy was still hugging Vera, though his sobbing had eased.

"I know he will never grow into the man who committed all those murders."

"I think you're right," Tom said.

"Are you ready to go?

"Go? Go where?"

"To Paris," Jim Anthony said. "We have another killer to catch."

Tom started for the door. "Brother, I'm driving to the airport. I can't wait to see this burg in my rear view mirror."

As they walked out of the house, Jim heard the familiar bellow of Inspector O'Donnell.

"Hey, where's Anthony? That guy owes me a steak dinner!"

The End

Chronicling A Super Detective

When faced with the challenge of writing a Jim Anthony story, I first had to decide which Jim Anthony I wanted to write about.

As some of you may know, the Anthony stories fall into two distinct eras. First, there was what I think of as the superhero stories in which Jim, clearly patterned after the successful Doc Savage series, demonstrated amazing feats of physical strength and mental acuity as he faced off against larger-than-life super villains. Later, most likely as a result of disappointing sales, Jim was downgraded from Super-detective to just plain detective.

Both periods produced some good pulp yarns, but I'm partial to the superhero tales. Once I decided which Jim Anthony to write about, my next hurdle was finding a challenge worthy of the scientific superman.

I picked a time-traveling antagonist (gee, I hope you finished the story before reading this essay) because I wanted a threat that seemed beyond Jim's skills, something that would appear to be supernatural but wasn't.

(Here's a solid pulp fiction rule of thumb: the super science hero cannot battle a supernatural nemesis. It doesn't work. It's oil and water. It's like Tom and Jerry facing off against The Terminator. It may sound cool in the planning stages, but the result somehow diminishes the characters.)

Remember when good ol' Doc Savage sort of went to Hell and sort of battled the devil? I always imagined that after an adventure so far out of his wheelhouse he did the walk of shame back to his 86th floor headquarters. Out on the corner in front of the building he bumped into his fellow crimefighter, The Shadow.

The Shadow: What's up, Doc?
Doc Savage: Um, not much. You?
The Shadow: The usual. Breaking up crime syndicates. Busting heads in Chinatown. That sort of thing. What have you been doing?
Doc Savage: (Mumbles)
The Shadow: Excuse me? I didn't catch that.
Doc Savage: I said I just got back from Hell. I fought the devil
The Shadow: O-o-o-kay....
Doc Savage: I'm serious.
The Shadow: Sure, sure. (Tries unsuccessfully to hide his snickering).

Doc Savage: What was–Are you laughing at me?

The Shadow: What? No. I, uh, got choked on this scarf. That's all.

Doc Savage: It's not so crazy. You fought dinosaurs once.

The Shadow: That's so not the same thing.

Doc Savage: Is too!

The Shadow: Whatever. I'm late for lunch at the Cobalt Club.

Doc Savage: Yeah. I've got to do...something. I guess.

The Shadow: (sniffs) What's that smell? Is that sulphur?

Doc Savage: Hey, you can smell it!

The Shadow: Naw. Just messing with you. Sucker. Hahahaha!

Doc Savage: (I really hate that guy.)

So, once the menace had been nailed down, I had to pick a setting. Since Jim Anthony inherited his father's business interests, I thought it would be fun to show him actually tending to business. That got him where he needed to be, and the adventure could begin.

Writing "The Resurrected Killer" was blast, even though it was delayed for several months due to some rather boring circumstances. I appreciate the patience of the editor in letting me finish the story. I hope you enjoyed it.

That's it, except to say I know what happens to Jim Anthony and Tom Gentry when they get to Paris to pursue a mysterious murderer. I would like to tell the story of that adventure some day.

Hey, Ron, will the company pay for a research trip to France?

MARK JUSTICE - writes The Dead Sheriff supernatural western series, which debuts in 2011 from Evileye Books. *Looking at the World with Broken Glass in My Eye*, his first collection of short fiction, will also be published in 2011, from Graveside Tales. He is the co-author of *Dead Earth: The Vengeance Road* (with David T. Wilbanks) from Permuted Press. He also serializes new pulp fiction and blogs at http://markjustice.blogspot.com. Mark Justice lives in Kentucky with his wife and cats.

SOME HEROES NEVER QUIT

Welcome to the fourth Jim Anthony Super Detective brought to you by Airship 27 Productions. Jim Anthony was always one of those B characters we wanted to promote when starting up this new publishing venture and we got off to a rollicking start with our first three books, featuring both awesome stories and amazingly beautiful artwork. All was moving along a great pace.

Then, as often happens in life, we hit a publishing speed bump that almost derailed us. Note, I said almost. This book should have come to you, our loyal readers, many, many, many months ago. Upon soliciting stories, we quickly received four truly fun stories by Joel Jenkins, Frank Byrns, Erwin K.Roberts and Mark Justice; each one of them a gem to our rapidly growing canon of new Jim Anthony exploits.

Next we recruited artist Michael Neno to do the interior illustrations and Michael jumped right on board, delivering twelve wonderful pieces of pulp style art that truly enhance each of the four stories. It sure seemed like we were on a rocket to a quick publishing finish for book number four.

Which is of course when we crashed headlong into the wall marked.... NO DECENT COVER ARTIST! You see, we here at Airship 27 take our covers very seriously and over the eight years of our existences have produced cover images that our readers have applauded and come to recognize us by. We hold that reputation of putting out the best looking New Pulp titles on the market today sacred. So recruiting an artist for this book would demand some serious consideration. A process that began to drag on over a lengthy period of time as each new candidate was either not up to the standards we were looking for, or those that had the talent were unavailable to us.

Naturally, some of our writers, and Michael, became a bit annoyed and they all had every right to be. Finally, after almost two years, I was made aware of Eric Meador, an artist who lived right here in my own town. Yup, that's how life works. A fellow writer put me on to Eric and when I saw his work on-line began to hope we'd finally found our guy. I wrote Eric, introduced myself and began to explain Airship 27, what we did and how we were desperate for someone to paint a killer cover for this book.

Lo and behold, after so many set-backs, Eric simply said, "Sure, I'll do it for you." Just like that. And now, at long last, you are holding JIM

ANTHONY SUPER DETECTIVE Vol. IV in your hands and it sports an awesome cover that far exceeded our wildest imagination. Trust me when I say, in large part, the wait was worth it and we have every intention of giving Eric lots more cover assignments. Who knows, maybe even the next Jim Anthony project; which, by the way is a truly original crossover adventure that teams him with a very popular modern day adventurer. But hey, I'm giving things away here.

Suffice it to say, like our ever stalwart protagonist, some heroes never do quit and we want to thank our four writers and Michael Neno for staying the course. We hope they are happy with the results.

Thank each and everyone one of you for your continued support, we couldn't do this without you. Be looking forward to that "special" Jim Anthony project I hinted at before, and keep your fingers crossed it doesn't take another two years to reach you. Ha.

Ron Fortier
9/6/2013
(www.airship27.com)
(airship27@comcast.net)

Airship
27

JIM ANTHONY SUPER-DETECTIVE

Airship 27 Productions is thrilled to present the all new adventures of one of pulpdom's most cherished two-fisted action heroes, Jim Anthony Super-Detective. Half Irish, half Comanche and all American, Jim Anthony is the near perfect human being in both physical strength and superior mental intellect. He's a scientific genius with degrees in all the major fields. Operating from his penthouse suite, which also houses his private research laboratory, he ventures forth into the world at large as a champion of justice, a modern knight righting wrongs and defending the helpless.

Follow the "super-detective's" all-new adventures in these three volumes written by today's best New Pulp Authors. Brought to you by Airship 27 Productions:

PULP FICTION FOR A NEW GENERATION!

For availability go to: Airship27Hangar.com

AN AIRSHIP 27 PRODUCTION